Night Fire

Also by Vonna Harper:

Surrender

Roped Heat

"Wild Ride" in *The Cowboy*

Night Fire

VONNA HARPER

APHRODISIA

KENSINGTON BOOKS

http://www.kensingtonbooks.com

APHRODISIA are published by

Kensington Publishing Corp.
850 Third Avenue
New York, NY 10022

All Kensington Titles, Imprints, and Distributed Lines are available at special quantity discounts for bulk purchases for sales promotions, premiums, fund-raising, and educational or institutional use.

Special book excerpts or customized printings can also be created to fit specific needs. For details, write or phone the office of the Kensington special sales manager: Kensington Publishing Corp., 850 Third Avenue, New York, NY 10022, attn: Special Sales Department, Phone: 1-800-221-2647.

ISBN-13: 978-0-7582-2217-6
ISBN-10: 0-7582-2217-3

First Kensington Trade Paperback Printing: December 2007

10 9 8 7 6 5 4 3 2 1

Printed in the United States of America

1

Feeling more than a little disconnected from the crowd, Hayley McKeon stood off to one side taking in the large, brightly lit event room. Maybe she wouldn't have felt out of it if she hadn't worked late last night—Friday, of course—but then maybe being alone among so many chattering groups was responsible.

You can't do anything about it, kid, she reminded herself. *Getting divorced means turning into a "one" again.*

Determined not to go down that road today, when singlehood was what she'd wanted emotionally, financially, and in every other way, she took a deep breath. Unfortunately, the air was warmer than she liked and smelled too much of people and whatever they were offering at the food booth. Still not moving, she concentrated on her surroundings. She hadn't been to a gems and minerals show for a couple of years and had forgotten how exciting yet overwhelming they could be.

As a rough guess, she estimated there were at least forty separate booths in addition to the elaborate, glass-enclosed displays in the middle of the cavernous room. People filed slowly past the central displays while some of those in front of the booths showed no interest in moving on. Much as she wanted to see what was for sale on the various tables, getting close enough to do her own gawking and purchasing was going to be a challenge.

A challenge she had to meet unless she wanted to spend the foreseeable future and beyond gritting her teeth every time her boss at Galpan Enterprises asked/ordered her to work late.

It's your fault, sis. If you were here, we'd be pushing folks aside and damn the consequences, and I'd be filled with courage, not fear.

However, not only was being scared of her future an all but permanent condition, Saree had called her on her cell phone just as she was arriving to say she'd be a little late—something about needing to pick up a new outfit. Laughing under her breath, Hayley imagined what would happen if her knock-'em-dead younger sister walked in wearing a red latex bodysuit with openings for her breasts and crotch. No doubt about it, gems and minerals would come in a distant second to that little show. Thinking about the difference between the way she and her sister paid their bills got her moving. She had no—well, probably no—interest in becoming a porn star. Of course, if she could make enough baring everything she had to get out of debt—

Forget debt today, damn it! Take chances, take control!

Now that she'd joined the milling throng, she took increased note of the throng's composition. Not only did there seem to be equal numbers of men and women, but all ages were represented, including children, who were repeatedly being told to keep their hands to themselves. A large number of older couples were in attendance, and although her parents had been dead for two years and nearly one year, respectively, Hayley still mourned what she'd lost. At least they hadn't had to see her marriage implode or explode, depending on how one looked at it.

She hadn't paid much attention to where she was heading since she figured that as long as she went in one direction, sooner or later she'd see everything there was to see—and hopefully make some *put your money where your mouth is* purchases. When she'd first heard about the show, she'd told herself to go to it with her mind and imagination and creativity open, that her love of and skill in jewelry creation would guide her.

Well, maybe. However, at the moment, she was stuck behind a noisy group of six women, and waited for them to move away from a booth in the far right corner. Sure, she could come back to it later, but something indefinable kept her in place. Other attendees were interested primarily in what was on display, but going by the women's animated conversation with whomever was manning the booth, something important or educational or entertaining was being said.

She'd just about given up when a man with a toddler in a stroller backed away, and she took the vacated place. The moment she looked down, she was glad she'd waited because the table was devoted to fire opals. Some had been made into jewelry, and necklaces, earrings, and rings were arranged on a variety of displays, but the majority of the opals had been spread out on velvet in cases with locked glass tops. Lighting had been designed so each box was touched by a slightly different hue, adding to the presentation. For the most part, the boxes had been arranged in color groupings ranging from a translucent crystal to opaque milky white to bold red with a predominance of the orange that was so common to fire opals.

Was it the fire lurking deep in the stones that had always drawn her to opals? Probably, since there was something sensual about finding so much color in such small stones. True, the stories about opals' place in history was fascinating, particularly the ancient Persian and Central American belief that they were symbols of fervent love, whatever that was, but even without the legends, she'd always loved working with them. Creating a faceted or cabochon piece to display the most fire possible gave her a sense of satisfaction she doubted would ever get old, and she loved holding the finished product in her palm, becoming part of it.

Unfortunately, she hadn't done as much work with opals as she wanted to, both because she hadn't had enough time what with life's recent curves and because she'd been discouraged by the large number of inferior or manufactured stones on the market.

There wasn't a single marginal gem or opal figment held together in a clear plastic cast here, nothing but the real deal. A virtual gold, or should she say fire, mine.

Excited, she leaned over for a closer look. As she did, she almost swore heat was coming up from the cases and touching her with warmth and energy, calling to her. If only the owner or distributor or whoever hadn't locked them up, not that she could blame him. Unlike her ex, she'd never taken anything that didn't belong to her, but Lordy, did her fingers itch to hold one, or more. For the gems to become part of her.

"Be careful," one woman said as another slipped on a ring. "You don't want to wind up with bad luck."

"You don't really believe that nonsense, do you?" the ring wearer asked of her companion.

"All I know is, I'm not taking chances. What about it? Do you think there's anything to that business about opals bringing bad luck?"

For a moment, Hayley thought the woman was talking to her. Then she realized she had to be addressing the man behind the table.

"Quetzalitzlipyollitli were sacred to the Mayas and Aztecs," a deep, strong voice said. "Gifts from the gods."

Almost of its own will, Hayley's head came up. The voice—that rich, strong voice—settled in her. More than that, the masculine tone seemed to be spreading out, seeping into her veins and racing through her.

"What was that you said?" the woman asked. "I can't begin to pronounce that word."

"Quetzalitzlipyollitli. It means the stone of the bird of paradise."

Forget birds of paradise and tongue-twisting syllables. Forget everything except deep eyes, eyes as dark as the darkest cave, and yet filled with a rich glow. Forget the crowds and noise. Absorb this man's energy and the look of raw disbelief and desperate hope in his gaze.

Even as her body heated, Hayley told herself this wasn't happening. Hell no. She didn't believe in like at first sight, let alone love in that particular instant. Fine. Fine and good. But what about lust? What about a communication that went beyond words?

Now her arms and legs were going numb and what was that buzzing in her lips? Just because the owner of what might be the world's sexiest voice was a good six foot three with shoulders that would make a football coach drool and a lean, hard body encased in a skin-skimming black shirt and faded jeans that more than hugged the territory they were responsible for was no reason to—to what?

The women were still talking to him, but if he heard, the man gave no indication. To her disbelief, his eyes had found hers, latched on to them, bonded with them. He'd cocked his head to the side as if trying to convince himself that he was truly looking at her, maybe wondering whether she was getting whatever message or order or command or tidal wave of sex appeal he was giving out. If he did that much longer, she just might melt.

Either that or jump over the display and launch herself at him.

Fuck. That's all there needs to be, fucking. Mating like a cou-

ple of animals in heat. Whether he or she was expressing those sentiments, she couldn't say. Didn't give a damn. Neither did she know how the hell she was going to keep her legs under her and her pussy from melting. Disconcerted, she dropped her gaze from pure magnetic power before said power ripped her to shreds.

Her attention snagged on a display she hadn't noticed before, probably because it was at the back of the table and near him. None of these stones had been cut and polished, but she saw their potential within their plain host rocks. Her heated fingers truly itched to touch and turn and explore, briefly distracting her from the man's unnerving eyes—either that or she'd found a connection between the opals and him.

"Blacks," he said and ran a strong, dark finger over the case.

"I, ah, I know." Much as she wanted to, she didn't risk looking up.

"What else do you know?"

About what? Wondering if he was referring to the connection already forged between them, she nevertheless refused to bite. Some things a woman needed to keep to herself—like the wet heat between her legs, like her tightening nipples and the pressure on her chest. "Blacks are rare, and thus quite valuable," she heard herself say. Then she lifted her head.

Looking slightly more relaxed, he gave an approving nod. "Yes, they are; I'm delighted you know that. Your knowledge says a great deal about many things."

"What kinds of things?"

The way his head came up, she knew he wasn't going to answer. Instead, he took a deep breath. "The most valuable have deep red captured in the black. They're considered depth instead of light, mystery over glow."

She'd never heard it expressed like that before, but he was right, so right. "Where are they from?"

When he didn't answer, she surrendered to the pinpricks of fire spreading over her spine. Animal magnetism was a buzz term, right? Then what the hell was this?

"They're from the Mexican highlands, on the site of an extinct volcano. The Indians call the area Pico de Orizaba. These"—he indicated the spectacular case—"came from a labyrinthine passage that winds through the open-cast mine there."

"Oh." She'd seen pictures of opal mines carved from isolated and desolate-looking land, and of the Mexican Indians who toiled there. Those laborers were short and solid, their bodies protected from the relentless sun by broad-brimmed hats and ragged clothing. They'd seemed part of the land, as if hardened by it.

This powerfully built man was larger and taller with dark, deep eyes undimmed by physical labor, and yet he made her think of those native workers. Maybe it was his rough-looking hands, his sun-weathered skin. And maybe it was because, like men who made a living from the earth, he seemed to be part of something ancient and enduring.

Don't do this. Don't get carried away!

But how could she help it? This man was passionate about some of the same things as she was, and his voice was like a strong wind surrounding and burrowing deep inside her. She couldn't remember when she'd last had sex or wanted more than her vibrator. She wanted him, now—rough and raw and loud and messy.

"Am I the only one feeling the heat?" one of the women asked.

"Hell no," another laughed. "Enough to burn down the place."

Vaguely wondering what they were talking about, Hayley tore her gaze off the ageless man. All six women were dividing their attention between her and him, smiling, fanning themselves, one pulling her blouse out and blowing down her front. "Don't worry about it, honey," the first speaker said with a giggle. "We aren't scandalized, just jealous."

It took every shred of civilization in her not to clamp her hand over her crotch and push against the hungry heat there. Maybe it would have been easier if *the man* was looking at something else, doing anything except leaning toward her with his beautiful strong hands resting on the table and his lips slightly parted. Thank goodness, the table hid him from the hips down. If she'd been able to see—

Knock it off! You want to catch fire?

Well yeah, truth be told, she did.

His gaze intent, his breathing deep and rapid, the man called Mazati studied the woman. It was too early to know whether she was *the* one, his reason for living. But if instinct bore him out, his desperate and determined search had come to an end.

Before entrusting her with his knowledge, came stripping her down, exposing her deepest vulnerabilities, teaching her how much she needed from him.

And once he'd accomplished that . . .

2

By the time Hayley had gotten a modicum of a handle on her nervous system, an extremely overweight man had pushed past the women and was confronting the object of said nerves. In a loud and obnoxious tone, the fat man demanded to know why the opal he'd bought here had cost so much when just a few tables away, he'd gotten no less than three for the same price. He held a total of four opals in his beefy hand as example.

"Not only that, these three"—he jabbed with a manicured nail—"are a hell of a lot brighter than what you foisted off on me."

"If you don't like it," that nerve-heating voice said, "I'll buy it back."

Hayley looked at the opals. "May I?" she asked, indicating she wanted to pick them up.

The fat man's skeptical gaze turned to a grin as he gave her the once-over. "Sure thing, girlie," he said as he dumped them into her palm. "You'll back me up, I bet. Look at these three. Loaded with fire."

"Yes, they are," she agreed. "But the one you bought here is naturally dry while the others have had artificial heat applied. Unfortunately, that dried them out and fatally weakened them."

"Huh, how do you know that?"

"Experience. I haven't worked with fire opals as much as I'd like to, but I know enough that I wouldn't have that trio at any price. Take a close look. Do you see those tiny fissures in them?"

"Like spiderwebs? I thought that was part of the design."

"Sorry. Fire opals consist of silicic acid with a relatively high water content, while the color itself comes from traces of iron oxide. The moisture is unevenly distributed, which means that if it dries out as a result of too much heat, the stones will crack. That's what you have."

"No shit?"

"No shit. Oh, they're all right if all you want to do is display them, but they'll never hold up as rings because of everything rings are subjected to. Cleaning products are deadly to opals."

"Damn it. I've been taken."

"Not necessarily," said the deep voice that had come too close to turning her inside out. "Like the knowledgeable young lady said, they're fine for displaying. Besides, you didn't pay much for them."

Grumbling under his breath, the fat man nodded. After she dropped the opals back in his hand, he spun around, nearly knocking her off her feet when his shoulder struck her, and stalked off, perhaps to give the other dealer a piece of his newly educated mind.

"I was right. You do know a great deal about opals."

Feeling a bit too much as if she was responding to a magnet, Hayley faced the tall, dark, killer-intriguing man. He held out his hand, and in his gesture she sensed a challenge—maybe the greatest challenge of her life. After a momentary hesitation and a prayer to the god of women in over their heads, she placed hers in his. Because she'd warned herself to expect a *zap*, she was ready for that to happen—at least a little.

But how could she possibly prepare for a zing along with a sharp zap, to say nothing of a little short-circuiting between her brain and the rest of her body?

"I'm Mazati," he said.

Just Mazati? "Hayley McKeon."

"Hayley. I've been looking for you."

You what?

He was still holding her fingers, palm, even her wrist, making it impossible for her to formulate a response or question or whatever the hell a rational human being would be doing about now. The physical-and-more connection went on and on, uncomfortable and incredible at the same time, pulling her out of herself and into him. They weren't shaking hands, weren't filling the air with small talk, weren't doing anything except holding on. Exploring.

"That's too much for me," one of the women said. "I'm out of here before I embarrass myself."

"You know what they say about three being a crowd."

"Hell, those two don't know whether there's a crowd. As far as they're concerned, they're alone."

Although she had no doubt the conversation was about her and this man who said his name was Mazati and spoke with a strange, faint accent, she couldn't conjure up any interest in responding. As for being embarrassed, she was too far gone for that. Only when the space around her cleared did she take note of her surroundings. The women were wandering off, looking back over their shoulders at the linked hands, envy and outright longing darkening their gazes.

Feeling the weight of that longing, she turned her attention to what she could see of her hand surrounded by male strength. She'd started dating her ex-husband because Cal had melted her bones, had married him for reasons that had dimmed with the months, divorced him in part because she'd forgotten what bone melting felt like.

No longer.

I've been waiting for you. Suddenly scared, she pulled free. Resisting the urge to cradle her hand between her breasts, she dug deep inside her for the courage to face those incredible eyes. But courage was a sadly lacking commodity because her skin still retained the imprint of his fingers and palm and her panties were getting a little more than damp, which were extremely distracting conditions.

Standing in a dark room waiting for the door to open. Hearing the sound of hinges working, sensing another presence, listening to approaching footsteps—naked footsteps, the first kiss of a man's fingertips on her exposed breasts. And then—and then those same fingertips sliding past her labia's wet barrier and coming home. Belonging.

"You understand," he said.

"Ah, understand what?" Oh no, her throat was closing down! And on fire!

He didn't immediately answer, the heavy silence more electric than words could ever be. The fantasy that had hit her demanded she enter it again, but she didn't dare because she might not survive. "Opals," he finally said. "The magic and power in them."

This isn't about opals, is it? Not just *them anyway.* "Not—not as much as you do, obviously." She punctuated her comment by sweeping her trembling hands over the display. If she wasn't careful, she might vaporize.

"You're right, but then no one does."

"No one?"

"You'll understand, Hayley, eventually."

"I—will?"

"Don't be afraid."

Oh shit! "Why should I be?"

"Because you've never been on a journey like this." He sighed. "Neither have I."

He'd come from behind the table in order to shake hands

but shouldn't he be taking up residence back there again? Talking to the other show-goers? Trying to sell his wares?

Even more important, shouldn't she be keeping her attention on his face instead of letting—letting?—them range lower?

Oh yes, the jeans. Faded by loyalty and use, molded to him almost as if fabric and skin were fucking, cradling and protecting his cock, holding it up for her inspection. The mound was impressive, proud, unapologetic, and challenging, all in one. He wasn't erect, but why the hell did she think he might be when all they'd done was shake hands and exchange names? Yes, she had an okay body, but she'd never delude herself into thinking she was anyone's gift to men.

Heat slapped her cheeks. *Oh shit!* How long had she been staring at his crotch? Even worse, how long had he been watching her watching him?

"What did you say earlier?" she demanded, hoping to—to something. "That you've been waiting for me?"

He responded with a short nod.

"What do you mean? We haven't met, have we?"

"Not in a way you understand, yet."

"How can you say that?"

"Because in some ways I've been looking for you forever."

Exhaust from the vehicles coming in and out of the parking lot drifted to the picnic table where Hayley had been sitting for the past five minutes and counting. She hadn't yet addressed the question of why she was out here instead of inside demanding Mazati explain himself, because getting a handle on her breathing and overloaded nerves still took all her concentration. Although it wasn't yet noon, it was hot, and she was grateful for the spreading oak that the table and bench seats had been placed under. She was even more grateful that she was the only one in this particular spot. As for whether some part of her wanted Mazati here—

Not yet. Not until I've gotten a grip on myself.

As if reinforcing that she was nowhere near a grip, her pussy muscles clenched. Not bothering to look around, she spread her legs and rocked back and forth trying to stimulate her crotch without getting her fingers involved. Unfortunately, she couldn't make a connection between her crotch and the wooden bench. As a result, the pulsing itch continued. Hunching forward, she slid her hands between her legs and pressed.

No good. No itch scratched. Only the wanting.

"What is it?" she chided herself, her tone less composed than she needed it to be. "You're so damned turned on your brain cells have melted?" After a deep breath, she treated her cunt to one more stroke and then reluctantly removed her hand. Oh shit. Things were getting more and more hot and bothered down there. "Damn it, it's not like you don't know how to deal with a little matter of abstinence and the consequences. After all, you've been doing it ever since Cal was arrested—and before."

No! She *wasn't* going to bring her ex into the mix. So what did that leave?

Mazati. A man with only one name and eyes that made her think of caves at midnight and some secret knowledge about her and a mound between his legs that—

Careful! Dangerous territory.

Swallowing, she berated herself for not bringing something to drink, but damn it, dealing with thirst had hardly been on her mind. Instead—

Instead what, old girl?

"He's beautiful," she whispered to the nearby robin working the sad excuse for a lawn. "And no, I don't know why I'm saying that instead of calling him handsome or manly or a hunk. Maybe because he's so much like those stones. Depth and fire. Shadow and light."

Depth. Shadow. Was that true or was her imagination responsible? Maybe he was nothing more than a tall, solid man wearing old jeans, and she only had her prolonged celibacy to blame?

"So get off your ass and go back inside."

Soon, damn it. Don't rush me. Besides, what he said about looking or waiting for me for a long time scares me.

Okay, she'd sit here until the robin was done hunting worms or whatever it was doing, but once it had flown or hopped away, she'd get off said ass and make her way to the front of the crowd around Mazati's booth and buy as many black fire opals as her skimpy pocketbook could afford because she *needed* that depth and fire in order to fashion the jewelry her creativity ached to wrap itself around.

And not just in the stones.

Leaning back and rocking against the bench again, she looked up into the tree where countless leaves provided the sun with a playground. The colors were infinite, the shadings stretching from light to dark incalculable. Life was like that, ever changing, beautiful, and mysterious. Full of challenges. And possibilities.

Mostly challenges and hard decisions these days.

Still studying the leaves, she acknowledged a simple fact. She was coming back to life, looking forward to tomorrow despite the unknowns instead of wallowing in yesterday's quicksand. Sexuality was a basic and welcome part of that re-established life, and she should be embracing it instead of turning tail and running the way she'd just done. If there indeed was something, or the possibility of something, between her and the mysterious Mazati, she needed to grab hold. And if she wound up getting burned or conned or who the hell knows what, at least she'd be alive.

So fine. Get up and get going. And if I'm lucky, maybe I'll get fucked before tomorrow.

Instead, she sat and stared, her mind easing down so she was no longer aware of it. And although she kept her eyes open, she was no longer looking at an ordinary summer day. Instead, a mist was taking over, red, not bright and brilliant like the fire in an opal's depth but muted and quiet and ill-formed. Fog? Burnished fog?

For maybe a half second, she gave serious thought to jumping up and running, but she didn't. Despite the mist's cool nature, it warmed and lulled her and took her ill-functioning mind off sexual frustration. Feeling as if she was sinking into a spa, she simply sat there with her arms resting on the table as the haze settled around her. It was so peaceful in here, soundless except for a faint humming, and the aroma of roses and violets added to the conviction that she was exactly where she wanted—no, needed—to be.

The haze pushed closer, making it impossible for her to see more than a few inches in any direction, but even that didn't bother her, maybe because the humming was turning into a beat, a steady and hypnotic rhythm. It was like, what, the build-up to a long, easy-listening music set? As for the haze, yes, the longer she remained in it, the less intense it became with the result that she was beginning to make out shapes and color shading.

Interesting. Beyond interesting. Fascinating. Overwhelming.

The variations between palest pink and blood red was almost more than she could absorb. If there'd been anyone in here with her, she'd ask them how the initial monochromatic red had defused like this and was there any way she could capture the vast array, but she couldn't pose those questions because she was alone.

Alone in a swirling, musical world.

The sound of her heartbeat snagged her attention. Although she felt utterly relaxed, unable to move in fact, her heart's sudden hammering warned of something. Instead of being alarmed, she accepted that she might be dying.

Dying? No. Despite her puny one hundred and ten pounds, she was strong as the proverbial horse. Sometimes scared shitless about her future but physically strong.

Easy, old gal. This is seriously weird, but how about we let things play themselves out? Besides, what choice do we have?

Her heart must have gotten the message because it started slowing down and now no longer felt as if it was trying to fight its way out of her chest. Dismissing the distraction, she went back to studying her surroundings. Yes, there was music all right, mostly drums now but also flutes and other instruments she didn't recognize. It was simple and clean and ancient-sounding, no electronic inventions. Swaying in time to the steady cadence the drums provided, she blinked several times. The reds were still there, no longer front and center but serving as the backdrop for other colors. Most prominent were browns and greens, the honest colors of trees and earth.

And now something gray was taking shape, a rising mass taking over the *world*, not rocks but some other stones all seamed together and resembling—what?

Something or someone grabbed her shoulders and hauled her to her feet, severing her interest in colors. Not only couldn't she see whoever had entered her fantasy, neither could she move a muscle on her own. Standing there like some old nag waiting for saddle and bridle, she continued to sway to the drums, waited for her role in whatever this fantasy was to be explained.

Something new now, a tugging sensation on her hips, the sound of a zipper being pulled down. Helpless to do or say anything, she watched as her slacks slid down her legs, stopping when they reached her ankles. She no longer had shoes on so when a voice that really wasn't a voice ordered her to step out of her slacks, obeying was easy. More than a little curious but still not alarmed, she lifted her arms in response to another command. Up went her top, static zinging through her hair. Cool/warm air caressed her skin now, touching everything except her breasts because she still wore her bra.

No bra. Not after reaching behind herself and unfastening it and sending it flying.

Nice! More than nice! Wind-fingers danced over her breasts and teased her nipples into hot knots. Eager for nudity, she wriggled out of her panties and sent them after her bra. Even more heat slid between her legs and played with her labia, causing her to widen her stance to give the warmth greater access to her sex.

Turned on. Swirling like some leaf in the fog and wind.

Hands again, not closing around her shoulders this time but sliding down her arms to her wrists and drawing her hands behind her. The sweet lethargy or building need or whatever had enveloped her faded a little to be replaced by, not fear, but a whispered warning to take back control of her body.

But then it was too late because something was closing down around her wrists. She heard a snapping sound and then another. The controlling hands were gone, but it didn't matter because she couldn't move her arms.

Caught. By some kind of cuffs, not police metal but softer, maybe leather?

Determined to see who had done this to her, she spun around, then backpedaled because she was looking at a column of red mist at least a foot taller than her. The longer she stared, the more distinct the mist became until it assumed the shape of a man.

What are you doing? she demanded in her non-voice.

What must be.

Before she could begin to make sense of that, fog-man held up something in his big hands. Leather. A strip more than two inches wide with metal clasps or clips on either end and a ring woven into it. Once again she couldn't move, couldn't twitch, could barely breathe. Helpless in a way she'd never imagined possible, she stood and watched and felt as fog-man placed the leather around her neck and snapped it in place.

With the sound, something shifted deep inside her.

Changed.

Good, Mazati acknowledged as Hayley's emotions played out over her body. The first step had been taken. It didn't matter that he hadn't touched a woman in hundreds of years or that the fire raging through his cock threatened to burn out of control. His aloneness and silence had to end; if it didn't, it would destroy him, and with his death, a complex and rich world would truly die with him.

She was his hope, maybe his only hope. His salvation and maybe his hell.

3

Speaking quietly and with animated eyes, a dozen nearly nude men made their way to the wooden seats on either side of the hard-packed path. At the end of the path were four steps leading to a raised platform. A massive man wearing nothing but a black, full-face mask with cutouts for his eyes, nose, and mouth stood waiting on the platform.

Leather still circled her wrists, forcing Hayley's hands to rest on her ass. What she now acknowledged was that a collar brushed her neck, the ring no longer hanging loose in front but attached to a rope she hadn't had the time or courage to study. Much as she wanted to demand or beg for an explanation, she couldn't because her mouth had been forced open by yet more leather. The gag fit securely, pressing against the back of her head with her hair caught under it. More curious than frightened, she turned her head to look behind her but stopped when she felt a tug on her collar.

Another tug, this one more insistent, got her moving, and she belatedly realized that she'd been walking, naked, along the path. And that the pace of every step had been dictated by the stranger holding her leash.

Male eyes bore into her, burning her and balancing her between fear and raw anticipation. Bondage fantasies and a little role play weren't new to her, but nothing she and Cal had experimented with had been this intense. This real. Imagining loss of control and reality were widely different, and how was she supposed to make sense of any of this when she couldn't ask questions and didn't know how she'd gotten here—or what was going to happen?

Ah, listen to footsteps. Measure the too-rapidly shrinking distance between where she was and the waiting masked man.

Not Mazati then. But who? What?

Her footsteps and pounding heart now provided the music, not distracting but involving her even more than she'd been a few moments ago. Equally involving was the slide of skin against skin as her inner thighs kissed with each step. No longer contained by panties, her labia absorbed the day's heat, and the rhythm of her bouncing breasts rolled through her.

Although she wanted to keep her head high so she could hold on to some measure of pride and sanity, she wound up looking at the seated men as she passed. Hunger filled their gazes, but although she thought they might reach for her, they didn't. Instead, they appeared content to challenge her with a superiority born from the simple fact that they were here of their free will while freedom had been stripped from her.

Walk. Give your keeper or whatever he is no reason to haul you along like some misbehaving dog.

Walk because otherwise you'll never know why this moment exists.

"Stop."

At the command, her handler stood in place, forcing her to do the same. She watched as one of the sitting men stood and positioned himself beside her. Without so much as a by-your-leave, he captured a breast and hefted it.

"Heavy," he announced. "Her own."

"What about responsiveness?"

On a grunt, the naked man ran his free hand between her legs. She tried to back away, but the leash stopped her. When she twisted to the side, he snaked an arm around her waist and cinched her against him. The hand against her crotch stayed. The longer it remained there, the more confused and over-whelmed she felt. On a level she couldn't begin to measure, she knew this wasn't happening. She also knew, without a doubt, that there was more going on than an out-of-control imagination, and she was sliding deeper and deeper into whatever this was because she wanted it. But those things were secondary to the reality of a strange man's hand claiming her sex, confidently owning it.

Maybe owning her.

Still holding her against him like some just-captured horse, he began stroking her cunt. With each pass, her ability to concentrate on anything else faded a little more. His thumb and fingers became her existence, loosening her and sending her down a heated path. The ropes on her hands, the leather caressing her neck, the gag, all that and more became part of a whole now dominated by her response. Yes, this was right, good, strong. Wanted and necessary. Although his hand was fleshy with rough finger pads and he smelled of sweat, she didn't care.

Sliding, sliding, the journey made smooth and easy by her pussy's lubrication. Even as things were falling apart for her and Cal, he'd demanded his rights, jamming his cock against her dry lips. She'd responded by letting him know in no uncertain terms that she'd file a rape charge if he went any farther and, cursing, he'd let her go.

So different this time. Helpless and hungry and surrounded

by strangers. A stranger herself in a strange world. And her body wanted this. Craved this man's hands, a thumb sliding between her labial lips and whispering over her clit, drawing wet heat out of her, making her moan behind the gag.

"Yes," the man holding and handling her said. "She's responsive."

"Instinct's working?"

"Oh yeah. The animal's there all right."

Animal?

The answer played out in her ever-widening stance and the way she pressed her breasts against him, her sex scent mating with his sweat.

"Good enough," the masked man at the top of the platform said. "Bring her on up."

Gone. No more fingers doing what she needed doing. No flesh sealed to hers and no arm holding her fast.

Shaking, she struggled to deal with the loss, but how could she when her *handler* was drawing on her leash again, and her feet once more slapped against dirt? Aware of how soon she'd reach the stairs and from there be assigned to some insane fate, she willed whatever this was to end. It had started with the mist, hadn't it? If she could find her way back to it, reverse the process somehow, get rid of these damnable pieces of leather, put her clothes back on—

No. No clothes. Nothing except summer's heat on her back and breasts and the top of her head while she forced her frightened body up the four stairs. Afraid to look at the masked man, she whimpered. This was no longer her body, her world. Instead—instead what?

Her handler turned her leash over to masked-man. Then her handler was gone, maybe sucked into a vortex because he was no longer needed in her fantasy/dream/nightmare.

"She's made for this," masked-man announced. He pulled up on her leash, forcing her onto her toes. "Raw material but filled with promise. She'll fight and fear and will need a firm hand, but you know what you need to do."

Raw material? Need to do?

"All of you"—he indicated the watching men below—"have been selected to bid on her because you are among those blessed by Huitzilopochtli. You've seen into your future and know how much depends on your success with her and what happens if you fail. Now, who has the courage to accept this challenge?"

With his words, the air seemed to grow heavier and darker. The men's expressions were all somber, putting her in mind of America's political and military leaders in times of crises. But what did this have to do with her? And what—

"Begin."

Stifling a cry took all her concentration. By the time she'd gotten a fragile hold on her emotions, the bidding had begun.

Yes, bidding. On her.

But although she understood the men's gestures and the pace of what was taking place, she no longer comprehended a word of what anyone was saying. They spoke in clicks and grunts. Fear threatened to swallow her. Weak, she took a chance on coming down off her toes. Masked-man didn't stop her, and in an insane way she wanted to thank him for his kindness. Unable to look at those who might soon command her future, she studied her surroundings.

A pyramid dominated the landscape; it stood between her and the afternoon's sun and cast a great shadow over everything. It had to be well over a hundred feet high, flawlessly constructed as far as she could tell, with two identical houselike structures at the top accessible by so many narrow, steep stairs that just thinking about climbing them made her legs ache.

Flawless? Incredible workmanship? New, or nearly so?

The why and how of what she was doing here defied comprehension; it was easier to admire the pyramid. She'd seen pictures of ruins in Egypt and elsewhere and drawings that supposedly duplicated what they'd looked like originally, but this was form and function.

And she was standing not far from its base.

Being auctioned off.

A cold shudder ran through her. Her mind numb again, she watched as one of the seated men got to his feet and walked up the steps. When he held out his hand, masked-man turned her leash over to him.

"You belong to me now," the newcomer informed her in flawless English.

That voice! Shaking, she focused. *Mazati!*

She waited for his touch, his taste and smell. He'd claim her breasts and pussy, paint her belly and thighs with his incredible fingers, and teach her the meaning of ownership. Of belonging.

What's happening? she begged with her eyes and body language. *What are you doing here? What am I?*

I have no choice. Otherwise I am sentenced to an endless half life. As for you, only the gods know if you have the magic.

Before she could reply, Mazati of the midnight gaze began to fade, as did the platform, pyramid, and her bonds. Everything sank into the swirling mist, reminding her of leaves being borne away by a creek or slow-moving river. *Don't leave! Please, don't leave.*

But why should she want to stay in a world where she was considered a commodity, a piece of merchandise?

Drifting formless as he'd done so many times, Mazati mentally replayed the scene he'd just handed to Hayley. He'd taken so many chances because so much was at stake. But although she could and maybe should have rejected the images, he had no choice but to try. Otherwise . . .

Shaking off what could wait for the night, he concentrated on how she'd looked. She was soft, smooth flesh, warm breath, fear, courage, and curiosity. He loved the sound of her voice and her long, capable fingers, but he'd be a fool if he let those things distract him from his mission. To begin he would make her his and mold her as he needed to mold her. If nothing was left of her at the end, maybe it didn't matter as long as she served as his link to the present.

But maybe it did.

Slender fingers topped by expensive acrylic nails closed around Hayley's shoulder and shook her. "Wake up. Oh, kid, back to the here and now."

Gasping, Hayley looked up to see her sister standing over her. Although Saree was real, lush flesh and blood as only Saree could be, nothing else really made sense. The world she'd been sucked into was still easing into the fog, and if she reached out, could she force Mazati to remain with her?

No, you don't want that!

Smiling her full-lipped smile, Saree perched rather than sat beside her on the bench. "Damn, you should see the look on your face. You need to get some sleep, kid. Either that or cut back on the vino. You were sure as hell out of it. If you were dreaming of getting bonked, let me in on it."

Good old Saree, nothing conservative about her. Of course, given the way she earned her living, being conservative was hardly an asset. And right now Hayley needed to connect with the world she shared with her sister. "I didn't hear you coming," she not too intelligently came up with.

"No shit. What are you doing out here? I thought you'd be inside blowing the family fortune, such as it is."

"Huh, oh, no reason."

"Bull. I know what those flushed cheeks of yours are saying. Something, or rather someone's, got you turned on. You waiting for some stud to join you?"

"I wish." Giving up on her lame attempt to sidestep her sister's curiosity, she grabbed Saree's hand. "There's, ah, there is a man in there. He's running one of the booths, one with some incredibly beautiful fire opals, especially the black ones."

"Then I repeat, what the fuck are you doing out here?"

"It was—hell, it was overwhelming."

"What was? Getting turned on?"

Once again Saree had nailed things, at least the turned-on part. All that was left for her to do was nod.

"So let's go gawk at him." Saree stood, tugging on Hayley's shirt sleeve in an attempt to get her to follow suit. "I wanna see. Do a little drooling of my own."

"I don't—"

"The hell you don't."

When Saree tugged again, Hayley got to her feet but couldn't convince herself to take a step. "I've never felt like that just from looking at a man," she admitted. "Like I was poleaxed or something." *Tell her about the dream or fantasy or whatever the hell it was.*

Yeah, right.

"Not poleaxed. That's what they do to oxen, I think. Fucking on the brain's more like it."

"Enough!" Startled by her tone, Hayley squeezed her sister's fingers. "I'm sorry. I'm just not as, ah, unrestrained as you are."

"Occupational hazard. Did you talk to him?"

"Yes. Briefly. About opals." *And he said he knew me and maybe I had magic in me—or something insane like that.*

"Hmm. A start. So do you want to talk opals some more or get down and dirty?"

Down and dirty, in spades. Bonk. Fuck. "That'd be jumping the gun but—hell, maybe I'm crazy, but I think he was sending out vibes. Not quite coming on to me but—"

"Did you get any vibes?"

She fanned herself with her free hand. "Sure did."

"Then he was sending. Look, sis, you've been through hell in a handbasket thanks to my ex- and unlamented brother-in-law. As a consequence, you're wondering what went wrong between you and the opposite sex and asking yourself if you ever want anything to do with them again, right?"

"Yeah."

"Damn that Cal! If you believe nothing else I tell you, believe this. Nothing went wrong on your part and you sure as hell deserve to spread your legs and have a certain hole filled again."

This time Hayley didn't try to tone Saree down because the truth was, her beyond-liberated sister was voicing what she'd been working up to on her own over the past few weeks. "So how do I let him know, assuming he isn't an ax murderer?"

"That's why you have me as your one and only sister," Saree said as she started dragging her toward the building. "I'll modestly point out that I'm a pro when it comes to the male animal. Part of the job requirements and perks."

"You're a pro at getting tied up and having climaxes forced out of you," Hayley pointed out, careful to keep her voice down. "Are you sure that makes you an expert when it comes to men?"

"Who the hell cares? It beats pounding a keyboard for some shit of a boss."

Ouch. Ouch and good point. Buoyed by Saree's in-your-face approach to life, to say nothing of the return to reality, she opened the large door and led the way into the showroom. With her silicone-enhanced, flame-haired sister as backup, she no longer felt overpowered by the crowd, although maybe the truth was that anticipating another look at the mysterious and erotic Mazati was responsible. Mazati? What kind of name was that?

And what had he and his companions been doing during whatever the hell she nearly believed had happened to her?

"Don't tell me," Saree said. "Let me check out the merchandise and see if I can figure out who's soaking your pants."

"Gee. It's a good thing our aunt can't hear you."

"That's why I'd make a good actress. I know what role to play when. With you, I can be earth-slut."

Not a word. Don't give her anything to play off of.

Hayley kept a step behind her sister as they made the rounds. She could have pointed out that picking out stud-studly wasn't going to be difficult since about half of the vendors were women and most of the men were hardly capable of soaking anyone's pants. Still, she wanted to study Saree's reaction since, as a submissive role player in the porn industry, Saree had been manhandled by countless men and had developed an instinct about who could be trusted and who couldn't. Hayley had seen most if not all of Saree's bondage videos and would be the first to admit that the men her sister worked with were out-and-out hunks.

And if truth be known, she'd lost too much sleep wanting the same for herself.

"Oh, shit." Following the line of Saree's finger, Hayley found herself looking at Mazati, who at the moment was leaning forward with his hands braced on the table as he listened to the man talking to him.

"Shit on a shingle." Saree panted. "The real deal."

"A stud?" Hayley ventured through suddenly numb lips.

"Nah. Stallion. Bull elk. Damn, if he ordered me onto my back with my legs gaping, I'd probably break my neck getting into position. Shit, shit, shit."

There might have been more than three shits strung together, but Hayley wasn't counting. How could she since Mazati had just lifted his head, and their eyes were truly meeting across a crowded room?

You're back, his gaze said.

Y-es.

What did you think of what happened?

Are you talking about that—that dream?

Not a dream, an introduction to what I have to offer you.

You mean being restrained and sold?

I mean tapping into your primitive nature and letting me become your world.

Letting? You forced me.

Did I?

4

"He's coming on to you," Saree whispered. "You and you alone."

You think so? No, she wasn't going to play stupid when she had no doubt of the truth. "This is a first. Usually I play second fiddle to you."

"Another occupational hazard, unfortunately. How do you feel about being first in line this time?"

Concerned that Mazati might be a lip reader in addition to the rest of his talents, she placed her hand in front of her mouth. "Like he's walking over my skin."

Grinning, Saree too shielded what she was saying. "I get the physical reaction. Hell, sis, I can smell your you know what. I'm talking about emotionally."

"I'm not sure what I'm feeling. I've never had this intense a reaction to a man I just laid eyes on."

"No shit? That's a damn shame. Well, you know what they say about jumping into the deep end. Don't make the poor man wait for you."

Hayley had the unsettling thought that Mazati was absolutely positive she'd close the distance between them and that the net he'd thrown over her would hold. But then what was wrong with nets? Or leather cuffs.

Cuffs? Letting someone else take the reins?

Knees knocking more than a little, she wove and ducked her way through those currently looking at what Mazati had to offer. Saree of the bold and fearless approach followed in her wake.

Close enough to hear Mazati's rolling, deep tones now, Hayley planted her feet so she could absorb both the words themselves and the energy behind them. He was advising the man looking up at him that because of their fragility opals weren't the best stones to buy for his teenage daughter who'd recently expressed an interest in jewelry making.

"I appreciate your honesty," the man said, "even if it means you missed out on a sale."

His expression unreadable, Mazati glanced at her. "It doesn't matter. I've accomplished what I needed to, finally."

"Hmm. Then you've done better than most of the vendors. I've heard some grumbling about slow sales."

"For me, it isn't about money exchanging hands."

Looking confused, the man put down the opals he'd been holding and wandered off. Hayley would have been content to go on staring at Mazati, but obviously Saree didn't feel the same way because, after planting her hand in the small of Hayley's back, she shoved. "Go get him, tiger," she hissed. "Although to be accurate, he's the tiger."

Yes, he is, Hayley admitted as she stared up and into those arresting eyes. She vaguely recalled that the big cat's eyes were yellow, but that was splitting hairs and she certainly didn't care about hairs at this moment. In truth, beyond calling up memories of what his hands had felt like on her body in her fantasy, she couldn't say she cared about a single thing in this big old round world.

"Sis," Saree snapped after who knew how long. "You said you were going to introduce me to your new *friend.*" Not giving Hayley time to react and respond, Saree held out her hand indicating she expected Mazati to shake it. "Never mind my suddenly stupid sibling," she told a bemused-looking Mazati. "I'm capable of doing the deed." She waited for Mazati to close his fingers over hers. "I trust you won't think I'm being too bold. Even if you do, I don't much give a shit because I had no intention of leaving here without meeting you. To state the obvious, I'm Hayley's sister."

"I know you are, Saree."

Suddenly tense, Saree pulled her hand free. "Hayley, did you tell him—"

"No, she didn't." Mazati lowered his arm to his side, his gaze taking in both women. "I'm an intuitive man, Saree. Also committed and determined. I trust Hayley mentioned that."

"Some—something like that."

"You're flustered, Saree. That doesn't often happen to you."

Squaring her shoulders, Saree planted her hands on the edge of the display table. "You don't know me at all, whoever you are. If you did, you'd know that nothing about men intimidates me."

"I'm not *men*. I'm me. You're right; you have no delusions about men because your career brings you into contact with them when they're stripped down to their most primitive. The same thing happens to you, which can be unfortunate because too much of the time you fail to see them as more than cocks."

Ignoring Saree's hiss, Mazati turned his attention to Hayley. The moment he did, Hayley knew she'd become the core of his interest and that nothing, not even the sexy Saree, mattered. The question of why he'd choose her over a knock-'em-dead-gorgeous gal like Saree surfaced only to be swept away. His eyes did more than study her. They sucked her into his world, a world which existed in a time and place she couldn't begin to comprehend but right now didn't question.

Are you ready for the next step? he asked.

Yes.

As her silent word fell away, the red mist rose from wherever it had been waiting, lapping first at the edge of her vision but quickly and smoothly drifting out in all directions. Hot and cold at the same time, it wrapped her in anticipation. Where was it taking her this time? And would she survive?

The large, crowded room slipped away. For several moments she knew nothing, waited, breathed. Her heart beat. Lightning slid over her skin. Then the thick red veil lifted, sliding slowly away as if understanding that she needed time to take everything in.

A different pyramid.

At first it took everything she had simply to comprehend and accept that she was standing at the base of a massive stone structure that looked as if it was reaching for the sun. Like the other it was gray with shades of brown thrown in, hard and harsh and lifeless in contrast to the wealth of green vegetation surrounding it. She couldn't begin to count the number of steps, and when her neck started to ache from looking up, she stopped trying to see the top.

Heavy vines and thick, moisture-fed trees? If she could believe her surroundings and limited understanding of pyramids, this wasn't Egyptian.

Tropical.

Mexico?

Blood pulsed against her temples as she reached out and touched the nearest stone slab. She expected it to be cold so the heat startled her. Then she became aware of the sun on the back of her neck and acknowledged that not even rock remained untouched. There was no breeze, and no sound stood between her and her thoughts. It had taken thousands if not tens of thousands of people to build the pyramid, but it was deserted—except for her.

Why is this happening? What's the meaning and why am I part of it?

Although she knew neither the sun nor jungle would answer her questions, she repeated them before giving up. The first time she'd been sucked into the past had been frightening enough, but maybe this was worse because she was so utterly alone. Caught someplace with no way of knowing how to get out.

When her thigh and calf muscles tightened, she half expected to start running away. Instead, she watched almost dispassionately as she lifted her right leg and planted her foot—her bare foot—on the bottom step. The stone felt rough. Hands now pressed over her breasts, she took a second step and then a third. Because she couldn't bring herself to contemplate how much effort it would take to reach the top, she concentrated on her feet. Maybe it was nothing more than her suddenly acute hearing, but a drumbeat seemed to announce each time her sole came in touch with whatever the pyramid had been made out of.

Climb. Climb. Keep going.

But although she could stay on her feet almost indefinitely in the world she knew and understood and had always inhabited, what she was doing here stole the air from her lungs and left her gasping, scared and disoriented, excited.

Hot. It was so incredibly hot. How could whoever had built the pyramid have worked under these conditions?

Two steps later she faced facts; the heat came from her, not the sun. Anticipation rolled through her to ignite nerves and speed the blood coursing along her veins. Did she really expect her reaction to be less intense? After all, the first time she'd been pulled into the past, she'd wound up being sold and bought.

Would that happen again? Was that why—

As if drawn by an invisible force, she looked up and to her

left. The sun was behind a male figure, making it impossible for her to make out features. But she didn't need to because her body knew whom that form belonged to. As she stared at the height and breadth of the man dressed only in what she took to be a loincloth, she sensed a reaching out on his part that had nothing to do with hands and arms. Instead, his energy, his force, circled her. He *touched* her throat and the space between her breasts, spun down and around them, came up on the outsides, pressed against soft and electrified flesh until her breasts nearly met. He stroked her hips with hot and rough fingertips, closed in on her belly only to slide lower. Whimpering, she widened her stance and arched her pelvis toward him. Rough heat worked between her legs.

"Oh god, god."

"I'm not that," he replied with his fingers quiet against her labia. "Listen to me, Hayley. Listen and believe, at least try, please. Open your mind and welcome what comes to it. You didn't have to come here. If you hadn't wanted this, you would have fought the mist, and it would no longer exist."

How? she wanted to ask. *Why?* But she couldn't speak with her cunt weeping and her strength dying.

"With your presence here, our journey has begun."

"I don't understand." Was that faint whimper her voice?

"You will, in time. Feel me. Feel and understand. Trust." With that, he slipped a finger into her.

She was going to collapse! On the brink of a climax. Housing a stranger's finger and drenching it in her honest fluids. Letting him, letting him—

No!

He'd pulled out of her, no!

"What just happened is a taste of what's ahead of you, if you have the courage for it. Do you?"

Crazed with need, she struggled to focus. The sun was blinding, her body screaming. Caring about nothing except an end to this agony, she started to slide her hands between her legs only to discover that she was wearing the slacks she'd put on this morning.

"Do you have the courage?"

"I'm—I'm trying."

"Thank you. And you're ready for the next step?"

Shit, shit, shit, what's happening? "Y-es."

"Thank you, woman of today. Your slacks, take them off."

Whether he'd spoken or she'd sensed what was a cross between a command and a request didn't matter as she reached for the button at her waist. Her numb fingers trembled so that it took several tries to complete the task. The zipper came easier, and she started to slide the fabric down her hips, then stopped.

Insane!

"I won't hurt you."

"I know you won't." Her words came from a place she'd never before tapped.

"Because the stakes are too great for me. Now, your sandals."

Once again blind obedience spun over her. As she crouched to unfasten the buckles, she pondered how she could have felt the rough steps while wearing shoes, but the answer would have to wait for later—if ever. Straightening, she kicked out of the flimsy footwear. How tall he was, how strong.

"Finish what you started. Take off those slacks, for both of us."

Sucked into his tone, she hurried to complete the task. If she thought while exposing her stomach and buttocks, she was unaware of it. Not until she started sliding her thumbs over her thighs did self-preservation and dignity return to still her hands.

"Now."

"I'm not yours to command."

"Maybe not, but a part of you wants to turn control over to me."

How could he possibly know of her fantasy about letting a man call the shots in her life, a man who put her first? Unnerved, she obeyed. After stepping out of the garment, she stood with her hands dangling at her side, her head lowered, alive and weak.

"The blouse."

Technically speaking, it wasn't a blouse because there weren't any buttons, but as she pulled the fabric over her head, she only wondered if she'd ever wear it again.

He held out his hand so she gave him the top. Then, as she'd done before, she waited with her arms useless at her sides and her nipples pressing against the practical white bra. Did he find her beautiful? At least attractive? Desirable?

What would happen when he was done with her?

"Panties."

Because she'd known this was coming, she should have been prepared, somehow. But exposing her sex was something she'd done only selectively as an adult and never in front of a stranger.

Made of soft cotton, her panties offered no resistance against her skin, and when she sucked in her stomach, they might have slipped off if it hadn't been for her hipbones. As she worked the cotton over her prominent bones, she ordered herself not to touch herself more than necessary, but her nails kept kissing her skin. The sensation dug in and buried itself in her pelvis. Shouldn't she be nervous, angry, confused?

Too late. You're in too deep.

Frightened by the thought, she stopped with the fabric bunched around the joining between pelvis and legs and her sex still hidden but far from safe.

"You can't fight this. It's going to happen."

"How can you say that? I don't want it to."

"Yes, you do."

Swimming in an erotic sea, drifting while his arms kept her safe and alive, desired. Trusting as she'd never trusted before and surrendering ownership of her body as a gift to the man who'd earned her trust.

Was that possible?

Incapable of thinking, she gripped the twisted fabric and tried to ignore the way her breasts strained the bra's seams. He was waiting her out, challenging her to doubt or disobey him. Could she stand like this until he'd given up on his insane mind game and released her?

Where would she go? Could she pick up the frayed fragments of her mind and life?

Did she want to?

Tell me what you want from me. Let me know where this is going and why. Help me, please help me.

Maybe he'd heard her plea and had decided to silence it because degree by degree her pussy heated. It was more than simple heat, an increased sensitivity, pulsing somewhere deep in her womb, juices escaping to coat her panties' crotch and slide down her inner thighs. She started rocking, moaning hopefully, silently, praying her legs would continue to support her, all but blind and the roaring in her head making her want to scream.

"Don't do this to me! Damn you, don't!" Her voice echoed against the pyramid.

"You're doing it to yourself."

"I'm not! Damn it, I'm not."

"Finish what we've begun today, Hayley. Prepare for the next step. If you don't, you'll have destroyed me."

"What are you saying?"

"Something I pray you'll understand, eventually."

The inescapable and maybe desperate words ricocheted in her mind. More frightened for him now than herself, she gripped her panties with such strength that she bent a fingernail backward. Wincing, she nearly released the cotton so she could suck on her injured finger. Instead, after a moment, she leaned forward and worked the fabric down her legs. Inch by inch she gave up all but the last of her modesty, and as the air rolled over her newly naked ass, she felt as if she was being caressed by a new breeze. When she couldn't bend over any more, she straightened and let gravity finish the job. Head down and yet feeling a new freedom, she stepped free.

"Pick them up. Give them to me."

Why not? After all, was this any more submissive than what she'd already done? And yet as she closed the distance between them so she could hand him what she'd just picked up, power surged through her. This was her hungry body! Let him see her like this, let him deal with it.

"Bra."

Maybe because she already felt naked, it took a moment for the word to register. Once it did, she could barely wait to free herself from the painful restriction. Her fingers had stopped shaking, and the moment she released the snaps, her swollen and hot breasts all but pushed the fabric away. She didn't linger over revealing her breasts as she'd done with her pussy. Instead, pride and challenge ruled as she flipped the useless garment at him.

Then she threw back her shoulders and held her head high. "Is that what you wanted?"

"Touch them. Caress them."

His words were both a promise and a challenge. Not sure which to address first, she closed her eyes and reached for the harder-than-usual orbs. The moment her fingertips touched the sensitive flesh, her mouth parted, allowing her to draw in a deep breath. She'd touched herself like this before, of course; foreplay was, after all, an essential element in bringing herself to climax now that she had no one to do it for her. Familiar with her body's wants and needs, she trailed her nails lightly over the outer edges. Her nubs tightened and cramped. Still, she drew out the moment when she'd satisfy their demands. Molecule by molecule, she came closer, bringing her fingertips into play as she did. The contrast between her own flesh and nerveless nails provided a tantalizing sensation. She could handle that all right, could please and pleasure her breasts and light them on fire. What she had less control over was her cunt's desperate demand.

My body. Mine to do what I must to it.

Following in the wake of that mind-expanding revelation, she sent her right hand between her legs.

"No!"

Startled, she struggled to remember that she wasn't alone in her bedroom after all. A stranger in a strange land had somehow convinced her to strip and that same stranger was responsible for the hand on her breast and the hunger between her legs.

My body. Staring at what she could see of him, she pressed the side of her hand against her pussy lips and rubbed. Once, twice, three hard—

"Stop it!"

With a whimper, she obeyed. The hand on her breast stilled; she tried not to think about the wet warmth she'd collected.

"That's not the way it has to be, Hayley." He sounded almost apologetic. "I hope you'll eventually understand and fully embrace it, but for now, you'll do what I must tell you to."

"Why?"

"It isn't important yet. You're turned on, aren't you?"

Much as she needed to deny her vulnerability, it was too late for that. Nodding, she looked down at her pebbled nub.

"And you'd do anything for a climax, wouldn't you?"

"Damn you." Hearing herself whimper again made her wince.

"What you think of me doesn't matter. I wish it did, but— you want to climax, don't you?"

"Y-es."

She thought he might laugh. Instead, he sighed. Long seconds later, he stepped closer. Bit by maddening bit he extended a hand toward her breast. A series of shudders ran through her, and once again she wasn't sure she had enough strength in her legs to go on standing. Maybe if she locked her knees or spread her legs a little.

His hand stropped moving. Crying under her breath, she leaned toward him. Inches still separated them. "Be still. Wait for your orders."

Not going to happen. In today's world, men didn't order women around. The sexes were equal, women in control of their bodies.

Then why wasn't she telling him that?

Because this wasn't her world and she desperately needed what he was ordering/offering.

Stay with me, Mazati thought. *I'm learning just as you are. More than learning, I'm rediscovering what it is to be alive, and I have no guidelines.*

5

Either the sun had lost some of its brightness or her eyes had finally adjusted. Whichever it was, she could now clearly see his features. His eyes held her, of course, but that wasn't all. He had an animal quality about him, a rough and wild air that both frightened and mesmerized her. Part of it, of course, was his near nudity marred only by that tantalizing scrap of fabric—or was it leather? Even his feet were bare. His hair looked as if it had been whacked at instead of cut, making her wonder whether he did it or if a woman had been responsible.

Although he'd been conservatively dressed at the gem show, he seemed more at ease here. Insane as the thought was, she now fully accepted that he'd had a hand in creating the pyramid and knew the surrounding jungle as well as she did her own home.

"Smell the air," he ordered. "Take the rich, ripe aroma into you. Make it part of you."

Filling her lungs gave her something to concentrate on, and as she did, she noted that the lush vegetation had a dankness about it, but wasn't much of Mexico—if that's where she was—

dry? Where had this rain-fed vegetation come from? On the brink of asking for an explanation, she clenched her teeth because she could only absorb so much at a time.

"You are no longer in your present," he told her. "I've taken you to where I began. Other things will be made clear to you once and if I believe you're ready, but first I must have compliance. Submission. Do you understand?"

A small part of her mind screamed defiance and denial and questions, but she barely heard the cry. Instead, her awareness began and ended with her nerve endings. Naked, she was naked. Standing before a magnificent and masterful man. Waiting and hungry.

"Good. Kneel."

No! Don't give in! If you do, you'll be lost.

"Kneel!"

Something hot and heavy wrapped itself around her, squeezing and embracing, holding her captive. She couldn't breathe and her heart pounded erratically. Fear lashed her, but it wasn't that simple, not with him so close and his eyes boring deep into her.

"This must happen, Hayley. My salvation depends on it."

"I—don't understand."

"Because you can't possibly, yet. Kneel, slave."

Slave? A whimper stuck in her windpipe, forcing her to rub her throat in an attempt to ease the sensation. As the terrifying feeling of not being able to breathe subsided, she discovered yet something new about herself. She was beginning to accept Mazati's command of her body. If he chose to prevent her from breathing, she couldn't and wouldn't try to stop him.

And if he wanted her to kneel . . .

She sank onto the step she'd been standing on. The rough surface dug into her knees. Suddenly she didn't know what to do with her hands or where to look; what, if anything, she could say. Confused and yet disconnected, she rested her hands on her knees and waited. She lacked the courage to lift her head.

"Good. You have taken the first step."

To what? she nearly asked, but did she really want to know? All she could see now were his legs, so she lost herself in studying the dark skin and even darker hairs; the strong, straight knees and powerful calf and thigh muscles. Then sharp pain in her own thighs drew her attention, and she discovered that she was digging her nails into herself. She'd give anything to be caressing him instead, anything!

"You are on a journey. We both are. I don't expect you to believe me, but the stakes are higher for me than they could possibly be for you. No matter what happens, you'll survive." He paused. "Today's lessons are powerful and vital and won't be easy for you, but I don't believe I have a choice. Do you understand?"

"I don't understand anything." Why did she sound like a lost child when she'd never felt more like a woman? "Are you saying you might not survive otherwise, might die?"

"I've been the same as dead for a long time. Look at yourself, slave. Tell me what you have done."

Wondering if he intended to shame her, she again pressed her nails into her thighs. This wasn't happening. No, it wasn't! No!

Grabbing her hair, he yanked her head up and back so she was forced to stare at him. Pain brought tears to her eyes, causing her to reach for his hand to force him to release her.

"No!" Capturing her wrist, he stepped behind her and twisted her arm up behind her back. "This is no longer your body, slave. It belongs to me."

"You're hurting me!"

"I bring both pleasure and pain." His grip on her hair and wrist held her in place, and although maybe she could have clawed him with her free hand, she didn't. "Sometimes the two sensations are separate. Sometimes, like now, they exist in the same space."

"Let me go."

"What did I just say, that your body belongs to me."

Any other time or place and she would be screaming for help while fighting with every bit of strength in her, but she was in his world—and didn't want out. Willing herself to remain still, she focused on the strain in her captured arm and the top of her head. Despite what he'd said about pain, that didn't accurately describe what she was feeling. True, these weren't sensations she would have chosen for herself, but they brought her to life and in the moment, focused on her body. The heat and energy she'd felt in her pussy earlier had returned. Plain and simple, her sex was waiting to see what he intended to do next, waiting and anticipating.

"I am still waiting for your answer. What have you done to yourself?"

"I—what do you want me to say?"

"Look at yourself. Speak the truth."

The truth. If she did as he commanded, would he release her? Did she want to be free? "I, ah, I took off my clothes."

"Did I force you or did you do so of your own free will?"

"I can't remember."

"Yes, you can."

He wasn't about to release her. She felt his patience and determination in the taut muscles so close to her. He was standing tall and proud and free while she'd placed herself on her knees before him, the difference between them simple and telling. Undeniable. "You, ah, you told me what to do, but I didn't object."

"Why not?"

Oh god, did she really have to say it? "I wanted to please you."

"Just me or did stripping yourself bring you pleasure?"

Her back was starting to ache, making it difficult for her to concentrate, but that wasn't the only reason she had to struggle to find words. Being a modern woman meant standing on her own two feet and fighting her own battles; dealing with everything life threw at her; paying her bills and being scared she'd never get out of the debt that had been imposed on her; and failing at her dream of having her own business. Now everything she'd believed about her place in the world had been turned on end. This man was in charge—of her.

"I—I was getting turned on."

"Are you still turned on?"

Yes. No. I don't know.

"Are you?"

"Nothing like this has ever happened to me. I don't know where I am or even what year it is. How do you expect—"

Before she could finish, Mazati released her. Determined to lessen the strain in her back, she lowered herself so her buttocks rested on her heels. The burning sensations backed off, which left her marginally more clear headed and even more aware of her body. It was almost as if her body was singing to her, not a gentle melody but a hard-driving rhythm that sent her temples to pounding.

"What are you feeling?"

Words gathered themselves, but if she told him the truth, she'd be even more exposed than she already was; and yet maybe it didn't matter because he'd already triggered her reaction and responses, and she had no doubt that he could do whatever he wanted to her, keep her here.

"What? Is trust really this hard for you?" He punctuated his question by stroking her right temple.

Trust, not surrender. Leaning into his caress, she looked up. Her gaze skimmed over his loincloth, then stopped. Until now she'd been afraid to study what little she could see of his cock because she sensed it would only fuel his power over her. He was, after all, in control while she—

Not total control. Not physically removed from what he felt compelled to put her through.

Her mouth dried and she started trembling, but she now knew she would look at his barely covered cock for as long as he allowed. The solid bulge beneath the simple and nearly inadequate covering made it absolutely clear that Mazati was erect. Aroused. She couldn't say whether his cock was simply large or off the scale, or if she could trust her conclusion. All that mattered was, somehow, housing it inside her. Whatever it took for that to happen, she'd do it.

"I've never wanted a man to take charge." She forced the words past her dry throat. "Not consciously at least."

"But subconsciously?"

"I don't know." Shocked by the whimpering tone, she tried again. "This isn't easy for me to say, but maybe you know anyway. Do you?"

"The truth needs to come from you."

Yes, it did. "I've sometimes had dreams, fantasized. I'm, ah, I wouldn't be surprised if most women do."

"What kind of dreams?"

He was pulling her deeper into something, someplace, but instead of fearing that dark cave, the challenge was restoring her, opening her. And it was already too late to turn back. "There are ropes on me, sometimes chains. I'm wearing a gag and have on a blindfold. I can't see what's happening or ask questions, but somehow I know."

"What do you know, slave?" He ran his hand under her hair and pressed against the back of her neck.

Electricity, lightning, even thunder ripped through her. "That I want this."

"To be someone's captive?"

"Not—not a captive." Speaking was so much work.

"What?"

"Owned. All right, owned! Surrendering responsibility. Letting someone else take over and trusting that person." Wrapping her hands around her upper arms, she started rocking back and forth. She didn't understand how things had come to this and had no knowledge of how to find her way out, if that's what she wanted. All she knew were her knees on the pyramid step and Mazati standing over her; being naked, her cunt soft and swollen. "Both of my parents died not that long ago. I had to be strong for them. And then my marriage fell apart. Hell, it more than fell apart. Can you blame me for wanting something other than the reality I've been facing?"

"But even if those things hadn't happened, a secret part of you wants to trust someone with your body, heart, and mind."

How can you possibly know that? "You sound pretty sure of yourself."

"Don't be afraid of the truth, slave. It's how it needs to be."

"Why? Why?"

"Many reasons."

She might have demanded an explanation if he hadn't positioned her arms down by her side. A strong, simple squeeze left no doubt that he expected her to leave them like that. Standing in front of her, he gripped her shoulders and pulled her toward him until her face was scant inches from his cock. Breathing raggedly, she opened her mouth.

"Not yet," he warned. "First, answers. What are you feeling?"

Thinking she'd already told him that, she looked up at him with her eyes filled with questions.

"What's happening to your body?"

"I told you; I'm turned on."

"Why? Have I done anything to stimulate you?"

Being near you is nearly more than I can handle. "You made me strip."

"How? By threatening or hurting you, forcing, maybe?"

"What do you want from me? Please, I don't know what—"

"For you to be honest with yourself, slave."

No more calling her a slave; she couldn't handle it! Still wondering how she might tell him that, she again opened her mouth. As she did, her lips brushed the loincloth. She was now almost certain it was made of leather, but she'd never felt any that was so soft, so supple. Her head started to roar again, and her pussy clenched. Caring about nothing else, she again ran her lips over what separated her from his cock.

There it was, the one thing that truly and fully proclaimed him as a man! The simple and yet complex organ not only ruled and controlled and drove men, it also commanded women.

Today Mazati's cock commanded her.

Lost in the roaring and her desperate pussy's needs, she began exploring his penis's contours. Her husband had wanted her to suck cock, and during the first few naïve months of their relationship, she'd enjoyed having him get off inside her mouth, but all too soon pleasure had become a duty and then repulsive. As a result, she'd believed she'd never want to have a man's cock against her teeth and tongue again, but Mazati had changed all that. If she thought it would do any good, she'd start gnawing on the loincloth. And if that didn't work, she'd tug and pull until she'd ripped it off him.

Licking, opening her mouth as wide as she could and trying to draw both his cock and the covering into her, fingers clenching, squeezing her butt cheeks together, she wanted to cry because so much of her own juice was flowing from her. All that and more swam through her awareness but none of it really mattered; only his hard heat did.

And his quick, harsh breathing.

He wasn't immune, wasn't completely in control. She'd gotten to him and could, maybe, somehow, bring him to his knees as she was.

Buoyed by possibilities, she moistened the inside of her lips and closed them around the straining, struggling organ. He leaned closer, then rocked away. A moment later, he rose onto his toes, but she came with him. If only she could use her hands, how simple it would be to rip his clothes off him.

But he'd ordered her to keep them by her side.

The corners of her mouth ached from being stretched so wide, and the leather was threatening to make her gag, but she couldn't bring herself to let him go. Shoving everything else from her mind, she turned her head to the side and raked her teeth over him. Even with the barrier, she relished the hard contact. Mazati jerked upright and then leaned forward, looming over her.

Ducking and turning her head even more brought her to the edge of the loincloth, which hung nearly to his knees. Much as she hated releasing what she had of him, she pushed the leather out of her mouth. The moment she did, he again grabbed her hair. No! She wouldn't be denied!

Eyes closed so she could concentrate, she shoved the loincloth aside with her chin. Then before it could fall back in place, she brought her mouth to the joining between thigh and pelvis. Her mouth filled with moisture, and she coated her tongue with it before licking his satiny flesh there. Again, he jerked upright. His breathing rasped. She was certain he'd say something, warn her or order her to stop, but he didn't. Was it possible he wanted this as much as she did?

Driven by something she didn't understand, she gripped the loincloth in her teeth and positioned it on the far side of his erection. Yes, this was what she needed, what she had to have! Leaning back a little, she studied his exposed cock. Full and hard and promising, it jutted out as if struggling to free itself from the rest of him. How she'd love to stroke the tip with her tongue, but that would have to wait until she had more self-control. Neither did she trust herself to mouth his balls or bathe the long, strong organ. Soon, yes, soon, but first—

She caught his rich, male scent. This was the smell of pre-cum and excitement, a hint of sweat, energy even. Personal grooming products proclaimed that everyone's goal should be to smell like their product, but they were wrong, so wrong! This was real, earth and sun and man.

The revelation swirling through her, she concentrated on what her body was trying to tell her. Yes, the caution that usually ruled her acknowledged that she was in dangerous territory and not just because she'd been ripped from her world. If she brought him into her mouth so his tip found the back of her throat, she'd never be the same. The memory of that intimacy would remain with her for as long as she lived. She'd be branded somehow, changed yet again, stripped even more naked than she already was, dangerously vulnerable.

It's worth it, her usually dormant submissive nature insisted. Yes, it was, she agreed. Whatever happened afterward, whatever the consequences, she'd always mourn what she didn't go after if she quit now.

Her decision made, she licked the side of his cock. Doing so forced his organ away from her, and she would have lifted her hand to hold him in place if her arms didn't retain the imprint of having been placed where he wanted them. His breathing had barely settled, and he was still holding on to her hair. Did he consider her the enemy, dangerous?

Too many questions, too much thinking.

After wetting her tongue again, she concentrated on bathing his scrotum, marveling at how smooth and warm he was there. Every time she ran her tongue over and under him, her cunt tightened, and it was all she could do not to sob in need. She was in heat, no doubt about it, a bitch in heat.

Gone where she'd never gone.

Amused by the thought that hormones had rendered her stupid to any need except breeding, she began running her lips over him so the sensation became silk against silk, raw breath against raw breath, hot energy flowing into more of the same. She now rocked back and forth with her belly and buttocks tight and her pussy trapped and inflamed. There was no rhythm to the way he jerked on her hair; maybe he didn't know what he was doing. She wondered if he was aware of the way he was breathing or that he'd turned toward her, giving her nearly complete access to him.

A gift, the gift of him.

Her mouth opened, stretched. She didn't know whether her eyes were open or closed or even whether she was still breathing because she'd started to draw his cock into the only home she could offer him until and unless he allowed her to open her legs to him. Filling and invading her, becoming part of her and demanding that she become part of him. Even as she continued to work him deeper, she acknowledged the shudder running through her. This was fucking, giving and surrendering, becoming vulnerable.

Calling on the strength in her thighs, she rose off her haunches and deepened her hold. Settling down again, she leaned back, drawing him with her. She thought he'd arched his spine, but unless he pulled free, she didn't care whether he was trying to distance himself from her. After pushing him out a little, she shifted her focus to his head and repeatedly tightened her lips around him. Every time she slackened her hold he sighed.

When her jaw muscles protested, she let him slide free. Her legs were growing numb and tension had clamped hold of her shoulders, making it difficult for her to concentrate on anything else, but she couldn't bring herself to ask permission to stand or even change position. And did she want to? Her cunt was alive, wet and insistent but not so much so that she couldn't retain control over its needs.

She needed to fuck, to wrap her arms and legs around him

and ride his cock until they both exploded, but as long as she didn't take the risk of moving, she could draw out the anticipation, play with him, tease him as he was teasing her.

Was he? Yes, he'd compelled her to strip and kneel before him, and now his finger pads pressed against her scalp, but she was free, white, and over twenty-one. She'd chosen to mouth-fuck him, and a moment ago, she'd decided to let him go. If he didn't like that, she'd head on down the road.

What road?

6

Something swirled in Hayley's mind. Electric fibers seemed to bounce against the sides of her skull and then tangle together, becoming hotter with each contact. She didn't want to fear what was happening but couldn't help it; thinking only further unnerved her. One thing she knew: the sensations were tied in to what was happening between her and a man that, only yesterday, she hadn't known existed.

"What are you thinking?"

"I—nothing." She started to look at his cock, then closed her eyes. He was huge! Dominating.

"You're again questioning what's happening, aren't you?"

"Can you blame me?" she snapped with her eyes still sealed shut. "This is insane. Where are we? What are you doing to me?"

"Open your eyes."

Angry at both of them, she did as he commanded. Something that wasn't quite a smile worked its way across his mouth. She lacked the strength to free herself from his harsh glare, and when he cupped his cock and aimed it at her mouth, she pressed her tongue against the tip. Then, although he still held his cock ready for her, she drew her tongue back into her mouth. The sweet, heady taste of pre-cum sent a charge through her.

"I don't like this! It's insane."

"It's necessary."

"You said that before but it makes no damn sense. My knees are killing me, and I'm getting a sunburn and we're supposed to be anywhere except here."

"You want to fuck me."

"I do not!"

"Yes, you do."

Arguing wasn't going to get her anywhere. Besides, she'd had more than enough of kneeling before him like the slave he insisted on calling her. Strength surged through her as she planted her hands on the step in preparation for getting to her feet.

"No." Clamping his hands over her shoulders, he once more kept her in place. The loincloth slipped back in place, which should have comforted her but didn't. Had she already been trembling when he placed his hands on her or was the pressure on the nerves at the back of her neck responsible?

"What do you want?" She was whimpering again.

"You, Hayley, you. I need you to belong to me."

"No, no." Suddenly, no matter how much she willed it, she couldn't muster the fortitude to try to stand. How could she with the way he was holding on to her, his again-hidden cock inches from her mouth? He was standing over her as if he owned her. As if his life depended on his control over her.

"Don't move," he ordered. "I'm going to get something." With that, he released her, turned his back on her, and strode away. Instead of taking advantage of the unexpected freedom, she knelt where he'd left her and studied the way his naked buttocks rolled with every step. He wasn't Native American and she didn't think he was Hispanic. What was he? More importantly, who and what had he turned her into?

When he reached the end of the step, he turned right and kept walking. A moment later he was out of sight, making her wonder if he intended to walk all the way around the pyramid. If that was his plan then she had more than enough time to get the hell out of here.

But where would she go, damn it? And how could she ever make that decision when she didn't know where she was?

She was still trying to answer these incredibly complex questions when he appeared again, carrying what looked like a leather bag that was filled with something. After everything she'd been through a simple bag shouldn't unnerve her, but it did because she knew it was intended for her. He didn't appear surprised to find her where he'd left her. Neither did he say anything about what he had in mind.

After placing his burden on the step, he opened the drawstring and reached in. Fixing his gaze on her, he drew something out and held it up so she could see. A strip of leather maybe two inches wide with a loop woven into it and some kind of buckling or fastening, long enough for—what?

Even before he started to place it around her neck, she knew: a collar. Not a twin of the one she'd *imagined* on herself before but close. Although instinct screamed that she needed to run, she struggled to remain motionless. The instant the leather and metal lightly caressed her skin, she relaxed. Despite its weight and undeniable purpose, she responded to the sleek, soft leather. Perhaps he was deliberately slowing his motions to give her time to accept what he had in mind, but it wasn't enough because how could any woman comprehend going from freedom to slavery in a single gesture?

Run. Kick him where it counts. Get the hell out of here.

But none of those things were going to happen because the

touch of leather against flesh was seeping into her, calming and gentling and protecting her. And if she was honest with herself, the impact went far beyond wiping away her nervousness. A restraint around her neck couldn't possibly reach all the way to her cunt; the human body didn't work that way.

Hers did.

"Straighten. Throw your shoulders back and arch your spine. Accept your submission with pride."

He wasn't just speaking words, wasn't simply giving her a command, because the impact went far deeper than obedience or defiance. If she took this single step, she'd never be the same again. For the rest of her life, she'd be tied to this man, and although she could only guess at the depth and breadth of those ties, only one thing mattered.

Did she have the courage to obey?

No, the modern woman she believed herself to be insisted.

Yes, the slave she needed to become begged.

Memories and impressions blipped through her consciousness. She recalled the day she'd graduated from high school, the night she'd come across an accident and held a traumatized woman's hands until the ambulance arrived, the mix of awe and fear and longing during that week when she'd thought she was pregnant, the phone call from her father telling her that her beloved grandfather had died, her parents' lingering illnesses and funerals, holding her sister while they'd both cried. Those realities and thousands more made up the fabric of her life, while Mazati and his collar challenged her to enter a new one.

Learning why he'd chosen her was vital. What he needed and intended her to do and become were questions she needed answers to, but the answers wouldn't come today. Only proof of his control.

Sis, you understand this stuff, this bondage business. Help me!

But Saree had no experience in—in—what was this?

It didn't matter. Nothing did beyond the crying need between her legs.

Trembling and yet deep down peaceful, she did as he'd commanded, taking pride in her ability to dismiss her sore knees. Stretching her neck as best she could to fully accommodate this proof of his claim on her, she waited. The strong, supple strap closed around her. He hadn't fastened it yet, maybe because he understood she needed time to adjust to each change in her world, and if she could think how to form the words, she would have already told him that it was all right. She was ready.

There. A faint click in back. The metal ring now rested against her throat, making her wonder if it could somehow sense when she swallowed. Releasing the collar, Mazati rested his hands on her shoulders, which made her wonder if he was concerned with calming her. After a moment, she lifted her hands and fingered her new *jewelry*. She loved necklaces; of all the jewelry she'd created and hoped to create, necklaces were at the top of the list, but she would have never chosen something like this. Not only did the leather lack any distinctive pattern, it was too solid. Jewelry should be a fashion statement whether it be fun or serious, offbeat or pretentious. This said one thing: *ownership.*

Mazati owned her?

No, she amended, it hadn't come to that, yet. But the journey had begun and her sex still wanted nothing else.

"Stand."

Easier said than done, she was forced to admit, but he must have known that her legs had gone numb, because he helped her up. He was so close that she felt his heat all through her body, and although that unnerved her, she couldn't bring herself to move. Standing here was like sharing the same air, the same space, the same thoughts even. He was feeding her new reality to her one small piece at a time, and the only way she'd reach the end of the journey was by taking it at his pace and under his direction.

"There's more I must do."

She nodded. And when he pulled a length of rope out of the bag, she nodded again. He took hold of her right elbow and turned her so her back was to him, but instead of tensing and looking behind her to see what he had in mind, she let her head sag and waited. From waist to knees a fire burned. She desperately needed to press her legs together, to rub her crotch, to do whatever it took to quiet the flames. One more second, maybe two. And if he didn't bring her a measure of relief by then, she'd jump him. Mount him. Fuck him.

Perhaps oblivious to her screaming hunger, perhaps ignoring it while he did what he had to, he looped the rope around her elbows and drew them together. Feeling the strain in her shoulders, she straightened. He kept tugging until she was afraid he intended to force her elbows to touch, but just as she was forming her protest, he knotted the rope in place. Then he spun her around so she was facing him again.

"Feel it, slave. Accept."

Oh god, she was! It had taken only a single rope to render her arms useless. Her hands were free; there were no restraints on her wrists, nothing like handcuffs. Instead, he'd given her no choice but to arch her back, which thrust her breasts toward him. Maybe it was seeing herself predominately displaying her breasts with their hard-as-hell nipples revealing so much that turned her inward and downward. She'd become a sexual object, a naked, tethered, and collared sex toy in the hands of a master.

"What do you feel?"

"Hungry." The admission burst out of her. "Turned on."

"Scared?"

"I don't know."

"Are you afraid of me?"

She should be absolutely terrified of this man, shouldn't she, but she'd never needed to be more honest than she did at this moment. "No."

"Of yourself?"

Ah, there it was, the core of everything. Sucking in hot air did nothing to clear her mind, and the heat too quickly found its way to her pussy. Moaning in sexual pain, she ground her thighs together. "I've never felt like this before, so—so horny. What have you done to me?"

"It's not me. You're responsible for this."

"I can't be! Damn it, I know my body."

"Do you?"

The truly honest answer would be that she didn't know anything about anything today, but she'd just given him as much as she could. Any more and she'd feel as if her skin had been ripped away, leaving her totally and irreparably exposed. "What do you want from me, sex? You didn't have to do this." She tried to move her arms.

"What I need goes far deeper than sex, but you're right. That's the trigger."

Maybe a cloud had drifted over the sun because his features darkened. The mystery unnerved her. Her cunt was alive, her clit aching, nipples so hard they hurt. Sweat drenched her and her lungs kept demanding more oxygen. Maybe she was going to explode!

"No more! Damn it, I can't handle any more of this."

"You can and you will."

"No!" She backed away, careful not to get too close to the edge of the step, but before she could put enough distance between them, he looped a forefinger through the ring in her collar and dragged her back to him. She tried to reach for him but of course the elbow tie made that impossible, and he was forcing her head down, threatening her balance. "Stop it! Damn you, stop!"

"This is what you need."

"The hell it is!" Pressure on the back of her neck from the leather brought tears to her eyes, but she could still see her now-hanging breasts. Everything came down to this, didn't it? She'd become a sex object.

"This battle and others to come are necessary for me, slave. Otherwise, I'll remain in hell."

"What are you talking about?"

Not answering, he released the ring, but before she could fully straighten, he clamped his fingers around her nipples. Pulling up, he forced her to meet his eyes. She read hunger in them, a sexual starvation of his own that fed her need.

"Do you want me to feel sorry for you?" she asked.

"I don't expect that, certainly not until you understand. But before that can happen, you need to know more about your body. That's my first task."

He was throwing too much at her, expecting her to think when her nipples burned and a flood had erupted in her. She could smell herself. Her inner thighs were drenched and she would have given years of her life for his cock to be buried deep in her.

"I've waited long enough," he told her. "It's time to begin."

What did he call what they'd been doing? she wanted to throw at him. But she was too deep inside herself, too tapped into craving for words.

"First, we have to finish climbing."

From where they were standing, she could barely see the top, not that it mattered because she had absolutely no interest in taking in the view up there. Determined to change his mind, she closed the distance between them and rubbed her breasts against his heat. His hands knotted, and his breathing left no doubt that she'd gotten to him. It didn't seem possible, but she could have sworn his cock was becoming even larger as it prodded her belly. If only she could work it between her legs and then clamp down, trapping him against her pussy!

Growling low in his throat, he shoved her away and again reached into his bag. She stared at the rope with a clip on the end. Closing his free hand around the back of her neck, he forced her to lean forward. Then he easily secured the clip and rope to her ring. A dog on a leash! She'd become his pet!

"Don't do this, please."

"You want it. I need it." With that, he grabbed the bag and began climbing, dragging her behind him. Maybe she could have resisted but then what? With her arms useless, she was hardly in a position to run down the pyramid, and she wasn't foolish enough to think she could outrun him.

But those weren't the only reasons she trailed meekly after him. What was it he'd said, that the time had come for her to understand her body? She might not have reached the level he wanted her to, but she'd never felt more alive or needy. She didn't know whether to fear her clit's desperate demands for satisfaction or bury herself in the promise of what it was capable of experiencing. A climax. Her kingdom, her life for a climax!

By the time they reached the top, her hunger had lost its intensity because trudging up one step after another using nothing except her leg muscles was exhausting. The sun stroked her back and buttocks and thighs. Not once had she looked at anything except Mazati's ass and legs. Much as she wanted to know why they had to do this, she didn't speak. Everything about their time together was happening at his pace and under his direction, and she had no hope of that changing. Even more important, she wanted him as she'd never wanted another man. Whatever it took to receive his gift, she'd do it.

Somehow.

"For the lesson to take hold and become part of you, I need

you to concentrate fully on what I'm doing and your body's reactions." When he released the leash, it settled between her breasts. The end brushed her mons. If only it was longer! If only she could rub it over her labia, anything!

By the time she realized that he was once again reaching into the bag, it was too late to do anything except stare and accept. This time he'd retrieved a short length of doweling with thin straps fixed to it. Because she'd seen a number of her sister's videos, she knew what it was: a gag. She reflexively turned her head to the side when he pressed the doweling against her lips, but he kept after her until she was forced to open her mouth. Once it was securely between her teeth, he quickly and efficiently buckled it in place. She could growl and moan and cuss, but whatever she said would be unintelligible. He'd rendered her silent because he needed her to concentrate on her body.

What are you going to do? Oh god, what!

Closing his thumbs and forefingers over her breasts, he pulled her close. "Not many women have your courage, or needs. That, in part, I believe, is why I finally found you through the opals. If you didn't have this capacity for submission, I'd fail. Whatever it takes, for both of us, I must succeed."

Unnerved by his less-than-steady tone, she tried to swallow but the wood made that impossible, and she started to drool. Compared to what was happening in her crotch, it was nothing.

"You believe you want many things from life—financial security, the means to create something of beauty, love, and health—but first and foremost you are a woman. A sexual creature."

She could hardly deny that. Even helpless and under his control, she wanted to fuck him more than she wanted to breathe.

"You'll do anything for a climax, anything."

No. She shook her head. *No!*

His features impassive, he clamped down on her nipples.

Tears sprang to her eyes. At the same time, her cunt clenched. A climax, close! Pain spinning into need. "What's happening to you, slave? You're alive, unbelievably alive." Still holding tight to her nipples, he started moving her breasts in circles. Sensation plunged through her, and like everything else that had happened since she'd lost her grip on reality, response centered in her cunt.

"This is your weakness, and your strength."

She continued to shake her head as he forced her to make one and then two circles around him. Being led by a leash had made her feel less than human, while this reminded her of how purely female she'd become. Maybe she could have pulled free, but the thought of the pain that would cause kept her trotting—that and the hot clenching. He was right; she felt both weak and strong, helpless and strangely in control.

His movements slowed, which allowed her to lift her head a little. Now that she was no longer staring at her artificially elongated breasts, her attention fixed on her captor's chest. Captor?

"You want to have sex with me. Not just my putting my cock into your mouth but you spreading your legs while I spear you."

Although she still plodded after him, she was no longer thinking about her breasts. Even the fury buried deep in her moved to the back of her mind as she concentrated on his words. Yes, she wanted to be skewered on his cock. Yes, she would lie on her back and spread her legs for him. And if he commanded her to stand on her head while he penetrated her ass, she'd find a way to do that too.

Oh god, what was he doing to her?

Suddenly, as completely as she'd turned into his puppet, pride and independence claimed her, and she glared at him. She was biting down so hard on the wood in her mouth that her jaws ached.

"What is it, slave? Rebellion?"

"Go—to—hell."

"What's that? I can't hear what you're saying."

No, she wouldn't say anything that would goad him into humiliating her. Neither was she going to play his stupid and dangerous games. As for the turmoil churning through her— well, to hell with that too. Planting her feet, she glared up at him. To her relief, he didn't increase the pressure on her nipples. Maybe he thought she should be grateful because he'd started rolling them between his fingers, then returning circulation to them.

"I don't want to fight with you, but I don't have any choice. Hayley, I understand what's happening to you, the desire to retain control. If there was any other way . . ."

Insanely, she felt sorry for him. If it wasn't for her gag, she would have kissed him.

"You want your life back, don't you?"

Fighting tears, she nodded.

"You don't want to give a damn about me, do you?"

Again she nodded.

"I understand," he said and she believed with all her heart that he did.

7

She was pondering whether he could see into her soul when he took hold of her upper arms and walked her around the top of the pyramid. By her guess, it was at least five but not six feet square, which did nothing for her sense of security. Even more unsettling, she could see for miles in all directions. The jungle-like growth didn't exist far beyond the pyramid. Soon rich vegetation was replaced by rocky ground punctuated by scraggly trees. Nowhere did she see any signs of civilization, not even a road. There were no jet trails, no telephone poles, nothing. Of course, she tried to tell herself, parts of Mexico were pretty remote, but that didn't explain the pyramid. Instead of appearing crumbling and decayed, it looked as if it had been recently built.

Perhaps sensing her disquiet, he drew her to his side and put his arm around her. "It's beautiful here. Even with everything it represents, there's beauty and grace both to the pyramid and the land."

She nodded.

"You see it, don't you? At least the peace that hides the reality of what happened here."

Not knowing what he was talking about, she waited for him to continue. At the same time, the press of his body against hers became an erotic caress. As aware as she was of his masculinity, his warm substance quieted her a little.

After several seconds, he turned her toward him, the intensity in his gaze saying he felt the same way. They could stand like this for a long time, speaking in ways that didn't need words, their bodies becoming familiar with each other, promising and anticipating. Even restrained, she easily accepted the rightness of their being together.

"You're a remarkable woman. Sexy and alive. This isn't going to be easy." He seemed to be talking to himself.

What wasn't going to be easy and was he talking about her or him? Damn, damn this gag! Determined to make her questions known, she tried to twist away. He gave her a little freedom but didn't release her.

"You don't want to fight me up here," he warned unnecessarily.

He was right, but did he really expect her to be able to think about anything except him? When he ran his hands down her arms, she forced herself not to move. Drawing her wrists together, he held them in a single paw while unsnapping her leash. Guessing but not being sure what he intended to do nearly drove her crazy although, she forced herself to admit, maybe sexual hunger was what had brought her to the brink of insanity.

That's what it was, she was losing her mind!

Now rope pressed against her wrists, circling them twice. She didn't think he'd used a knot to secure her, but because of her elbow restraints and the way he'd wrapped her wrists, there was no way she could get free. Why had he added to her helplessness? And why did it feel so right?

When he once again roughly spun her toward him, she became dizzy. Instead of giving her head time to stop spinning, he looped his fingers through her collar and lifted, forcing her onto her toes. Keeping her there, he ran his hand between her legs. Frightened and excited in ways she'd never known were possible, she tried to look at him, tried to make sense of this latest change.

"Whether we're ready for this or not, it's time for the journey to being possessed to begin."

What had happened to the gentle tone she'd clung to earlier? Now his voice was rough and commanding, even superior.

"You know what's meant by the thin layer of civilization." Using the side of his thumb, he started rubbing her crotch. "I'm sensing you're already at the limit of yours, and now it's time to step over the edge."

Under his caresses, what she could see of the world took on a crimson haze. Her calves started to ache, and she had to work at breathing, but those things were unimportant because the movement against her crotch kept changing. One moment the pressure was enough to force her as high as she could go. The next, his thumb caressed and loved. When that happened, she settled herself over him and rocked back and forth. The sounds behind her gag were somewhere between moans and mewing, and she couldn't stop. Her entire body was softening and heating, melting a little, becoming undone.

He commanded her, ruled with touch and sensation on the one part of her body no man should touch without her approval, and yet she'd never needed anything more. Never felt more helpless or desired. This was letting go, casting off her fear of the future and living in a single precious moment.

Just when she wondered if she was capable of floating, he released her collar, allowing her to settle back onto her feet, but except to widen her stance a little and roll her pelvis forward, she didn't move. As long as he kept his hand on her sex, she'd stay where he needed her to be. And she'd sob out her need.

"You're with me, aren't you? No existence beyond what I give you."

Too far gone for anything except the truth, she lowered her head and nodded.

"You'll accept whatever I do to you, crave it. Do anything I want."

A small alarm broke through the heat swirling around her. Lifting her head, she stared at him. And despite the cost, she forced herself to stop massaging her pussy against his hand.

"There's still resistance in you, good. Useless but necessary." With that he grabbed her wrists and lifted, forcing her to lean over at the waist. "Spread your legs."

What do you think I am, your pet?

"Spread your legs." Bending her even farther, he forced obedience so she wouldn't fall. When he had her where he wanted her, he again turned his attention, his manipulations, to her pussy. Open and exposed and vulnerable, she allowed his finger into her. Welcomed. He took her slow, maddeningly slow, penetrating inch by intimate inch. She wasn't sure but thought he was using his forefinger and would have been grateful for his smooth, trimmed nail if she hadn't waited so long for this moment. Having her head lower than her heart contributed to her dizziness, but in truth, his bold mastery was almost everything. She, who had always had the ultimate say under what conditions a man's cock was allowed into her pussy, had become his possession.

And in her helpless hunger, she lived for him.

Deeper and deeper he explored until she would have gone onto her toes again if she'd been able. But he'd easily rendered her helpless in ways she'd never guessed a man could, so she simply presented herself to him. Her breasts dangled and saliva dripped. Her nostrils flared, not that her desperate breaths brought enough air into her lungs. She'd watched wild horses being roped and restrained on TV. Seeing their helpless fear had filled her with sympathy and regret for their lost freedom, but she wasn't a wild animal. She was a woman in the hands of a man who understood her body better than she did.

"Lessons, slave, lessons. Surrender." With that, he pulled out of her, bringing her hot juices with him. Keeping her bent over, he wiped his finger on her cheek. "If you weren't gagged, I'd make you drink yourself."

Despite the loss, a spark slid over her cunt. Close to climaxing, so close! An instant later a second spark touched her nerves, but it carried less promise than the first. If he didn't run his finger into her again, she might spend forever hovering near but not reaching release. "Please," she whimpered. "Please. Help me."

"What was that? You want something from me?" He held his hand in front of her face and then ran it over her chin, down her neck, between her hanging breasts, over her belly. He stopped when he reached her pubic hair and then cupped his hand over her mons and shook it almost fiercely. Fire licked throughout her pelvis and sent her cunt to shattering. Whimpering, she struggled to rub her shoulder against him in gratitude and encouragement.

Ignoring her silent message, he gave her mons another fire-inducing shake before releasing her. Frustration roared through her, forcing her to repeatedly clench her pussy muscles. She was becoming more and more lightheaded, and the crimson veil over her vision was getting darker, but it didn't matter. Only fueling the flames did.

Sensing that he had repositioned himself, she lifted her head as much as she could and tried to locate him. A moment later, he pulled down on her wrists, causing blood to race through her veins. The resultant pins and needles sensation gave her something other than her clit to think about, but the reprieve didn't last long because he lifted her arms again and slightly to the side. Holding her there, he leaned away, his burning gaze raking over her. Did he see her as what she needed to be, his sex object, his human artwork?

"I didn't know how I'd react." His tone low, he enunciated each word. "The power—and frustration."

Frustrated, him? Oh, of course, of course and good. Yes, that's what she needed to do, somehow keep him emotionally off balance. Once she had—

What was that? Oh, shit, he was pushing his cock between her legs from the rear. Sensing he was bending his knees, she stood on tiptoe in a silent but undeniable welcome. Animal to animal, mating. It didn't matter! Only relief and release did.

Either he'd deliberately pushed his loincloth to the side or his erection had forced freedom. Whichever it was, his cock now glided over her loose and swollen labia. She couldn't stop mewling. Neither could she so much as think how to hold back from rocking her pelvis in a primitive attempt at stroking him. Their bodies were dancing with each other, cock caressing pussy, pussy kissing cock. His breathing was as ragged as hers, and each time his groin pressed against her buttocks, his taut muscles spoke of ragged self-control. At this angle, he couldn't penetrate her, but she'd take what she could. A little more, just a few more wet strokes and she'd climax!

No! Not again!

When he pulled himself out from between her legs, she ground her teeth into the wood gag to keep from cursing. How could he be so cruel when she was dying, raw and barely human, debased but too far gone to care.

"Hard. So damn hard."

His words rolled off her and might have faded under the hot weight of her frustration if he hadn't run his fingers over her buttocks. Gentle and rough at the same time, the touches seeped into her. She longed to tell him that it didn't have to be like this, that they could call a halt to whatever the hell lessons he was trying to impart to her and simply fuck, but of course only garbled sounds came out. She didn't know she'd started crying until her eyes began burning. Although she'd always taken pride in keeping her tears private, she no longer cared about anything except release and relief.

"Time for something new," he announced as he brought her arms down so she could stand upright. "I'm offering you a proposal. If you do exactly what I tell you, I'll give you what you need. Understand?"

Instead of nodding as he obviously expected, she studied his expression. Hard spots of color highlighted his cheeks, and his nostrils flared. Under her relentless observation, confusion followed by comprehension passed over him. "Trying to read me, aren't you?"

Allowing herself the slightest smile, she nodded.

"Which wouldn't be possible unless you're not as far gone as you've been pretending."

You think I was pretending? Much as she'd like to act as if she didn't know what he was talking about, she couldn't, so she lifted her chin. It wasn't much of an act of defiance but what else could she do?

"But you're close." Cupping his cock, he aimed it at her. "Monitoring what I feel gives me a good indication of what's happening to you."

But you can do something about your frustration, damn you!

Her silent profanity stopped her. She'd never been much for swearing, because she saw cussing as a lazy way of expressing oneself and because stringing out profanity left her feeling out of control. Still, cursing him even if he couldn't hear had released some of the pressure.

The truth was, beneath everything he'd subjected her to and everything she'd embraced, she'd never felt more alive, or closer to a man. Regardless of his motivations, they'd both sunk into rawness. Civilization's conventions no longer mattered and had nothing to do with them.

Her dip into reflection died a swift death when he unfastened her gag and drew it out. Instead of working feeling back into her mouth, she pressed herself against him and rose up on her toes, her head uplifted and lips parted. "Kiss me," she ground out. "I dare you to."

His already taut body became even more so, and although she couldn't be sure, she thought he'd started to tremble. Despite her burning calves, she continued to lean against his strength. He looked down, but they were too close for her to trust her reading of his expression. Hunger, yes, anger, maybe. As for confusion—

Throwing off all concerns for her sanity, she stretched even higher and touched her lips to his. One of them shuddered; it didn't matter which. He could break this off whenever he wanted, but he didn't, and his mouth was soft and filled with promise. His cock, trapped between them, prodded against her belly, making it all too easy to imagine it elsewhere—in her.

Kissing her captor, sealing her body to his, rubbing her hard nipples against his heated skin, feeling his hands close around her buttocks as he took over the task of keeping them together melted into a sensation that brought her to the edge of some great cliff. A semirational part of her mind questioned whether she was climaxing in a way she never had, but she didn't care. He was holding her against him, embracing her from lips to hips and that's all that mattered, maybe all that ever would.

The touch of lips against lips intensified; she couldn't say which of them was responsible. Determined to let him know how much she needed this, she parted her mouth and ran her tongue against his teeth. Instead of granting her entrance, he replied with a tongue probe of his own that forced her to retreat. He kept after her, his tongue pushing past the barrier of her teeth and demanding she accept him. She did of course; how could it be otherwise?

And although she didn't want him to know how exposed

and needy she was, she couldn't quiet her guttural cries. Neither did she have the strength to stop herself from repeatedly driving her groin into him. Heat spun through her from belly to thighs. She couldn't get or keep enough air in her lungs!

Answering her thrusts with powerful ones of his own, he fucked her belly. And when it became too much and she tried to pull free, he closed his arms around her and held her against him. "Damn you, damn you," he chanted.

"No, damn you!"

Hissing, he shoved her away. "I shouldn't have ungagged you."

"Why did you?"

"Because I need to hear your frustration and surrender."

There it was again, that reference to what he needed from her. Later, somehow, she'd make him explain why, but not now with need threatening to melt her. Settling onto the balls of her feet again, she risked a look down at herself. His cock had left rub marks on her belly but even more telling was the sheen of moisture on her inner thighs. Trembling waves rocked her, and although she knew it wouldn't do any good, she strained to free herself. If he wasn't going to fuck her, she'd do it herself!

"Why? Why?"

"The reason isn't important, yet. Only the journey is." His fingers clenched and released, clenched again and stayed.

Her hair was sticking to her damp temples and obscuring her vision, but when she shook her head, she only made herself even more dizzy. She was a mess, her skin rubbed in several places, sweat trapped under her arms and running down the small of her back, smelling like a woman in heat, the restraints forcing her breasts out like some whore. Most of all, only her ties kept her from jumping him like a mare needing to be mounted. "Let me go."

He shook his head.

"Why not? Are you afraid of me?" The question nearly

made her laugh since he outweighed her by close to a hundred pounds.

"Maybe."

That she didn't expect. Neither was she ready for the change taking place in his eyes. They were darkening again, losing humanity and becoming feral. The insane thought that he was turning into a jungle cat distracted her from his first step toward her, and it was too late by the time he'd taken the second one. She'd barely had time to tell herself to back away when he looped a forefinger through her collar ring and again pulled down.

Once more she was staring at the pyramid with her legs spread for balance. Even more disconcerting, he was rubbing the back of her neck much as a cowboy might gentle a just-captured bronc. "I'm sorry, Hayley, sorry I have to do this to you."

"Then don't!"

"Quiet, quiet. You've taken the first step. It's time to make sure you don't ever regret it."

What was he talking about?

"You need a climax, don't you?"

"Yes, damn you, yes."

"There's been enough foreplay, hasn't there?"

Nearly laughing, she tried to straighten. "Foreplay? That's what you call—"

"Quiet!" He slapped her buttocks, sending a quick sting through her. Residues of sensation rested in her cunt and added to the damnable unquenchable fire there. "I'm the source of your pleasure and before we're finished, your entire existence. Forget what you've experienced with other men. They haven't come close to the lessons you're going to learn, starting today."

Fascinated instead of frightened, she compelled herself not to move. That accomplished, she wondered at the tension she was willing to subject herself to in order to experience everything he was promising. The first time he'd bent her over, the resultant head rush had hindered her ability to concentrate. Maybe she'd already learned one of his lessons because instead of trying to clear her head and vision, she focused on the hand now roaming over her spine. He was gentle and slow, the touches calming her while keeping high her awareness of his leg occasionally brushing against hers.

Long before he'd worked his way down her back to her crack, she knew that was his destination, but waiting for that moment became a delicious agony that drenched her in fresh sweat and turned her breathing into shallow gasps.

"Spread yourself, slave. Make yourself accessible to me."

She'd started to blindly obey when she realized he'd released her collar. Unsure of the message behind the change, she lifted her head a few inches.

"No. Stay as I commanded."

His voice was low and calm, and the fingers making their way to her ass represented promise, not invasion. Still, self-control was so difficult that if she hadn't vowed to please him with her obedience, she wouldn't have been able to lower her head again.

"Good, good." He patted her buttocks, his nails gliding over full flesh and helping a moan break loose. "You're learning. I'm going to take control here." Pulling her ass cheeks apart, he made room for much of his hand. Now his thumb rested over her puckered hole. "But I can't expect you to keep your balance while focusing on what I'm doing to you. Do you agree?"

She didn't know anything except his touches and words and promises.

"Do you?"

"I, ah, yes."

"Hmm. I'm not sure I have your full attention." The pressure increased and, thinking he intended to invade her asshole, she tensed. "Yes, I rather believe you're more interested in what I intend to do than my explanations of the why and how. Is that right?"

"Y—es." *Don't clench there! Let him know I welcome him.*

"That's what I thought. In preparation for the answer to your prayers—you do want to let go more than anything, don't you?"

Your thumb! Pressing repeatedly at my rear opening! "Yes, please!"

"Please *master.*"

"What?"

The act of switching from slow and deliberate probes to rapid-fire strokes against her asshole nearly sent her into spasms and made hearing next to impossible. *Tell him! Somehow, tell him.*

"Hold still, slave. Quit shaking."

"I—can't help it."

Her sad admission was still echoing when he reached between her legs. Now that his fingers were well lubricated, he had no trouble working his forefinger past her sphincter muscles. "Yes you can and you will."

"Please! I can't—"

"Quiet! You need to listen carefully because if I have to tell you again, I'll punish you to make sure the lesson holds. For now you are to call me *master.* Repeat after me. This body belongs to me, master."

"I, ah . . ."

Oh god, what is he doing? Almost before she'd finished her desperate question, she had her answer. He'd again lubricated his fingers, but this time he wasn't content with penetrating her ass with just one finger. No matter that he'd ordered her not to move, when two fingers slid in, she arched her spine.

"What did I tell you to say, slave?"

"I, ah, oh, please!"

By wrapping his free arm around her chest, he easily held her immobile. She couldn't be sure but thought he'd buried himself into her up to his second knuckle. "Please what?"

"Master! Master."

"That's better. Now say it, all of it."

No man had ever done this to her. Yes, she'd wondered what having her rear hole drilled would feel like, but not once had her imagination conjured up it happening this way. To feel so utterly helpless. "This—this body belongs to you, master."

Suddenly she was again upright, her head spinning and her ass empty. Although she tried to look at him, he'd become a blur, like her body.

"It's takes time to take things to another level, one in which you allow me to do whatever I want to with you. Do you understand?"

But you're already in control. "Yes, master."

"Good. Keep your legs as far apart as you can. I also want you to close your eyes when I tell you to. No matter what I do, no matter what you feel or fear, you're to keep them shut."

This time he hadn't asked if she understood, and although she'd been a modern and independent woman a short while ago, she'd lost contact with that core element of her personality. He was molding her into what he wanted her to be, what he believed she needed to become, and to hell with whether she understood why.

And she was letting him. More than letting, she was starved for the next step to begin.

"Stand straight, slave. Put your shoulders back and turn so I can easily reach your breasts."

He hadn't yet commanded her to close her eyes, had he? Worried that she might have missed something, she shifted so she was facing him. Although her back was already arched because of the ties on her wrists and elbows, she struggled to present her breasts fully to him. Opening her stance would have been easy if her legs weren't so shaky. She prayed he wouldn't ridicule her awkwardness.

He didn't, but neither could she tell whether she'd pleased him, because his features were impassive when he folded his arms across his chest and looked down at her. Only his ridged and dark cock said anything about what he might be experiencing, but maybe he was capable of disconnecting his mind from his sex organ. He had no weakness?

"You're beautiful," he said softly, "expressive, open eyes. And your hands—"

"What about my hands?" He thought her beautiful?

"They're made for creating, as is your body."

Suddenly proud of what she'd always taken for granted, she looked at him with new eyes. With his probing, almost hungry gaze, she couldn't simply call his expressive. There was something old about him, and solitary. Although his body was in prime condition, it had an enduring quality as if it had served him for a long, long time. Sex between them would be a union of youth and age.

When he bent down, she struggled to see what he was doing, without moving her head. Fortunately, she didn't have long to wait because an instant later he was drawing her right breast into his mouth. Suction snaked over her sensitive, swollen flesh. Lost in the incredible sensation, she moaned. At first he concentrated on bathing her, his warm saliva controlling her own temperature. Still, the promise of more heat waited just beyond her consciousness as did the potency in his teeth. Keeping her stance wide became more than an attempt at obedience; it was the only way she could guarantee that she wouldn't fall.

Over and over he drew her deep into him much as she'd ministered to his cock—had she really done that or had the act gone no deeper than her imagination? Wondering if she'd ever have the courage to ask him that separated her from the moment's reality. By the time she found her way back to it, he was releasing her breast, rejecting it and her. Gasping in fear, she struggled to lean into him only to have him close his teeth around her nub and draw her breast upward.

"Ah, ah."

There was no pain, not so much as a hint of discomfort. Instead, she simply surrendered even more to this man whose mastery of her might know no bounds. Wet anticipation slid down her legs, the scent blending in with his mix of maleness and sweat. She now leaned back so far that maybe only his hold on her breast kept her erect, but along with a measure of fear came a heady letting go. She could fly, float, levitate. Everything else about her world had changed, so why not this?

Perhaps he understood how much she was depending on him for support because he kept gripping her breast until, finally, the hot current racing from there to her cunt changed. He was hurting her, damn it, his teeth undoubtedly leaving marks in her nipple and cutting off circulation.

"Please!" Jerking from one side to the other, she tried to shake free. "No more."

For a long, frightening moment he didn't react. She would have gone on resisting if she'd thought it would do any good and if she hadn't been afraid of hurting herself or toppling over. Then, when he'd truly let her know that he called all the shots, he released her, gripping her collar once again to hold her in place.

"Close your eyes. Now."

Taken aback by the sharp command, she nevertheless locked herself in darkness. The sun pressed against her lids to lighten the cocoon now surrounding her, but what did it matter?

"I'm on a mission to become more than your master, Hayley," he said with his mouth inches from her ear. "For now all that matters is that you embrace the journey, for your surrender to me to be complete and unquestioning. For trust to live between us. That's why I'm doing this, because the bonds between us must be stronger than any other ties you've ever experienced."

His words slipped into her, easily finding quiet corners to take root in, and yet she didn't understand what he'd said, only that he needed them to be welded to each other.

Then he slipped a hand between her legs, and she had no doubt how he intended to accomplish that—through sex.

"This is your weakness, Hayley." Fingertips both rough and satin sweet glided over her soaked labia. "And your strength."

What strength? She felt only the delicious hunger that came with the hot climb to release.

His other hand now pressed against the small of her back. Maybe she should thank him for steadying her, but she could only pant, only rock her hips and suck in oxygen as his strokes lengthened. He'd started with a nearly imperceptible movement just behind her clit. With each trip and retreat, he covered more territory until she was bleating like a lamb. How soft, soft and yet firm, firm and briefly penetrating, housing one finger after another in her sex, sometimes filling her flooded passage with two digits.

The first time he skewered her with all except his thumb and baby finger, she wondered if she'd pass out. Head back, eyes obediently shut, sagging against the palm pressing into her spine, she howled.

There! So close. Cunt muscles already clenching.

"No! Don't climax! I haven't given you permission." Roughly pulling himself free, he slapped her mons.

Again! Slap me again, please!

"Listen to me, slave! I own you here." His hand closed over her labia. "I control what happens and doesn't happen here."

"Please, please!"

"Not yet. Not until I give you permission to come."

Was he insane? Maybe she was the one who'd crossed the

line into madness. Whichever it was, she only wanted one thing in life.

"You wear my collar, slave. When that happened, you turned ownership of your body over to me. Say it, call me what I am."

More pressure on her flaming tissues! His middle finger pressing against the space between her pussy and anus! "Master. Master!"

"I say when you can climax and when you practice restraint and control, got that?"

"Yes, master."

"Do you?"

His tone, a mix of resignation and regret, penetrated the purple haze surrounding her, and she would have given anything to look into his eyes. Perhaps he'd sensed his vulnerability and was determined to keep his barriers in place because he unexpectedly licked the valley at the base of her throat. A sensation like kitten claws spiraled out from the contact. She was still mentally tracking the light touch when he bore down on her clit. Taken utterly by surprise, she struggled to stay on top of this latest invasion.

He didn't give her time. The pressure briefly let up only to return, to stay. Even *worse*, he started creating small and intense circles until she felt as if her clit was being taken on some frantic circus ride. How well he knew what the core and center of her sex was capable of, how sensitive it was, how close to being over the top he'd already brought her.

"Ride it, slave." His tone was calm and quiet, and if it wasn't for what he was doing, she might be lulled into sleep. "Accept and enjoy what I'm doing to you, but don't let go."

"Ah, please, please."

A gentle brushing stroke brought her down a step; in the next heartbeat, he caught her clit between thumb and forefinger. "Please what?"

Terrified and excited beyond all control, she tried to pull free. "No, no, no!"

"Yes, slave, yes. You're going to dance for me, dance until you're exhausted."

Her feet were under her, her knees locked. No matter how much she needed to get away, the only thing she could do on her own was shudder and sob. His hand grinding into the base of her spine became the strength she needed to keep from passing out. She was his puppet, his crying, shaking puppet.

His other hand, the one that had laid claim to her clit and the rest of her sex, by turns guided her deep within herself or threw her out into a dark, hot universe. Was she climaxing? She couldn't tell and couldn't stop, could only chant, "No, no, no."

"Are you dancing, slave?" The grip on her clit melted away; everything stilled. Then he came after her again, vigorously rubbing her labia this time. Even with so much lubrication, heat spiraled. "Becoming mine?"

"Yes, yes, yes!" There! Something different, a lifting up and in, muscles screaming and the top of her head about to blow.

"No!"

Shit, shit! When he went quiet again, she had no choice but to pant and sweat and hate/love him because he'd once again denied her. Was this what it was like to be in labor, the barest control over one's body and a massive force relentlessly shaking it? She wasn't in pain and yet, damn it, she'd never wanted anything more.

Only by forcing her mind to the complex task did she comprehend that although his thumb was still against her clit, he was no longer stimulating her. The touch was barely that, more like a whisper of contact, just enough to remind her of what he'd done. Pressure she couldn't name or control kept working through her. How little it would take for that pressure to become the ultimate pleasure.

But he didn't want that for her.

For reasons she couldn't fathom.

"That's all we both dare for the first time." His tone was seductive, faint and hard to grasp. "You need to return to your world, at least as much as possible. But you won't forget what happened between us, will you?"

"No, master."

"Good." He kissed one eyelid and then the other. "Good, my beautiful and necessary slave."

His words were still on his lips when a fierce shudder tore through Mazati. Weak and scared, he struggled to lock his legs in place. When he was sure he wouldn't fall, he tried to tell himself that sex in the forms he'd just employed on Hayley was responsible for his reaction but in his soul he knew better. Pouring so much of himself into forging a bond between them was draining him. It wasn't a simple matter of handling a woman after so long, not even the power in his cock, even memories he'd thought were long dead.

Why hadn't he considered the impact on his own emotions, his soul?

Even more important, could he survive what he still needed to accomplish?

And did it matter?

8

"Where the hell did you go?"

Hayley had known that voice her entire life, and yet Saree could have been a stranger for all the impact her question made. Everything that had happened since Hayley had walked into the room where the gem show was being held had the air of Alice in Wonderland about it. Maybe she should simply label it under *weird shit* and lay off the hard liquor, but that was a lot easier said than done. For one, she'd never in her entire life needed a climax more than she did at this moment.

"Did you hear me? Where'd you take off to?" Saree insisted. "We walked in together and were eyeing the two-legged merchandise who'd gotten you all hot and bothered when suddenly, you made like poof."

"What?" Was that her speaking?

"I swear you just disappeared." Saree grabbed her forearm. "Gee. You're sweating like a pig. Did you go back outside and stand in the sun?"

Every ounce of rationality at her disposal was begging Hayley to come clean with her sister, but if she did, Saree would be within her rights and responsibilities to call for the men with the butterfly nets. Until she'd had time to try to come to grips with the ungrippable, she had no choice but to lie. Easier said than done.

"I told you I needed to go to the bathroom," she tried. "But it was so noisy, and you were so intent on that male merchandise you were talking about that I'm not surprised you didn't hear. So, much as I hate to disappoint you, I didn't disappear."

Saree didn't look convinced, but thankfully the room was even more crowded than it had been earlier, which, hopefully, would make her sister believe they'd simply gotten separated in the crush. She just hoped Saree didn't grill her about where she'd been because she didn't know. Neither did she have any idea how she could begin to explain what had happened.

"You scared me," Saree continued. "I've been in the bathroom a couple of times looking for you, to all of the booths, out in the lobby. Where did you and tall, dark, and mysterious go?"

"What?"

"Come on, sis. He winked out at the same time. Spill! The two of you slip out for a quickie?"

If only. "I've barely spoken to him."

"Who says there needs to be chitchat when you're only interested in a certain part of the anatomy?" Frowning, Saree again took Hayley's arm and turned her so they were face to face. "What the hell is that?" She pointed at Hayley's neck.

Hayley didn't have to touch her neck to know what her sister was indicating. In fact, going by the amount of heat radiating from the encircling weight, she was surprised she hadn't been aware of the collar from the instant she *returned* to the showroom. Despite her skin's decidedly favorable reaction, she had to force herself to touch it, and she couldn't quite muster up the courage to meet her sister's eyes.

"Do you like it?" Even as the words came out of her mouth, she wondered what, if anything, she'd say next.

"I don't know what the hell you think you've bought," Saree said with an *I can't believe what I'm seeing* laugh, "but I've never seen a bondage collar outside of work. What prompted you to buy that?"

"You think it looks like a bondage collar?" Why was she trying not to blush when she knew it wouldn't do any good?

"Duh, I *know* what it is. After all, it's my business." Releasing Hayley's arm, Saree tilted her head to the side as she studied her sister's neck. "It's kind of sexy, all right—kinky but sexy. What booth was it at? I didn't see any specializing in leather."

Waving vaguely, Hayley ran her finger through the metal loop Mazati had used to manage and manipulate her. Of course it was only her imagination, but she could nearly swear she felt his heat still on it. A sudden thought froze her. What if she couldn't remove it? "Ah, I'm sorry I worried you. After I was done in the bathroom, I wandered around comparing the work I do with the pieces here, trying to decide whether I can compete or need to take up armed robbery in order to get out of debt."

"Don't you ever doubt yourself, got it? Believe in yourself and you'll more than make your mark. You'll be rich inside of a year."

"I wish."

"Look, being scared is perfectly understandable. If I was the one on the brink of bankruptcy, I'd be losing as much sleep as I'm sure you are."

Much as she hated hearing the bold-faced truth from her sister, it was better than pretending she'd come out of her wreck of a marriage on top of the world. "I'm trying to make things happen; you know I am. But I need to know whether I have a chance of succeeding or am just deluding myself."

"You aren't deluding yourself, honey. You've got the talent." Saree frowned. "That said, I don't understand something. Instead of picking up the gems you need to get your business off the ground, you grabbed this." She indicated the collar. "Doesn't make a tinker's damn bit of sense."

Although Hayley was used to her sister's earthy language, she held a finger to her lip. "Criticize me later, all right? So, what do you want to do before I buy myself into the poorhouse? Any looking you're interested in, now that you're no longer trying to chase me down?"

Saree's eyes glittered. "Let's find the hunk. I'm still not convinced you haven't been jumping each other's bones. In fact—" She leaned in close. "Shit, I smell your juices."

"What? That's—that's sweat." Thank goodness Saree couldn't see or feel the stickiness clinging to her labia and thighs.

"I know my smells, sis. You been in the bathroom playing with yourself?"

I wish it was that simple. "You need a vacation," Hayley retorted, careful to keep her voice down. "Get your mind off your job."

"It ain't me, sis. You're the one with the blotchy cheeks and bedroom eyes."

Issuing what she hoped passed for an indignant snort, Hayley spun away. Her intention had been to try to find something, anything to distract them, but the surroundings were all a blur—except for Mazati.

The first thing that registered was that he was in front of his booth. Next she took note of his height; he was even taller than she remembered. Broader across the shoulders with upper arms made for fighting and winning, thighs carved from hardwood that nothing he wore would ever diminish.

Then, although she'd never wanted anything more—well, almost nothing—than to go on imprinting him in her memory bank, sudden fear and caution stopped her. The *thing* that had taken place between them hadn't been her short-circuiting libido or a mental dive into fantasyland. It had happened. Her collar was proof.

"Don't drool," Saree hissed. "Not that I blame you."

Given the amount of noise and maybe six feet separating them, she was fairly sure Mazati couldn't hear, but if Saree had dialed into her reaction, so could he. Hell, wasn't that what he was telling her as he walked his gaze down from her captured throat to her crotch?

It's all there, isn't it, he was saying. *The impact of what happened when we were together.*

Yes, master.

A hard shudder all but sent her stumbling backward. At the same time, she all too easily imagined herself dropping to her knees in acknowledgment of his power over her. "Holy shit," Saree whispered. "Nah, the two of you weren't off humping each other. If you were, you'd be down for the count, not all hot and bothered."

"What are you talking about?" *Stupid question.*

"I get e-mail from countless horny men, and more women than I want to think about. Believe me, I know the condition when I see it."

Not taking her eyes off Mazati, Hayley punched her sister's shoulder. "Stop it. Someone might hear."

"They don't need to. You're giving off fireworks."

Much as she wanted to tell her sister that she was reading her dead wrong, Hayley knew better than to continue a conversation she couldn't win. Besides, she'd already lied more than enough today. "I, ah, I want to buy some of his opals."

"Sure you aren't interested in the family jewels? Okay, okay, you want me watching your back?"

Yes! No! I don't know. Before she could stumble through a reply, Mazati gave her the faintest of grins. Then he turned his back on her and walked away. She started to stumble after him only to stop. Maybe he'd overheard her saying she wanted to buy from him, because he was returning to his booth. Why had he left it and run the risk of getting robbed?

Because she was more important to him.

"You're sure?" Mazati asked, some ten minutes after Hayley had planted herself in front of his booth. "That's a lot of money to be putting out."

Swallowing did nothing for the lump in her throat and the swirling knot in her belly. "Yes, it is." Determined not to give in to the image of having to live in her car while she struggled to emerge from the nightmare of financial ruin, she concentrated on breathing. A strong, warm male scent seeped into her and filled her with courage. "But if my designs take off and the demand's there, I don't dare run out of supplies. I, ah, I don't even know how to get in touch with you when I'm ready for more."

Instead of giving her the information she needed, Mazati waited while she counted out her money, and if he noticed that she now had less than a dollar left, he made no indication. Neither did he comment on the way her hand shook as she placed the bills in his palm. Still silent, he picked up each unfinished opal and deposited them in separate plastic baggies. Mouth dry and the skin under her collar burning, she watched his every move.

Don't chicken out now. Saree believes in you and Mazati— Mazati has entered your life.

"About the two of you connecting again, what if she wants to come to your shop or wherever you keep your opals?" Saree spoke for the first time since they'd reached Mazati's booth.

"I'll know when she needs more."

"Yeah, right."

His only reaction was a shrug of those unignorable shoulders. Maybe Hayley would have asked her own questions if he wasn't staring at her throat, his eyes speaking of the secret between them and everything that went with that secret. Even when the vendor to his right shuffled over and offered his negative opinion of accepting credit and debit cards, Mazati's gaze held on the claim he'd locked on her.

"He could make it big in the biz," Saree said when at last Mazati turned his attention to the other vendor. "Absolutely big."

"The—are you talking about what you do?"

"Is there any other business?"

"To hear you, no." Hayley should have picked up her purchases, put them in her purse, made sure she had Mazati's business card, and gotten out of that too-warm, too-crowded place. Instead, she watched him.

"Damn but he's one fine specimen, exactly what Phil's looking for."

Phil, if Hayley remembered, was not just Saree's boss but the owner of the adult Internet site that provided her sister with a lucrative career. "You're not talking personally, are you?" she asked, appalled.

"What Phil does on his own time is his business, but no, he wouldn't waste prime talent behind the scenes."

The conversation, backed by what Mazati had done to her—real or imagined didn't matter—was throwing her off balance when she'd spent more than enough time in that condition today. In an attempt to regain her equilibrium, she glanced over at Saree, who was staring at Mazati like a hunter sighting down her rifle at a trophy buck. "Mazati isn't *talent*," Hayley told her. "And even if he was, he's not a submissive."

"Wait, back up a minute. Let's make sure we're on the same page. What are you talking about?"

Again Hayley hauled her attention off Mazati. This time Saree did the same. "You *act* on a bondage site. You can't possibly be thinking that he'd—no, he'd never let someone do to him what's done to you." *Believe me, I know where his interests lie.*

An unladylike snort accompanied Saree's punch to Hayley's shoulder. "Okay, I've got you now. You were thinking I wanted to recruit him to let someone tie him up, beat him, and force an orgasm out of him."

Pity anyone who's listening to this. "Isn't that what Phil's looking for? Don't forget, you tried to get me to contact him."

"I'd still like to seduce you into the porn business because I think you'd love it and it pays damn well, but that's for another time."

"Thanks, I think."

Saree leaned closer. "You haven't forgotten that drunken night when we spilled all to each other, have you? When it was your turn, you told me about some of the games you and Cal played. No matter how much wine I had in me, I remember how you let him spread-eagle you to the bed and—"

"Enough! Are you going to get to the point?"

"About today's hunk, you mean? Hell yes. Over here. We need a bit of privacy." Grabbing Hayley's shirt, Saree dragged her over to the nearest wall. Because there were no displays here, it was of minimal interest to others. Even better, Hayley could still keep an eye on Mazati who, when he wasn't waiting on customers, favored her with looks that said she wasn't to leave until she'd spoken to him. The thought of having to get his approval to do anything was both unsettling and natural and seemed to feed the heat running through her collar.

"So," Saree said. "Here's the deal. First, you've seen me at work."

"If you call it work."

"Whatever. How much attention do you pay to the dom handling me?"

Truth time. "Something tells me I'm going to flunk this test. There've been several of them, what, maybe five?"

"Seven to be exact. What, specifically, do you remember?"

Sudden laughter threatened to catch her cheeks on fire. "You have to ask? You aren't the only one who's naked, not by the end anyway. There's nothing left to the imagination."

"Then you've studied their cocks, have you?"

"Of course."

"And?"

"All right, all right! A couple of them, Sax and Deon, are damn well hung, not that I need to tell you that."

"You should feel how those cocks fit in my pussy."

"I've seen," she shot back, determined not to let Saree embarrass her. "And the way they fill your mouth."

"I'm glad you're following the various aspects of my career."

Careful not to look at Saree, Hayley debated confessing that watching her sister climax fueled her own imagination and sped her toward her own toy-aided releases. "You're talking about Mazati doing what Sax and Deon do, aren't you."

Saree's grin would have done the Cheshire cat proud. "Those aren't their real names, you know."

"I kind of figured that."

"Everything else about them is real, though. No matter how well a dom plays to the camera and no matter how expertly he handles the *talent* like me, if he isn't well hung with a lot of staying power, he isn't going to make it in this business. Mazati has those things going for him."

"How—how do you know?"

"I know men. Comes with the territory."

Giving up all pretense of being interested in anything except Mazati, Hayley stared openly at him. If anything, the comparison between him and a big cat was stronger than earlier. She half expected him to grow claws and leap upward to land on the overhead lighting. His lips would retract to reveal teeth made for hunting and when he howled—"He's magnificent."

"No argument there," Saree agreed. "But I don't want you forgetting you're vulnerable these days thanks to my fortunately former brother-in-law. I'd guess that anything with a cock and proof of gainful and honest employment would look good to you, especially if the specimen's cock was in prime working condition."

About to protest that she couldn't possibly know anything about Mazati's cock, she bit back the lie. "You're right. Thanks to Cal, my objectivity regarding the opposite sex is shot to hell."

"Just make sure you keep that in mind when you jump Mazati's bones."

"*When*? You sound pretty sure of that."

"I know the symptoms. Inject equal parts lust and opportunity and it's a foregone conclusion. You don't think all the fucking in my business takes place on the set, do you? You try getting sexually manhandled for hours and see if you can just shake hands and walk away when the shoot's over."

Although Hayley had wondered what went on behind the scenes, she'd decided to let her sister bring up the details. "But if that hunk has done his job, he's forced several climaxes out of you. I'd think you'd be done in by then."

"You think wrong. Coming's addictive. And if the session calls for the hunk not getting off himself, well, what's a sub to do but take pity on him."

What Hayley did know was that this particular conversation wasn't helping a bit when it came to putting whatever had taken place between her and Mazati in perspective. In truth, she'd always been a little uncomfortable watching Saree *at work*. This was her sister after all, the kid who'd trailed after her and her friends; who used to crawl into bed with her when she had a bad dream; her maid of honor. Sitting, or rather squirming, through a video of other women doing the submissive thing was all right because that's when her imagination and libido took flight and her sex toys took a beating. It was another story with Saree, personal and involved.

"Are you with me?" Saree demanded. "Damn, you're doing the glassy-eyed thing again. I'm going to have to get you a bib before you start drooling."

"Sorry."

Saree's delighted laugh snagged Hayley's attention. "You aren't sorry. How can you be, when you're occupied with the hot and bothered?" An unexpected frown pulled the light from Saree's eyes.

"What?"

"That *necklace*. I've worn some on the job that weren't half as professional looking as that." Reaching out with her long, manicured nails, she spun it around. "How the hell do you get this off?"

"It, ah, the clasp's hidden."

"No shit. Give it to me again. Why'd you buy it?"

I didn't. "You really think it looks like a collar?"

Saree responded by giving her another *no shit* look. "I can hardly see your neck, just this thing."

No longer trying to hold back, Hayley fingered the soft yet strong leather. After repositioning the ring in front, she explored every inch of what Mazati had fitted on her. Saree was right; there was no fastening. Would she have to cut it off?

"Now why the hell did you buy it?"

"Impulse." Then, determined to pull the conversation away from Mazati or at least try, she shrugged. "Memories."

"Oh shit. Are you going to tell me something I really don't want to know?"

"You already do."

Nodding somberly, Saree clasped her hands. "Oh yeah, the BDSM thing between you and Cal, such as it was. You never said, but did watching me working give you the idea? I got the two of you to experiment?"

Yes and no. Yes, to some extent because studying Saree pretending to be a sex slave or submissive or whatever her role of the day was called had expanded her mind. Before Saree had gone into the porn business, Hayley's imagination hadn't taken her any farther than wondering what forced sex was like. She had absolutely no interest in being raped, of course, but being seduced by a powerful and mysterious stranger was another story. Conditioned by Saree's videos and emboldened by a glass of wine, she'd brought the subject up with Cal. They'd only been married a few months at the time and were having sex almost nightly, and he was more than agreeable to the experiment; he ran with it. They'd bought Velcro restraints, vibrators, even light whips on the Internet, which had further expanded their imaginations.

Forced sex, small dildos in her ass, clips on her nipples, all those things and more had turned vanilla sex into capital letters HOT.

But of course, that was before Cal had betrayed a number of people, her included.

"That's all this is about," Hayley muttered as she stroked the leather against her throat. "Memory lane."

9

The ice in her soft drink had melted, diluting the flavor, but instead of pouring it out, Hayley remained at the table near the food booth. Too-hot grease and popcorn were doing unwanted things to her stomach, so why wasn't she getting up and leaving as Saree had done?

Because Mazati was still here.

Granted, she couldn't see him from here, but that was all right because at the moment that was all she had the nerve for. Her plan, as far as it went, was to finish her hot dog and then tell him how much she'd appreciated his help in her selections. If the stars were aligned the way she needed them to be, he'd indicate an interest in seeing the finished product, and she'd tell him where she lived, and somehow an invitation would be issued and accepted.

She didn't want to think about having to get in her car without those things having happened. Nor had she come close to working up the necessary courage to get through the night with his proof of possession around her throat and his hands not on her body.

"It belongs on you."

Just like that, Mazati's voice settled around her. Feeling as if she was floating in it, she slowly lifted her head to find him standing on the opposite side of the long table. He'd planted his big hands on the flat surface and was leaning over, looking like a panther staring down at his latest catch. "It?"

"The collar."

Why had she asked the question when she'd already known what he was talking about? Maybe, the answer came, because she was fighting for time. Swinging his legs over the bench, he sat down. An older couple glanced over at them and then went back to their conversation. If they'd caught the sexual tension building in her, they gave no indication.

"How was your meal?" he asked.

"Okay. Are you—you came to get something?"

"A burger. They'll bring it when it's done."

Chitchat was good, chitchat gave her time to get a grip on the energy that had come with him. At his question, she explained that Saree had wanted to go home and get some rest. She said nothing about how her sister earned her living. When she asked if Mazati was going to be here tomorrow for the last day of the show, he said no; he'd accomplished what he'd needed to. His attention locked on her neck.

"You're talking about me, aren't you?" she blurted, her lips and fingers tingling.

"Hayley, despite what you're probably thinking, I'm no more sure of myself than you are. What we're doing is something I wasn't sure I'd ever chance. But . . ."

"But what?"

"The stakes."

"For you, right?"

He nodded.

"Why can't you tell me what this is about?" A stab of pain in her temple briefly rendered her mute. "We wouldn't be hav-

ing this conversation if what I should call a break with reality—
a delusion, fantasy—hadn't really happened, would we?"

"No."

Shivering, she nevertheless acknowledged that she wanted to
see this conversation through. "What should we call it, a trip to
the Twilight Zone?"

"Call it whatever you need to."

"Thanks, I guess. About what *took place* when I wound up
with this around my neck: did it happen in real time or did you
somehow plant it in my mind?"

"What do you think?"

"Maybe a bit of both." Were they really having this conversation? "Did—we've never met before. How did you know—"
Seeing an adolescent boy approaching with Mazati's meal, she
fell silent. Mazati thanked the boy and gave him a tip, but didn't
start eating. Instead, he glanced at the older, oblivious couple.

"No, I've never seen you before today, but the moment I
did, I knew you were what I've been looking for for a long
time, what I believe I must have."

Must. There was that word again. "I, ah, see."

"Do you?"

To her surprise, she chuckled. "No."

"But you want to."

"I have to. Otherwise . . ."

Nodding, he picked up his burger and took a bite. Then he
set it down and drank deeply of his iced tea. Something brushed
the outside of her right ankle. The contact increased, warmth
against warmth, and she knew he was rubbing his ankle against
hers. Pinpricks spread up her legs and reached her crotch; she had
to work at keeping her breathing level. "What are you doing?"

"Do you want me to stop?"

Closing her eyes, she shook her head. The sensation continued and heat built. Just like that, things had again tipped from
the ordinary to the sensual between them.

"I want to learn about you, Hayley. What brought you to where you are in life."

"Does it matter?"

"Yes. Later I hope you'll understand why."

One winter morning she'd been driving to work when her car hit a patch of black ice, and she was suddenly spinning out of control, trying to remember whether or not to hit the brakes. With each drunken circle, she came closer to a raised cement divider. If she hit it, the car might flip over. At the very least, tires would flatten and metal crumple.

This *thing* that was happening between her and Mazati felt like that. As before, she had no say in the outcome. Maybe she'd wind up straddling the divider strip the way she'd done that morning, and maybe she'd crash into Mazati and total not a vehicle but her sanity.

"You want to learn things about me, do you? What about a fair exchange? For everything I reveal, you do the same?"

"I'd like to," he said softly. "But I have to be sure you can handle it."

"Handle what? What are you, a prison escapee? Political refugee? Disgraced politician?"

Her attempt at a joke—it was a joke, wasn't it?—died without a response on his part. She could have tried to wait him out, but he'd already made it clear that he kept huge chunks of himself private. "There's nothing remarkable about me," she began. "An ordinary woman living an ordinary life, at least mostly ordinary. I have a dream, a passion. I want to develop my own line of jewelry and see if I can make a living doing that. Your black opals in particular are what I've been looking for."

"You're looking for more than stones, Hayley."

Yes, I am. I just don't know what it is. Swallowing around the words she didn't dare utter, she nodded. "I'd say that was pretty perceptive of you except that could be said of almost anyone."

"I'm talking about you. You aren't happy with your life; I can see it in your eyes."

He'd stopped rubbing her ankle, and now his calf pressed against hers, adding strength to the sense of heat against heat. Straightening her spine reminded her of when his ropes around her elbows and wrists had forced an even more rigid position.

"There are things I'd like to change about it, of course, starting with no longer having to work for a large corporation, but I've already made one major change. Things are getting better."

"You got divorced."

Shocked, she leaned back but kept her legs within his reach. "I thought you said you didn't know me."

Smiling faintly, he took her left hand and held it up so they could both look at it. "There's still a mark on your ring finger."

"Oh, right. The divorce was final two months ago."

"Do you still love him?"

Only her sister had the right to ask something so personal and yet she didn't hesitate before shaking her head. "That died when I learned about his deception. For a long time I hated him for what he did, not just to me; but hate's a destructive emotion."

"Tell me about his deception."

Against all reason and self-protection, she did. Somewhere in the middle of the telling, the older couple left and two men and a teenage boy took over that end of the table. Other conversations flowed, and she trusted the sounds to keep what she was saying from reaching anyone else. Mazati continued to hold her hand and press his leg against hers, and as the words bled out of her, she sensed he was pulling them deep inside himself.

The story, minus only some of the numbness that had sustained her through the first nightmare days, was that she and Cal had been packing for the trip of a lifetime to Hawaii when police had knocked on the door and waved a search warrant at them. Although the police had refused to explain their intentions, she'd soon realized they were after her husband's business records. Cal had been an investment broker who, along with two other men, specialized in investments that appealed mostly to older people looking for stable dividends to supplement their Social Security and other retirement income. Before everything had fallen apart, she'd been proud of Cal because he'd never pushed high-risk stock. What she hadn't known was that his *picks,* as he called them, were made up of shell businesses and products that existed only on paper. He'd been able to produce the expected dividends by robbing from new clients, creating a house of cards that had started to collapse when checks began bouncing.

She'd believed Cal that night when he'd screamed at the police that if there'd been any wrongdoing, his partners were responsible. She'd continued to defend her man even when he was jailed. The first crack appeared when she tried to pull together bail money only to discover that their joint bank account had been drained, his two personal credit cards were maxed out, and he'd been unable to make the minimum payments on the latter. Perhaps most terrifying was learning that the house she adored was about to be repossessed.

"Don't say it," she warned when Mazati opened his mouth, "because I've already called myself every kind of an idiot you can. He was a financial expert, but I should have taken an active role in our personal finances. I should have questioned him when he blithely told me the Hawaii trip was a well-earned bonus." Using her free hand, she pressed her fingers against her forehead. "My mother was fighting breast cancer when we got married, and we never went on a honeymoon. After she died, I buried myself in what I'd always loved doing, creating jewelry, and Cal was spending all his time on his *business.*"

Coworkers, neighbors, and casual friends had prodded her with endless questions about the depth of Cal's deception, so when law enforcement came to her, she'd already known what to expect. Much as she'd wanted to hide under a rock, she'd made a decision she'd never regretted—to tell the truth. Now, looking at Mazati, she silently challenged him to say something she hadn't heard before.

"How did your family handle it?" he asked.

"My—my mother got sick just after my father died from kidney disease." She blinked away tears. "So other than an aunt living thousands of miles away, there was just my sister and me. I don't know if I would have survived without her."

"She believed in your innocence?"

"Totally." Did he?

"What about at work? That had to have been hard."

"I'm what's called an executive secretary, and as such, I sometimes handle funds, so yes, once the news broke, everything I'd done was scrutinized. They brought in an auditor and nothing turned up, so eventually I was able to breathe again. That's part of why I stay there; it's easier than having to prove myself somewhere else."

His hand tightened around her fingers in what couldn't be anything except understanding. Fighting tears she thought she'd put behind her, she studied his strong features. Cal was a handsome man, but as the layers of his deception came to life, she'd started seeing a chilling hollowness in his eyes. It was as if something had shut off, or maybe what she considered humanity had always been missing. In contrast, Mazati's dark eyes were alive with not exactly compassion but commitment. He cared deeply about something. She just didn't know what that was, yet. Eventually, his gaze and strong hand and the current flowing between her legs said she'd understand—and what drove him would do the same to her.

Wondering if it would really come to that distracted her from the tale she desperately wanted to put behind her. "Are you sorry you asked?" she came up with. "I'm more than happy to change the subject if that's the case. Any secrets in your life, something to match my sad tale?"

Maybe he was simply blinking, but then maybe he was deliberately throwing up a barrier. Finally, though, the light that had been there earlier returned. "Where is Cal now?"

"In prison, seven to ten years—not that that means much since it's a white-collar crime."

"But you won't see him when he's released."

It wasn't a question, so she kept her explanation short. She was moving on in life, trying to start over.

"Trying?"

"There never was a case against me. The D.A.'s office eventually connected Cal's partners to the scheme, but fortunately, I'd had nothing to do with the business." Not long ago her voice would have been tight with anger, but she'd learned that fury was unproductive and self-destructive. "Unfortunately, our creditors didn't see it the same way. I got saddled with a lot of the debts he'd run up. And I lost my home."

Silenced by memories of having to walk away from the yard and garden that had been her joy, the down payment financed by proceeds from her parents' modest estate, she struggled to keep her features impassive. But Mazati must have heard or felt the truth because he slid his fingers between hers, the gesture both comforting and erotic. Her hand looked small and safe in his, protected. "I'm living in a small rental, with a garage I'm turning into my work space."

"I want to see it."

It's nothing, just a roof over my head. "It's not very impressive, certainly not anything like what you're used to."

"What am I used to?"

"You're right; I don't know."

As silence ran between them, she gave her imagination the freedom to create what she believed Mazati needed in the way of housing. He'd never live in an apartment complex; being forced to would be a kind of death for him. Although he'd spent today talking to who knows how many people, he was a man who craved space and quiet, to be left alone with his thoughts.

Maybe the hunger in her made her think this, but she sensed nothing of a man in love about him. Sexual energy barely under control spoke of nights spent alone, not because the opportunities didn't fall at his feet, but because he chose his partners carefully. And when his nights were solitary, he surrounded himself with rustic, even primitive, furniture in rooms whispering of history. His neighbors were trees and open land. Windows remained open no matter what the weather. He seldom turned on the TV, preferring music. When darkness drove him inside, he read from his extensive library, mostly history. But much as his home satisfied his soul, he was seldom there.

"There's more to you than an opal broker," she said. "Other sides to you, other interests."

"Not interests, obsessions."

Nodding even as the word *obsession* scraped her nerve endings, she wondered if she had the courage to tell him about her fantasy about where he lived, but maybe he already knew. "Where did this come from?" She indicated her collar. "How did you get it around my neck, and how am I going to get it off?"

"I don't want you to try."

Even as she fought to pull enough air into her lungs, she acknowledged that he was telling her something she already knew. "Why not?"

"Because I need you."

A tremor briefly robbed her of the ability to speak. "I—in what way? If this is all about sex—"

"No, it isn't *all* about sex."

Mesmerized and frightened, she watched as he extended his hand toward her throat. His leg slid between hers, and he straightened his knee and rubbed it against the inside of first one thigh and then the other. As he hooked a forefinger through the ring at her throat, she drew back only to stop after a few inches, held in place by his strength. Strength of her own gripped her, and she stared back at him with a fierce message. No matter what his agenda or need, she wasn't his prisoner, his slave.

"What's going on?" a man asked. "Lady, you need some help?"

Mazati's grip held, forcing her to try to look at the man who'd been at the other end of the table without turning her head. The man was obviously uncomfortable but committed to coming to her aid if she asked. "It's all right. I can take care of it."

"Yeah?" the other man spoke up. "If that's the case then take it outside. No one's interested in whatever the hell kinky game the two of you are playing."

This is no game.

"Sorry." Smiling, Mazati held up both hands in an *I surrender* gesture. "Guess we got a little carried away." At the same time, the pressure against her thighs increased. The teenager with the two men stared at her so intently that she scrambled to her feet. "I have to go." Not taking a chance on looking at Mazati, she whirled and stumbled away. With every step, her panties pressed against her blood-engorged cunt. Could she bring herself to climax by breaking into a trot?

"Don't."

Stopped in mid stride, she slowly swiveled to acknowledge the man who'd turned her life on end. How he'd managed to overtake her so soon was beyond her comprehension.

"We aren't done," he said in the low and sexy tone that might take off the top of her head if she didn't throw up some defenses.

"I know."

"Tonight."

Words bunched inside her, but she didn't try to free them. After all, this was his agenda, his time.

"I'll be leaving around eight," he said. "I want you waiting for me."

10

The shadows from the regimented row of poplar trees lining one side of the parking lot had more than lengthened; now that the sun had set, they invaded the area in front of the building where the gem show was being held. Most of the spaces were unoccupied, proof that the visitors had left. Vendors were loading up their wares. From where she sat in her car, Hayley couldn't hear what was being said, but most of the faces illuminated by their vehicles' interior lights were smiling, which she took to mean that it had been a successful day despite what she'd heard earlier. So far she hadn't spotted Mazati or determined which was his vehicle.

She was tired and hungry and had no one to blame except herself for her empty stomach. Looking back at the hours since she'd left the show, she couldn't say why she hadn't gotten something to eat beyond the small hot dog, and why she had driven aimlessly with her newly purchased opals on the passenger seat.

Although she'd studied each stone, both when she was buying them and after she'd left Mazati this afternoon, she turned on the dome light and again took them out. Each unfinished stone rested in its plastic envelope, the sparkle seeming to reach out and caress her from just below the ring on her collar to between her breasts. The longer she looked at them, the more at peace she felt. Her desire to create things of beauty from nature's gifts wasn't just a pipe dream, was it? All she had to do was let each unique opal speak to her; the results would please most people who looked at the finished product.

Traditionally, most opals were molded into oval shapes, but she didn't want to force the ones she'd create into something nature hadn't intended. Her resolve to let their true shapes speak to potential buyers grew. That's where their mystique, their magic lay—being true to themselves. She was simply the means to that end.

Picking up a stone that had caught her eye, she held it up to the light. To the casual observer, its color wasn't that different from the blacks, but she'd detected something she couldn't put her finger on. After turning it one way and then the other, she rested it in her palm and leaned back.

"Boulder opal."

Brought alive by Mazati's voice, she faced the open driver's window. He was leaning over, his forearms resting on the ledge. Why, when she'd become acutely aware of everything about him, hadn't she sensed his approach? Shoving aside the ludicrous notion that he'd materialized out of thin air, she struggled to make sense of what he'd just said. "Boulder?"

"They come from a thin seam of opal on an ironstone matrix. The ironstone is very dark, which makes the fire stand out, resembling a true black opal."

What was it about his tone that shifted everything into high gear for her? She'd never been this energized by a man, not even back when she'd been discovering what the opposite sex was good for. "Then this is worth more than the other blacks I bought?"

Because he was surrounded by darkness, she sensed more than saw him nod, and even with her memories of what he looked like, she couldn't draw him out of the night. "But I paid the same for each one."

"Yes."

"Why?"

"Maybe it was my way of thanking you." Reaching in, he removed the stone from her palm and dropped it onto the seat. "You returned."

"I had to," she blurted. "I—I don't understand what's happening between us, and I need to."

"Why?"

Because my sanity depends on it. "Don't play games with me, Mazati; I can't handle it."

"They aren't games," he said and opened her door.

Taking courage and wanting in hand, she flowed more than stepped out of the car. He was only inches away, calling to her in a primal way, heating her collar and more, so much more. If she could speak, she would have demanded an explanation. Instead, she acknowledged his greater height and heft, a primitive strength she couldn't deny. The world was full of beautiful and uncomplicated women, so why had he chosen her?

Maybe he didn't have an interest in her beyond tonight, beyond whatever the hell spell he'd slipped over her. Even as she embraced the night's promise, she didn't dare forget that.

"This thing that's happening between us, Hayley. What does it feel like to you?"

He hadn't touched her. As long as she kept her distance— her barely perceptible distance—she was safe, wasn't she? "I keep getting tangled up in reality and fantasy."

"It's possible for them to exist at the same time."

What are you saying? "I—before today I'd have argued the point with you. If this is what being on drugs feels like, I'm glad I never tried them. It's too confusing." Determined to turn the conversation in a safer direction, she looked around. Her gaze fell on the opals. "You—you said they came from Mexico. Where? Unless it's a secret."

"It's not, but the mine is remote. You'd never find it on your own."

Blindsided by an image of him guiding her through the wilderness to a wealth of gemstones, she didn't realize he'd reached for her until he brushed her hair off her forehead. She could tell him she needed to get a haircut and was hopeless when it came to styling it, but did he care? Did she? "The mine: describe it, please."

"It's fairly shallow, long, and narrow. The excavation is done by natives and mostly by hand digging."

"Why?"

"Because only people who have been raised in the area understand and appreciate it. Outsiders can't grasp history's significance. The moment they see the pyramid, that's all they care about."

Pyramid! A wave of lightheadedness hit her and her legs felt weak. Determined not to fall, she reached for the door. Instead, she found Mazati's arm and clung to it. As she leaned against him, the feeling that she might pass out faded, to be replaced by a need so strong it took every bit of willpower in her not to rip off their clothes.

"What is it?"

He wasn't posing a question so much as encouraging her to be open and honest, and with his arms around her now, she couldn't be anything else. "Tell me about the pyramid."

"You're ready for this?"

"Yes."

"Thank you. It's Aztec, more temple than pyramid. Built to honor Huitzilopochtli, God of the Sun and War, and Tlaloc, God of Rain. It was started in what you would call the fourteenth century."

"The fourteenth century?"

"It has seven levels and rises over one hundred feet into the air. There's an inner passage that leads to a large cave housing underground springs. The cave branches out to four smaller chambers in a shape you would call a cloverleaf."

"Hidden chambers?"

"Rooms for the dead to rest in before journeying to the underworld."

It was too much! "Springs? Does that part of Mexico have much water? Isn't a lot of it arid?"

"It didn't used to be. Long ago, when Tlaloc ruled, rains fed the land and rivers."

And created the junglelike environment you showed me. No matter how hard she tried, she couldn't stop shaking. Thank goodness for Mazati's strong arms. Otherwise, she'd be on the ground. "How do you know so much about the pyramid? Has there been a lot of excavation? I thought you said that's discouraged."

"I know because it's part of me."

So much of what he'd said in the last few minutes was beyond her comprehension, so why was this even harder to grasp? "What do you mean, part of you? Mazati, damn it, what is this about?"

"I can't tell you yet."

"When, damn it, when?"

"Once you're ready."

Another lightning-driven spark roared through her, forcing her to increase her grip on his arm. Before she could regain control, he swept her into his arms, elbowed the car door closed, and started walking toward the adjacent area, a small city park popular with couples in large part because it lacked a playground. The surrounding trees, benches, grass, and three flower beds were touted as an escape from the city while still inside the city limits. Lighting came from solar globes driven into the ground that were just now coming to life. The park had been vandalized in the past but not since the arrest and conviction of a trio of lowlifes. Since then, apparently the area had been deemed off limits by those with more time than brains.

"I can walk," she muttered, her head resting on his chest and his heartbeat pulsing through her.

"Not now, you can't."

After making his way to the edge of a rose garden, he sank to his knees on grass. She remained in his arms, her buttocks on his thighs and her arms around his neck. This was insane, of course. She didn't know this man. He could be a criminal, a rapist, a crook, a murderer even.

No, he wasn't.

Dark and light coexisted here much as an opal's various hues created a color-filled mix. An opal's history and the mystique that went with the stone gave it its richness. The same was true with Mazati; without him, there'd be no mystery here, no depth.

Lids lowered, she wondered at her philosophical bent, since she'd never been one for much introspection, or rather she hadn't until she'd held her first opal and accepted the challenge to do something magical with it. Mazati was hardly a piece of rock waiting to be molded and enhanced. Instead, he was the artist, the master, and she his subject.

Where are you taking me? she wanted to ask. *Why have you chosen me?* Instead, she sank into him and let his heat into her.

And when he repositioned both of them so she was cradled in the pocket created by his spread legs, with her back resting on his chest, she accepted him with every molecule of her being. "I love places like this," she told him, somewhat surprised because she was content, simply content. "Like my mother, I've always needed flowers and other living things around me. It's as if I feed off them. They make me strong again, ready to face the world."

"Is facing the world hard?"

"Sometimes." She gnawed on her lower lip, trying to decide whether to be honest. But even if she said nothing, maybe he already knew what beat inside her. Maybe there wasn't anything she could keep from him. "I want this so bad."

"This?"

"To create."

"It will happen."

"You have no idea how much I want to believe you, but I might only *think* I can turn opals into something someone would buy."

"You have the skill."

Although she should know better than to blindly believe him, she was convinced he could see inside her. More than that, he understood her surfaces. Most of all, he'd tapped into the raw woman she usually kept hidden, the wild female animal who needed a mate, a strong and even more wild male.

Him.

A blip of thought prompted her to ponder what she might say about her blooming confidence in her talent, but his hands were sliding over her thighs and heading for her crotch. She placed her hands over his and joined him in the journey. His cock pressed against her tailbone to let her know how ready it was, how determined to house itself in her, to take control.

Too late to run, to hesitate, to fear.

Scooting closer to let him know she shared his readiness, she stared at the whispered reality of the rosebushes. Her pussy was like an opening bud, unfolding in answer to a message spoken by flesh.

Even as she shook her head at her poetic turn, she felt herself open even more. Yes, her labia was swelling and softening, but her response to his touch and mystery went much farther than her sex organ. Her muscles were weakening, her vision fading, her hearing oblivious to everything except his heartbeat and breathing. There was only this moment and his fingers strong over her crotch, only her head falling back and hungry sounds pushing past her lips.

The pressure on her pussy increased. Moaning her hunger, she gave her hips the freedom to move restlessly. Her cunt tightened repeatedly, and when she tried to slow the pace, she discovered she couldn't. His hands had done this to her, hands and arms and hot breath against her neck and his belly taut with his own need.

Sighing and sobbing at the same time, she pushed her pelvis toward his hands. "So fast, so fast."

"What is?"

"Us. This. I don't—"

"Yes, you do."

Was she ready for sex or was he sucking her into his need, molding her like a piece of clay? Yes, he was molding, she answered herself. Wasn't the collar proof?

But if she hadn't wanted it, she'd have taken a knife to it.

"You know so much about me," she said with her legs wide open and shaking as his knuckles ground against her clit. "Storm into my life and—"

"Quiet. Feel, only feel."

Her master had issued an order. Determined to obey, she clenched her teeth and dug her nails into the back of his hands and held on with what little sanity she retained. The snap and zipper on her jeans offered no resistance, and in seconds, he'd exposed her panties. Then he slid his hand against her belly. Instead of reaching for her pussy, he rested his fingers on her mons. His other arm now covered her breasts as he cradled her. Hard moments of concentration brought her silent whispers to an end, but she knew better than to try to calm her breathing. Raking in short gasps only fed her hunger, and because she had no choice, she let him know by repeatedly dragging her nails over his forearms and rocking from side to side. The pressure

on her breasts and mons increased, but she couldn't heed whatever message he was sending out. She was starving, release
clawing into her but not finding a home.

"Please, please. Fuck me."

"You're ready?"

"Yes!"

Was it her imagination or was he, too, now trembling? Telling
herself that she'd gotten to him increased her self-confidence. If
she could think of anything except the wonder and joy and
danger of taking him into her body, she might have tried to take
advantage of her newfound power.

And yet even as she soaked her panties and her hard nipples
prodded his arm, the reasoning, responsible woman she was
hissed her warning. "I can't. We can't."

"What?"

"Protection, damn it. A condom. I'm not on the pill."

Confusion rolled through him.

"Don't make me spell it out," she begged. Was that what it
felt like to be drowning, desperate for air but helpless?

"You're fertile?"

What a quaint way of putting things. Giving him the answer
they both needed called for concentration she wasn't sure she
was capable of, but at length the facts came to her. "No, not yet.
My period just ended. But there's more than pregnancy to—
damn it, you know what I'm talking about."

His silence made her wonder if he did understand. Instead
of asking, she spelled out what should have been obvious. She'd
been faithful to Cal and hadn't had sex with another man since
the divorce because fucking a man called for trust or affection
or lust or a combination of all three, and until today she'd been
too raw and wary for any of those conditions. But just because
she could promise Mazati a clean bill of health didn't mean she
expected the same of him. After all, look at what he had to offer
women!

"You must carry condoms," she finished.

"No."

What had she gotten herself into? "Why not?"

Slowly, so beautifully slowly, he stroked her labia. Wondering if she could truly flow into him, she let go of the tension that had seized her at the beginning of the conversation. "Hayley, I haven't had sex in many, many years."

Nothing he might say would have surprised her more, but instead of doubting him, she slid deeper into the warm cocoon of his body. Maybe he'd been a member of a religious order, in prison, on some kind of secret foreign assignment, in a coma.

No, it hadn't been any of those things.

"Do you believe me?"

"Yes," her heart answered. *Yes,* her body echoed.

When he sighed, a shudder accompanied the sound, adding to her sense that they were sharing something rare. His heated breathing enveloped her, quieting the sexual rage that had nearly turned her into a bitch in heat. The bitch still clung to her edges, ready to erupt, but for now she was content with the softness between them. As a girl, she'd thought that this was what romance would feel like: flowers and warm breezes, cuddling with a man while they shared a cup of hot chocolate, riding off into the sunset on matching horses, living in a little house with a white picket fence. Then the hormones had kicked in, and as she marched to their insistent tune, she'd laughed at her earlier naiveté.

Tonight she embraced her innocence.

"I want you to undress for me," he said, "this time."

As completely as lethargy had enveloped her, it washed away under his request. Because he gave no sign of letting her go, she was forced to pull out of his embrace. Getting to her feet was a monumental task, and she tackled it one step at a time, starting with settling herself on her knees. Instead of planting her hands on the ground so she could push off, she hauled her slacks as far as she could down her hips. Guided by night and need, she slipped a hand under her panties. He'd touched her here, claimed her mons and ignited her labia.

And because he'd done the same to her breasts, she reached under her top and ran her hand between her breasts. Her bra cups were too small, damn it, the constricting fabric pressing painfully against her swollen globes. Much as she wanted to bring her sex fully to life, getting rid of the impossible bra had to come first.

Scooting around so she was facing him was hardly the most graceful thing she'd ever done, but she wanted his eyes on her while she worked. He'd closed his legs and was leaning back with his arms behind him, a powerful and self-confident man waiting for what they both knew was his due. Shoving aside the desire to rip off his clothing, she pulled her shirt over her head and dropped it in his lap. He glanced at it, shrugged. "Keep going."

Noting that his words had changed from request to order, she swallowed away what she could of her nervousness. If she'd known this was going to happen, she would have worn a less practical bra—if she had one. Wondering if she still had the black lace push-up Cal had bought for their first anniversary briefly distracted her. By the time she'd remembered that she'd gotten rid of it during a memory-dumping session, she had the clasp unfastened. Halfway through a consideration of whether she should attempt a striptease, his gaze burned a path from her throat to her pussy. Eyes unfocused, she yanked off what she suddenly and totally hated. A flip of her wrist and the bra rested on top of her shirt.

When she tried to swallow again, a lump lodged in her throat, and her vision refused to clear. Still, she knew he was watching her, waiting, appraising. This man who'd called her a slave earlier today wanted to see her not just naked but with her body and soul ready for him. All her adult life she'd wanted larger breasts, but this was what she had to offer him. Cupping them, she lifted and extended them as far as she could toward him. *Yours, my gift to you.*

"No," he said when she started to stand. "Stay down here."

She indicated the front of her gaping slacks. "I thought you wanted—"

"I do. Make it happen without getting off the grass."

Now there was something kinky, or rather another kinky something, in a relationship that was already full of the unconventional. Responding to this latest command cloaked in a request, she closed her legs and sucked in her stomach. She managed to bring her slacks nearly to her knees before resting on first one hip and then the other to work them down to her ankles. Fortunately she'd worn flats, which she easily kicked out of, but it took stretching out on her back with her legs in the air to drag her slacks over her feet. She threw the discarded garment in his direction but from here couldn't see whether she'd reached him. Still on her back with the short grass prickling her spine, she turned her attention to her one remaining garment. If someone walked by—

Before Mazati, she would have been mortified to be caught stripping in a public place, but now she didn't care. The little park belonged to them; they owned it for as long as they needed; it claimed them.

Lifting her buttocks off the ground with her knees deeply bent while her shoulders and feet supported her weight might not have been the most efficient way of removing her panties. She managed to get the scrap of satin off her left foot, but the toes of her right got hung up in the wadded fabric.

It didn't matter, not with her ass back on the grass and her legs gaping and her hands again reaching for her sex. There! Wet. Ready. Awareness of Mazati faded as she spread her lips and ran a forefinger into her opening. A hot shudder flowed through her as she arched her back and plunged deeper. Her clit screamed its demand; she'd explode if she so much as touched her trigger.

"No."

A hard word, a word she didn't dare ignore. Her finger still in her, she rolled her head to the side. He hadn't moved, but his glare slapped at her. "I can't help—"

"That's *my* cunt, slave."

Shocked, she looked around half expecting to find that they'd been spirited back to the pyramid, but the quiet ground lighting still illuminated them. "What—did you say?"

"You heard. And you remember." His voice had turned silken, but beneath the smooth tone rode confidence and command.

"What do you want from me?"

"You, becoming what I need. For now, you are to take your finger out of yourself and lick your juices off it. When you're done, you will crawl over to me."

Where was she? What had happened to the peaceful park, her discarded clothing, the gentle lighting? They'd faded away to be replaced by his voice, his presence. Hot and cold lapped at every inch of skin as she deserted her cunt and ran her wet finger between her lips. Sucking took her full attention because she imagined *his* finger in her mouth and that he'd coated it with her fluids. Squirming, she waited for his next order. When it didn't come, she held up her clean finger for his approval. She nearly missed his slight nod.

"Do you want . . . I'm supposed to . . ."

Was he deliberately torturing her with silence? Maybe, and maybe he'd already said all he believed he needed to. Sitting up and then getting onto her hands and knees became an out-of-body experience. Even when she started crawling toward him with her ass in the air and her breasts dangling and her panties dragging behind her foot, it was as if she was watching some other woman submitting to a powerful man, her master. Knowing she needed time to absorb and accept the latest step in what was developing between them, she patterned her progress after a cat stalking prey. Every movement of arms and legs became a slow extension of one limb before bringing the other up to it.

Night air played along her spine as her ass swayed in rhythm with her legs. In her mind she became a sex kitten, her muscles and bones working together in an erotic glide she felt along her length and registered in his intense study of her. She loved knowing that her body was turning him on, and that made the waiting bearable. She wasn't his slave; under her own direction, she was becoming his whore, willingly accepting her new role as sexual object. As the weight of her breasts caused a pulling sensation, for the first time in her life she truly and without reservation worshipped that part of her anatomy. He was teaching her how to celebrate her neck and belly; thighs; and wet, loose labia.

He hadn't said where he wanted her, but because she craved his hands on her, she drew alongside him before settling back on her haunches like some obedient dog and resting her fingers on her knees.

"I have something in my right pocket," he told her. "Take it out."

Curiosity about how much preparation he'd gone to distracted her from his heat long enough to do as he'd ordered. The instant her fingers touched the soft cord, she knew where this was going. Pulling the white rope free, she held it up for both of them to see. *Yes,* her cunt responded. *Yes, I want this.*

"I'm saying this only once tonight, Hayley." His voice was leaden, as if the words were unwanted but necessary. "If you aren't ready, walk away."

Walk away? No! Never. Still, because she understood how much was at stake, she didn't hurry her response. Instead, she ran the rope between her breasts before looping it through the collar ring. Once he'd put it to use, she'd have given up something precious and fragile.

And in turn, he'd take her where she needed to go.

Eyes brimming with tears, she handed the rope to him. "Turn around and put your hands behind you," he commanded.

His instructions were simple, so why was it so awkward to present her back to him? Maybe it was no more complicated than wanting to study his expression, but maybe she wasn't as ready as she'd believed. But because she'd wrestled with the same emotions before, when she'd walked away from her marriage and fought her way through them, she presented her back and ass to him and then rested her hands against the base of her spine. He left her alone for the better part of a minute while she imagined he was studying her, maybe applauding his mastery, maybe preparing for his role.

When he crossed one of her wrists over the other and lashed them together, freedom bled out of her. And when he'd tied the last knot and ran his hands over her arms, she flowed into him.

"We're going to feel and experience as one. The position and pace will be mine but the journey shared. Do you understand?"

"Yes."

Maybe she should have guessed what he had in mind when he abruptly shoved her forward so her forehead was on the ground, but her thoughts went no farther than his strength. Then he pushed her legs apart and tapped her pussy with the flat of his hand, and she whimpered into the grass. His next tap to her sex was harder, more possessive. "Mine. Say it, slave. Your cunt belongs to me."

"My—my cunt belongs to you."

A slap this time, vibrations resonating into her belly and making her squeal. "You want this."

"I want—oh god, I need!"

Pushing her pussy lips apart, he buried his thumb where her

finger had been. His fingers closed over her clit. "I need," she mewled. "Shit, shit!"

"Quiet."

He expected her to say nothing? Gnawing on her lower lip, she prayed she'd have the strength to obey.

"I need you to exist inside your skin so your journey's complete. When you've learned certain things, you'll have earned the right to take as you're being taken, but you aren't there yet." His thumb went to work on her, plundering deep and fast as if foreplay was behind them and all he wanted was for her to climax. But what about him?

How to tell him, how to let him know she'd do whatever it took to release his tension? Hoping to distract herself from the energy swirling through her, she turned her head to the side, but she couldn't see him unless she lifted her head, and she refused to disobey him.

A wave of sensation beyond description ripped through her to arch her back and curl her toes. She sounded like a cat howling, her voice soft but barely under control. "Can't help, can't help," she repeated as he worked her. "Please, can't help."

"Ride my thumb and feel my power. Give it up, surrender."

Yes, yes, yes, she could do that! Hot webs snaked around her lower body and pulled her into something deep and fiery. Drooling, she fought her restraints without knowing why or wanting to. She'd never been handled like this, with a finger pumping inside her and her clit trapped. Helpless, not because of the rope but because only he existed in her world, she clenched her pussy muscles and rode his thumb, pulling his power throughout her. Strength radiated down her arms and legs and sent her toes and fingers to tingling. Fascinated, she wondered how long she could dangle at the edge of a climax.

Not long, if he kept after her like this.

Although it nearly tore her apart to resist, she sat up. The effort nearly caused her shoulders and belly to cramp, and if he'd done anything to stop her, she wouldn't have succeeded. Confused and with fire still licking at her cunt, she looked back at him. He thrust his gleaming thumb at her. Relieved to be doing what he wanted, she licked him clean of her and then pulled him as deep as she could into her throat. He nodded, and she smiled her gratitude and relief at him. Rescued from his mastery but wanting it back, she lowered her head. "I'm sorry," she muttered. "I didn't mean to disobey. I just—I don't understand—"

"What you don't yet understand is how deep you must go." After brushing her hair out of her eyes, he ran a finger through her collar ring and forced her head up. Once he had her in position, he began slapping her breasts with a slow, easy rhythm. "I'm scraping away at your walls. Revealing the you beneath the surface that you never knew existed."

Far from being painful, the slaps took her back to how he'd handled her cunt before finger fucking her. When he let go of the ring, she remained in place so her breasts were available to him. "Teach me, please."

Slap, slap, slap, measured beats seeped through her. "Earn the lessons."

Earn? What was he—"What do you want me to do?"

"No, it's not going to be that way!" A sharp sting on her right breast punctuated his outburst. "I need you thinking and functioning, not just experiencing. Much as I need to get inside your skin, the same must happen to me. Otherwise, I will have failed."

It was all too complex. On the brink of begging him to explain what he wanted, she forced back the words. He was still stimulating her breasts, but when she looked into his eyes, dark mystery and pain caught her in their grip. *Why so much turmoil?* "Let me fuck you, please. Let me see you naked."

His eyes closed, his hands stilled, and he leaned away. Watching his struggle, she cursed the bonds that prevented her from embracing him, but only he could take the next step. Long seconds marched between them, but finally he stood up and quickly, efficiently shed his clothes. With each garment discarded, her hunger grew, and when he stepped out of his shorts and presented her with his nude form, she loved him. The frighteningly vulnerable emotion faded away, and she embraced animal need. Even without the use of her hands, she'd find a way to have sex with him, and in the act they'd become one—briefly.

As he got down on his knees, she wondered if he was having the same thoughts. She, too, was kneeling but there the similarity ended because he was muscle where she was lean, hard in contrast to her softness. She possessed a womb, while he was owner of a red-veined cock pointing arrogantly at her.

When he reached for her, she feinted to the left. Then, straightening, she plowed into him, the top of her head connecting with his chest. Although he could have easily withstood the assault, he allowed her to knock him backward. Straightening his legs, he folded his arms under his head and gazed up at her, waiting. Instead of answering the message in his dark and needy eyes, her attention slid down his body. Once there, nothing else mattered, not her immobile arms or collar, not where he'd come from and what he was doing in her life and where he intended to take her, not even whether his plan was to guide or force her.

There was only his cock and her cunt and joining.

More scared than she'd maybe ever been, she forced her feet under her. When she was nearly sure they'd hold her, she swung a foot over him and straddled him with his cock under her. Looking down, she wondered if she'd been waiting all her life for this moment. Then the enormity of her question hammered into her, and she shut down. This was about sex, fucking, male and female parts molded together, and explosions—most of all the explosions.

Her leg muscles felt strong and sure as she lowered herself. She stopped when his tip touched her clit, adjusted and sank down another inch. Concerned that the alignment was less than perfect, she blocked out everything except welcoming him home, and when he ran his knuckles over her straining calves, she relaxed and experienced, simply experienced. His cock rode along her pussy walls, stretching and fulfilling her. The moment was alive and intense, her nerves short-circuiting even as they shivered. He wasn't just in her cunt; parts of him were spreading outward, entering her veins and swimming everywhere. Something she couldn't define found her heart. Heaviness was settling on her hips and breasts and thighs.

Skewered by him, she stared at nothing and lifted herself slightly. Having her arms behind her made her awkward; still, she went after the rhythm of sex. Then he closed his hands around her waist, and she no longer concerned herself with her balance.

Picking up the pace, she dove into the notion that she was the aggressor. His ability to thrust into her was limited so she did all she could to make up the difference. Her thighs burned, and she couldn't think how to relax her stomach muscles, but that didn't distract her from repeatedly filling herself with him.

Laughter punctuated her hard gasps as she fed off his straining muscles. His cock spread her wide and reached deep. Her pussy wept every time she withdrew only to weep anew when she filled herself with him. *Faster, faster,* her head and clit roared. *Harder, harder!*

She barely noticed when his hands moved up from her waist, and when he grabbed her upper arms and pulled her down, she continued her frantic pounding. Now he held her upper body immobile, which forced all her energy, strength, and desperation into her lower half. Thank god he was powering into her, his movements far from in sync with hers but fueling the burning.

There it was, the telltale shift from promise to fulfillment. The coming ride! Thinking she could speed the journey by changing his alignment in her, she fought his embrace. He might have started to grant her request before tightening his grip and forcing her breasts against his chest; she might have only imagined the momentary slackening in his domination. It didn't matter; she was too far gone. Too close.

Sweat streamed off her; she couldn't fill her lungs. Thrusting frantically, she pounded his body with hers, barely swallowing a howl because his cock kept powering into her. Promise again lapped at her, then danced away. Then heat from deep inside exploded. She was bleeding into him, emptying out. Fighting and accepting at the same time, she gathered her thigh and ass muscles and pushed against him with every bit of strength in her.

Her climax kept coming, coming. Levitating, she took him with her. Hissing, he shoved her upright, and she hammered her body against his until her muscles died.

And still she came.

So spent he wasn't sure his legs would hold him, Mazati stared in the direction Hayley had driven. Hopefully he'd kept his weakness from her, but he wasn't sure of anything where she was concerned. About to tell himself that his exhaustion was because he hadn't had sex in so long, he stopped the lie.

He hadn't expected this! Hayley was supposed to be his connection with the modern world, a woman with the ability to re-create what was beautiful about his heritage, nothing more. His goal had been to share his knowledge with her, but not before he'd forged an inescapable bond. In order to do that, he'd believed he had to make her so emotionally and sexually dependent on him that the reality of what he was wouldn't overwhelm her.

More dead than alive for countless years, he'd thought he'd be able to remain separate and untouched, as numb as he'd been back when his world collapsed, but he'd been wrong. When he heard her heart beating, his lonely one had responded. His body needed hers next to it, sheltering and housing what made him a man.

Shaken by his unexpected reaction and dangerous vulnerability, he visualized himself walking back into the fog that had claimed him for so long. Surrounded by the dense mist, he'd drift again, unfeeling and barely thinking, alone and safe.

But if he did, what had been entrusted to him would remain his alone. As lost as he'd been. And maybe that was worse than taking risks.

Maybe.

If only he knew.

11

"Where are you?" Saree asked.

"Ah, heading home. Why?"

"Home from where?"

"What's this, twenty questions?" Hayley had never been comfortable driving and talking on her cell phone. The light traffic should have made things easier, but getting her mind past the *just been fucked* feeling hadn't happened.

"I'm your sister. I'm entitled. Let's put it another way. When did you leave the gem show and did you and "dark and mysterious" exchange personal information?"

About to sidestep, Hayley decided on honesty, because quite frankly, she needed help. "It's moving pretty fast."

"Home run?"

Much as she'd like to close her eyes and replay the scene in the park, ending the day with an accident wasn't high on her list of favorite things to do. "We more than got to first base if that's what you're asking about. Oh shit, all right, yes. *It* happened."

Silence. Not good, because Saree not talking meant the wheels were going around. "That's not like you, sis. I know, I know, I've been encouraging you to kick loose and embrace the single life, but I did so because I never really thought you'd take me up on it. You're the conservative one, the good girl."

"I'm still good." She slowed as a car being driven by an elderly woman ahead of her started drifting over into her lane. "Let's just say I wasn't any good at self-control tonight."

"Hmm. How do you feel about that?"

That was Saree, all right. She didn't have a judgmental bone in her body, opting instead to push and probe until people were forced to reveal their own truths. "It was a hell of a ride. I'm still vibrating."

"Is that what you were after?"

"I don't know," she blurted, suddenly near tears. "It's pretty overwhelming."

"Pretty? I think something is either overwhelming or it isn't."

"All right! I'm kind of scared but in an incredible way, at least an exciting way. I've never—"

"You don't have to tell me that. What's got you scared?"

Concentrating on passing the old woman, who turned out to have a little dog in her lap, prevented Hayley from supplying a quick answer. "I'm in over my head; I'll admit that. It's like he has some kind of agenda and I'm a vital part of it, but I have no idea what his goal is."

"Not good."

"How do you know? You aren't in the middle of it."

"True, but I picked up some vibes from this Mazati guy. He's not, how should I say it, he isn't easy to read. Intense as shit, not exactly uptight but something along those lines. This should come as no surprise to you, but some seriously creepy people are addicted to porn. Thanks to the safety measures my employers have put in place, the only way I know anything about them is via their e-mail, but I've read some damn sick stuff. Sure, their blathering is a combination of fantasy and a certain amount of anonymity, but just knowing what people can dream up can be scary."

"You're scared?" Saree had never mentioned that.

"Let's just say I'm damn glad they don't know where I live. What I'm trying to say is, I didn't get that kind of a vibe off Mazati. If I thought he intended to kidnap you and keep you as his sex slave, I'd personally separate him from the equipment he needs to pull that off."

Where was she? Damn it, she knew this part of town and should be able to make the necessary turns without thinking. However, this street looked only vaguely familiar. "I don't doubt that," she came up with.

"Mazati, I'm fairly confident, doesn't need to come up close and personal to my largest kitchen knife to keep him from breaking the law, but he's unlike any man I've ever been around. Maybe I should be surprised that you believe he has an agenda involving you and you alone, but the way he homed in on you today pretty much spelled that out. The question is, is it right and safe and sane for you?"

For my body, hell yes. "I don't know yet."

Another of Saree's telling silences hung as Hayley spotted a street sign and realized she should be two blocks over. "What if it's too late by the time you have things figured out?" Saree finally asked.

"I don't know!"

"Then get the hell away from him. Tell him thanks for the wham-bam but you're going to live your own life from now on."

I can't! Whatever he's offering, I need it.

"Hayley? Are you listening to me?"

"I hear you."

"But are you listening? Damn it, stay in control!"

How?

* * *

Her landlord hadn't been crazy about her plan to cut an opening in the garage/workshop so she could install a window air conditioner, but when she'd offered to do the work and explained that it would make the space that much more desirable to the next tenant, he'd given in. He'd also caved when she brought up replacing the small single window with one large enough to bring in some real light. The two changes had more than strained her budget when it couldn't stand any more stretching, but she was well pleased with the results because she'd created a space she wanted to spend time in.

Today, two weeks after she'd met Mazati and the day before she was set to have lunch with her sister, she was leaning over her cutting wheel, but instead of polishing the roughly egg-shaped opal stuck to the end of her dop stick, she stared into the about-to-emerge color. At times she saw nothing except an uncomplicated opal. Then, suddenly, the rich hue would turn even darker and shift to a royal blue. Maybe she should keep this one for herself, make it into a large ring she could wear when calling on stores she hoped would carry her line. She could make sure the lighting hit the ring just right and then artfully flutter her hand, ready to smile modestly when whomever she was talking to exclaimed about it.

And maybe she was loathe to let go of this opal, like the others she'd been working with, because the stones were her connection with Mazati, her only connection except for the collar still caressing her throat.

Where was he? If only she'd pressed for his card, his phone number, something. But sex had gotten in the way of practical matters, sex and insanity. Starting with that first night, she'd given herself headaches and upset stomachs worrying that he'd walked out of her life. Just as he'd stormed into her world, he'd deserted it. No matter that he'd promised to keep on supplying her with opals; she'd forgotten to give him her phone number, and he didn't know where she lived.

Ships passing in the night? No, hell no! What they'd experienced was so much more than that. She'd been awake and sober when he'd lifted her out of the existence she'd always known and deposited her into a jungle, a jungle that had existed hundreds of years ago. He'd spirited her back in time, as witnessed by how new the pyramid looked.

"Enough!" Her voice echoed, reminding her all over again of how alone she felt. Determined to put an end to the unsettling sensation, she got up and turned on her stereo. Her favorite, all-music station came on. "Better. There's nothing to be gained by replaying one damn day and evening in your boring life. Now get to work."

Returning to her chair, she picked up the dop stick and aimed the opal at the cutting wheel. The fine grit sander slipped repeatedly over the stone's surface almost like a lover, and as had happened ever since she'd started her *hobby*, she became as one with her materials and machinery. There was more than a rhythm to cutting and polishing. And despite what it said on her business card, she wasn't just a jeweler; she was a liberator—because without her skill and patience and eye, an opal's deepest secrets and richness wouldn't be revealed. In some respects she became married to each stone, living with and for it until both she and the stone were satisfied. Once the initial process of letting free the opal's truth was finished, she'd place it on velvet and study it until it whispered to her of what it wanted to become. This had become her favorite part of the process. Fear of failure had no place during those introspective moments. Instead, a deep core belief that she was doing the absolute right thing with her life seeped into her. Creating beauty from nature was what she was about.

When she was satisfied that the opal had no more life left trapped inside, she leaned back and gazed at it. Within a minute she had her answer. Yes, it needed to be a ring, the setting all but invisible, and not for her. Opal rings were problematic because of the stones' delicacy, so she'd include her note to the potential buyer about keeping it away from chemicals such as dishwashing detergent. Given what she intended to charge for it, hopefully its owner would understand that wearing a Night Fire ring should be reserved for special occasions.

Night Fire. Before she'd seen Mazati's stones, she'd been struggling with what she should call her jewelry line, but the words had draped themselves over her consciousness as she was waking up the morning after having sex with him. As to whether she'd been thinking about the rare and rich black opals or the man when it had all come together, it didn't matter.

"What do you think, Mazati? Do you approve?" Sighing, she looked over at the shelf holding her finished creations. Just a few more days and she'd have enough necklaces, bracelets, earrings, and rings so potential outlets could see she had a full line. As often happened when she studied her growing collection, the need to go over and pick them up asserted itself, but if she did, she'd lose valuable time.

The strange thing was, she'd accomplished more in the past two weeks than she had in the two months before that. Some of her productivity came, she suspected, from sexual frustration. If she sat and contemplated, she'd wind up with her panties off and her legs spread, and as momentarily satisfying as masturbating was, her fingers and toys didn't come close to the real thing.

And because she couldn't have the real thing, she spent her time with what reminded her of Mazati: the opals.

"Are you responsible for this?" she muttered as she went back to work. "Are you in the background, pushing me, fueling my creativity?"

It wasn't the first time she'd pondered whether he somehow had a hand in her ability to look at a stone and know what it wanted and needed and deserved to become. She'd always had the desire to create jewelry, but so many times uncertainty had stifled her. Was this design the best choice, this free-form mold-ing of silver or gold appealing to anyone other than herself? Maybe she was kidding herself about her talent, and what the hell was she doing holed up in this little room when she could be working overtime so she could get out of debt before she was old enough for Social Security?

The questions and doubt were gone. Now she knew, *knew* she was doing the right thing. It was all good, except for miss-ing Mazati.

After removing the opal from the dop stick, she held it up to the high-intensity light aimed over her work space. Interesting. What she'd thought was blue now revealed itself as black. Spread throughout the deep red tones, the black had a quality that reminded her of Mazati's eyes. Wondering how much more of the midnight hue she could coax out of the stone, she placed it on a piece of black velvet and leaned back. Incredible! If she rimmed the stone with a fine bead of dark wire before en-casing everything in her trademark silver . . .

A shiver ran through her as she reached for her small plastic storage boxes. Not bothering to consider other possibilities, she picked up a thin, ebony wire coil and formed it around the opal. Then she leaned back again. Mazati's eyes, Mazati's en-ergy and mystery!

"Thank you," she whispered. Running her hand under her bra, she cradled her suddenly hard and hot breast. "My god, thank you!"

There was no sign on the door that led to the studios where Saree earned her living, and to the casual observer, the building looked like a factory or storage facility without windows. But as Hayley waited to be buzzed in, she knew what she'd see once she stepped inside. Behind the deliberate façade was a so-phisticated and complex operation that ran as efficiently and professionally as any business—any wildly successful business.

"Hi kid, your sister said she's expecting you," the man she recognized as one of the camera operators greeted her. "She's in the Cave. They're just finishing up. Go on in, just make sure the door doesn't slam behind you. Gotta be quiet, you know."

The first time she'd come to the building owned by Ecstasy Enterprises, she'd felt like a fish out of water, a conservatively dressed woman surrounded by other women who were either naked or jammed into corsets, leather, garish underwear, or see-through fabric. But beneath their heavily made-up faces, art-fully casual hairdos, and tanned, toned bodies were females who loved what they were doing and weren't shy about demonstrating their passion. Their no-nonsense conversations about lubes, nipple clamps, cock sizes, and the best places around for pizza had rubbed off on her, and when the woman in charge of talent recruitment asked if she'd like to do a test shoot, she wasn't offended. All right; truth was, she'd kept the offer at the back of her mind.

The Cave was one of Saree's favorite sets. Resembling a cross between something primitive man might have lived in and a dungeon, it nicely fed the bondage theme with its low ceilings and dark passages where men did wild things to their female captives. Easing the door closed, Hayley's attention was immediately drawn to the bright lights that lit up her sister and the man kneeling over her, while keeping the rest of the set in darkness. Naked, naturally, Saree was on what looked like a bear rug on the stone floor. She'd been wrapped and contorted into a classic hog-tie, complete with a cord knotted through her long hair and tied to her uplifted feet, which forced her head back, exposing her long, vulnerable throat. Her hands were tied behind her while more rope crisscrossed her breasts. The Neanderthal man who'd supposedly kidnapped her knelt between her knees, the better to torture her cunt with a large, electrically charged vibrator.

Despite her restraints, Saree was twisting from side to side, not because she was trying to get away but because the vibrator was forcing one orgasm after another out of her. The man was laughing; Saree was grunting and sobbing and obviously having a wonderful time.

Ignoring the two video and one still photographers leaning over the scene, Hayley slipped into her sister's mind and body. The ropes were on *her*, the vibrator stimulated *her* cunt. And most important, Mazati was responsible.

"Shit, shit, fucking shit, stop it!"

"I'll stop when I'm good and ready." Still holding the vibrator on Saree, the man started slapping her buttocks. "Think you can sneak in here and steal from us, do you? This'll teach you!" Reaching under her, he pinched her right breast.

"I'm sorry, please, I'm sorry!"

"You've learned your lesson?"

"Yes, please stop, please! I can't take—"

"Silence! One more orgasm and I'll let you go. You've got another in you, don't you?"

"Please, please. Oh, enough."

If she hadn't seen her sister at work, Hayley would believe Saree was being driven to the limits of sanity, but along with the purely sexual nature of the scene, Saree and the man were playing to the cameras. Oh yes, the forced orgasms were real, and undoubtedly her clit was on overload, but what a hell of a way to make a living!

Struggling ineffectively, Saree stared at the ceiling, her body drenched in sweat. Thank goodness for the shadows; hopefully no one would notice that Hayley's hand had slipped inside her slacks and was pressing against her own pussy. Her other hand stroked her collar. Her kingdom for a quick switch with her sister, and for her being given the relief of release!

"Ah, ah! Coming, coming! No more, no more!"

* * *

Ten minutes later Saree, wrapped in a white robe that she used to dab sweat off her face and throat, was sitting on one of the artificial boulders while Hayley occupied the one next to it. Ignoring them, the cameramen were looking at the video while a short, attractive young woman cleaned the sex toys. "I don't care where we go," Saree said, "as long as I can have a milkshake. Damn but I'm thirsty."

"I wonder why."

"What'd you think? One of my better performances, if I do say so myself." Unself-consciously slipping her hand under her robe, Saree lightly fingered her sex. "I'm still buzzing. Not going to have any trouble getting to sleep tonight."

"I'm happy for you."

"Oh, what's that I hear? A little envy?"

About to lie, Hayley took a deep breath and smelled her sister's cum. "Hell yes. At least you're getting some."

"And you're not. That's what this is about, isn't it?"

"He hasn't gotten in touch with me, nothing, not even a message on my phone."

"And that tells you what?"

If she wanted subtlety and sympathy, she should have gone somewhere else, since Saree didn't believe in the gentle touch. "Don't say it, all right? I was a fool to think anything would come out of that one-night stand."

"If you've told me everything, it was a hell of a lot more than a one-night stand. Maybe he's embarrassed by the way he treated you."

Although she didn't know the first thing about Mazati, she couldn't pin the word *embarrassed* on him and told her sister so. "He knew what he was doing every step of the way. Too bad I can't say the same about me."

"Put it behind you, then. What say we go to a bar tonight

and pick up a couple of guys, or maybe you'd like to open my little black book and start dialing numbers?"

"I can't."

"Because you're a good little girl?"

"No!" she protested although she'd always been the more conservative of the two. "I'm not interested in just getting myself around a cock. There's got to be more to it."

Leaning close, Saree hugged her. "The whole emotional thing, I know. Why do you think I don't call the guys who e-mail me their phone numbers? I can get all the cocks I want here. When it comes to the real thing, I need the whole package, not that I've found it yet. But sis, you're not going to get it from Mazati. Believe me, if he wanted to continue the relationship, he would have gotten in touch with you by now."

"I know."

"So get rid of that damn collar. It's not the most attractive thing you've ever worn. Kinky but not attractive."

Just last night Hayley had picked up a knife and started sawing on the leather, but she'd quit after three or four slices because, whether she wanted to admit it or not, Mazati had put it on her and now, except for the opals, it was all she had of him. "I will," she muttered, but only because Saree kept staring at her.

"You'd better, because if you don't, I'll do it for you. Look, I need to get a shower before we go anywhere. If you want, there's a shoot starting in the Dungeon in a few minutes. Might be entertaining, or frustrating."

Frustrating, no doubt about it, frustrating. Thinking to let Saree know in no uncertain terms that the last thing she needed today was another reminder of what sex was all about, she held up her hand. As she did, the bright lighting highlighted the ring she'd finished last night.

Saree grabbed her wrist. "Holy shit! That's one of yours?"

"You like?"

Contemplation and Saree had nothing in common, so her sister's silence caught Hayley's attention. Her mouth parted, she continued to study the ring.

"What?" Hayley demanded.

"Holy shit. When you told me you were going to name your line Night Fire, I wasn't sure you could pull it off. I mean, there's a lot of jewelry on the marketplace, a lot of competition."

"Don't remind me."

"And some of the stuff you've shown me . . . while the stones are spectacular, I wasn't sure that would be enough. But the black beading around the opal—beading's what it's called, isn't it?—really makes the stone pop. You've got a hit here, sis, a genuine hit."

Basking in her sister's compliment, she made a quick mental inventory of her finished pieces. No, it wouldn't take much to incorporate the thin black accent in some of them. A hit. Hopefully leading to financial success and creative expression and paying off her bills.

What did she need with a man if she had the things she'd been craving for so long?

What did she need with Mazati?

12

It was dark by the time Hayley arrived back home, and although she hadn't intended to be gone so long, the day couldn't have gone better. During lunch, she and Saree had pored over a list of the area's jewelry stores and upscale boutiques with a mind to which should be at the top of their list—not that the answer was that hard to come by. Despite its unpretentious name, Porters had a reputation as *the* place where the city's *in* women bought their *pieces,* as they were called. No socialite or successful businesswoman went to a public function without something she'd bought at Porters dangling from her neck, wrist, or ears, or on her fingers. Perhaps even more important, well-heeled men made Porters their first and usually only choice when it came to buying jewelry for the women in their lives.

Hayley had been hesitant to approach Porters because most of the store's suppliers were in places like Paris, New York, and Madrid, but Saree had threatened to storm the doors herself if Hayley didn't go there before the day was over.

Incredible, more than incredible! Even as she stroked the

contract dangling from her fingers, Hayley wasn't sure she'd fully wrapped her mind around the reality that Porters had agreed to carry the Night Fire line based solely on the ring she still wore and half a dozen photographs. The buyer had nodded approvingly at the ring, but had given her a jaded look until she'd explained that she intended to incorporate the thin black accent into almost everything she'd made. That, the buyer had assured her, made all the difference, and wasn't it amazing how a touch of ebony brought out a stone's depths.

Not just any opal, Hayley acknowledged as she headed for her front door. Rare black opals from a mine in Mexico, a mine she'd never have known about if it hadn't been for Mazati.

Spotting a rock on the walkway, she kicked it. Damn it, she'd come close to cleansing him from her mind and body this afternoon. He had no right coming back! As soon as she was inside, she'd get the hell rid of the collar, and not just because Saree had kept staring at it!

A package at her front door caught her attention, and she picked it up. Because she didn't have her front light on, she couldn't tell much but didn't think it had a label identifying one of the major postal shippers, and if it had come in the mail, she'd have gotten a slip telling her to pick it up at the post office, not this. It could be a bomb, she acknowledged without so much as a whisper of alarm. After all, she had no political or legal or otherwise standing that might turn her into the object of anyone's wrath, and Cal had much more important things on his mind than getting rid of her.

Despite her curiosity, she made slipping out of her shoes the first order of business once she was inside, after putting the box on her coffee table, of course. After retrieving a kitchen knife— might as well kill two birds with one stone—she perched on her couch and turned the small container over. From what she could tell, it was a wood box, but with the brown wrapping paper, she couldn't be positive. She'd been right: wherever this had come from, it hadn't arrived via a commercial service; it didn't even have her address on it, let alone a return address. The package was only about eight inches square, just big enough for a couple of sex toys or nippleless bra or crotchless panties. Thanks, sis.

It was wooden, all right, with a hinged top held in place with a small clasp. Releasing the clasp, she opened the box.

"Oh my god."

Instead of picking up one of the fabulous opals resting on red velvet, she stood and backed away. Only one person could have left this, and he'd done so in person, while she was gone.

"Oh my god."

Her knees warning that they might buckle, she plunked her ass on the couch again and leaned closer, discovering that she'd been wrong in her initial assessment of the contents. The box had three layers or shelves, each cradling twelve of the unfinished black opals that had played such a strong role in her life being turned on end.

"Why, Mazati, why?"

Because you know what they deserve to become.

Now doubly glad she was sitting, she leaned forward and rested her head in her hands because she'd go through the rest of her life believing heart and soul that Mazati had just spoken to her. It didn't matter that she couldn't see him; his presence now filled the room. Her hand went to her throat or rather to what he'd placed on her.

"Where have you been?"

Here, but giving you the space you need.

Not about to ask him what he meant or get into a prolonged conversation with an entity or ghost or whatever unbelievable thing he'd become, she wrapped her fingers around her upper arms and started rocking back and forth. At least twice before in her relationship with him, she'd slipped out of the world she knew and into something beyond comprehension, and although that wasn't the case right now, it could happen at any minute.

And maybe that's what she wanted.

Not sure whether she was hot or chilled, she concentrated on rocking until her room and the box with the opals came back into focus. Then she leaned forward and picked up the largest stone, half expecting to see a little dust from the mine it had come from. Mazati had touched this. He'd chosen the container and was responsible for every opal's placement. She imagined him thinking of her as he did, maybe wondering if she'd be able to feel the heat his fingers left behind.

"Were you here when it all came together for me? What do you think of the name Night Fire?"

It belongs.

"Thank you." Even after her voice had faded away, she waited for him to say something more. When he didn't, she put down the opal and ran her finger through the collar's ring. "I'm still wearing this. Are you part of that decision? You kept me from taking a knife to it because you aren't done with me?"

I pray I'll never be done with you.

Seriously spooked, she curled up in a corner of the couch with her feet tucked under her. "I don't like it like this! What kind of relationship do we have? Fuck, is it all me? I dreamed you up and sent these stones to myself without remembering? You're a figment of my imagination and I should be walking into one of those padded rooms? You—you don't exist."

Something brushed the side of her neck just below her right ear, causing goose bumps to chase over her skin. *I exist.*

Hayley had been certain she wouldn't be able to sleep, which is why she'd worked until after 2 a.m. She'd tuned in to a talk radio station and turned it up loud to keep from hearing voices in her head. And she'd created, fashioning a pair of earrings from four small opals that now looked as if they were free-floating in cobwebs made from spun silver and black threads. By the time she'd finished, her vision had been so blurry she wasn't sure she'd accomplished what she'd intended to, but at least she'd made it into her bedroom before collapsing on the coverlet. Her final conscious thought had been to wonder if she'd set her alarm, since the last thing she needed was to be late to the dreaded day job; but she'd drifted off before she could force herself to check.

Some time later a fresh thought worked its way inside her brain. Were there smells in dreams?

It had to be a dream since she was at home, in bed, wasn't she? But where had this aroma of rich vegetation come from? Even more crucial, why was she walking through it on a thin path?

No, not walking, running and stumbling with her arms stretched out in front of her because she was being pulled behind a large man via her roped-together wrists. As sweat ran down her throat to between her exposed breasts, she became aware of something in her mouth that forced her teeth apart. With each step, something pressed against her crotch, but she didn't dare take her attention off her captor long enough to see what it was.

Naked, she was naked.

So was he.

Either his pace slowed or she'd become accustomed to the path, because she now had the freedom to assess what had changed about her world since flopping onto her bed. The pressure on her crotch wasn't just relentless but erotic, made even more so because she didn't know how any of this had happened. She still wore Mazati's collar, and her feet must have become calloused because being barefoot didn't hurt. Her jiggling breasts created a constant rippling sensation, and although it was crazy, of course, she rather liked the way her arms looked stretched out ahead of her. Wherever she was being taken, adventure awaited.

Going from shadow to light and back into shadow rendered learning anything about her captor difficult, but as she became more and more alert, she acknowledged she didn't need to; she already knew that form.

Mazati, taking over her world and body again.

Smiling despite the leather in her mouth, she looked down at herself. Although she couldn't see her neck, she felt her collar against her veins. Her only other piece of *clothing* was a crotch rope that circled her waist before going between her legs. The rope, which consisted of two strands, rode low on her belly, vaguely resembling a bikini—but this was no flimsy piece of lace and satin. The knotting must be in back because she saw no way of untying it. The strands against her crotch had been placed on either side of her labia so her clit wasn't in danger of being abraded, just trapped. Sweat covered her legs, and her thigh and calf muscles burned, making her think Mazati had been pulling her through the jungle for a while. Did that mean they were nearing their destination, and what would happen then?

Although she wasn't satisfied with what she'd learned about her body, she dragged her gaze off herself. Mazati was no longer striding his long-legged strides. He'd stopped near a massive tree with vines wrapped around the many branches and was throwing the loose end of rope over a limb some twelve feet off the ground. Grabbing the rope, he pulled, easily forcing her under the limb and stretching her arms over her head. On her toes, she watched as he tied the rope to another branch.

Stuck. Right where he wanted her.

"You have every right to wonder why I'm doing it like this, slave," he said, his tone gliding over her. "Why I didn't come to you and ask you to accompany me here instead of resorting to force, but you could have refused to enter my world. I can't let that happen. The stakes are too high for me."

Giddy, because after endless days and nights of waiting for him, he was here again, she longed to tell him she'd accept him under any terms, but the leather prevented that.

"I'm sorry." He ran his fingers over her lips before checking the gag's tightness. "This isn't how I'd prefer it between us, but your fantasies and my needs must bleed together."

What was it about his voice and touch that sent her into a place where everything revolved around sex? She had no objections, of course; the handful of self-inflicted orgasms she'd managed to work out of herself hadn't done enough. Instead of being uneasy about his intentions, she could hardly wait for the next step.

"Master and slave, leader and willing subject, your needs giving you the courage to travel with me, that's what this is all about. For now."

What did he mean by this? Hoping to get him to supply the answer, she extended her right leg toward him. She managed to run her toes over his calf but couldn't reach any higher, and the effort made the crotch rope tighten. Frustrated by his impassive expression, she lowered her leg. Now she felt the strain of her up-forced arms down her sides, an erotic burning that then oozed over her belly and down to her pelvis.

Perhaps he knew what she was experiencing, because he ran his hands from her captured wrists to her knees. His touch on her taut arm muscles allowed her to forget, briefly, the burn there. To her relief, he didn't linger at her armpits, and the pressure along her ribs was firm enough that she didn't feel as if she was being tickled. His palms pressed against her hipbones, then let up a little before gliding over her thighs.

"A beautiful body, strong, graceful."

Don't care! I don't care. Just, please, don't stop!

"What about here?" he asked with a finger hooked through the crotch rope. "Too tight?"

When she shook her head, the collar slid over the tendons at the side of her neck like a lover's caress.

"But tight enough, right?" He tugged, released the pressure, tugged again.

Snorting, she rose even higher. Unable to maintain the position, she sank back down as far as she could, which of course increased her awareness of her trapped labia.

"Do you remember freedom?" he asked, tugging once more. "When your body belonged to you and only you knew what it was capable of?"

Alert now, sliding toward being afraid, she studied him. Why was he naked this time, when another time his loincloth had served as a reminder of the vital difference between them? She could keep nothing from him, while he exposed his sex only when it was to his advantage. If his intention now was to hammer home the message that he was still in absolute control, he was succeeding. And the sight of his hard and straining organ teased without promising, taunted. How could she fuck him with his ropes on her cunt?

"No freedom tonight, slave. Only sliding deep into the meaning of what I choose to call you."

Expecting him to pull on the crotch rope again, she wasn't ready when he ran his hand between her legs and pressed against both her pussy and the twin cords. His middle finger found her entrance. "Lift your right leg. Keep it there until I tell you different."

Fuck you! What do you think I am, your toy?

"Do it!" Grabbing a nipple with his free hand, he slapped her cunt at the same time. Need powered through her, and she greeted the fingers on and around her clit with a hot flood. "That's it, my slave. Show me how much you want this."

I don't, I don't, I don't.

But he must not have cared what she was trying to tell him because he pulled her breast toward him and closed his teeth over her aching nub. The slaps against her cunt kept coming, but instead of trying to squeeze her legs around his hand, she obediently lifted her leg. In danger of losing her balance, she leaned forward so her arms supported much of her weight.

He occasionally and briefly released her nipple, but only so he could bathe her breast with his saliva. Intent on keeping her leg up, she rocked from side to side. With his access to her cunt now unobstructed, he drove home lesson after fresh lesson about his intimate understanding of her body.

"Swing for me, slave. Hang in my ropes while I play with you." He paused to nibble at the side of her breast. "Sweat and beg and wait because I give you no choice."

Yes, yes!

Fingers moistened with her hot offering slipped inside her. She gave an instant's thought to how he'd found space with the crotch ropes there, then it no longer mattered because he was once more finger fucking her. Sagging in his restraints, she listened to not just her body but the echo of what he'd just said about hanging in his ropes and sweating and begging and waiting.

Waiting?

Yes, she was helpless to do anything except what he commanded. The fingers were gone now as were the teeth on her breast. She'd just blinked away her blurred vision when she felt something being looped over her head. Whatever it was pressed against her eyes and thrust her into darkness. Although she tossed her head, he had no trouble tying it in place.

Locked in darkness with no way of knowing where he was, she lowered her leg and waited. As the seconds ticked away, she wondered if she'd displeased him by standing on two feet again. Maybe he'd left.

No, he wouldn't do that, would he? Not leave her alone and blind and helpless and hungry.

"It's been a long two weeks, slave, long but necessary."

Guessing that he now stood to her left, she turned her head in that direction.

"I've been watching you, with you nearly every minute, but keeping my distance because I needed to learn how you function on your own."

Touch me, please. Let me down so I can wrap my body around yours.

"Well; lonely and horny, but well. You're not used to being dependent on a man, are you? The desire is there. You got married because you expected him to take care of you and make the decisions, to tell you that you're desirable, his precious property."

No, she hadn't wanted that! Had she?

"But he failed both you and himself, and now you're afraid to admit you still need certain things from a man. To be dominated."

Am I? Do I?

"You don't need to admit anything, because I already know. That's my power, my damnable but necessary power."

There was nothing except his words carving holes in the walls she'd erected around herself. Nothing except him, and waiting.

"You aren't alone in this. Even with all the risks I'm taking, I feed off dominating you. Doing so brings me back to life after barely existing for so long. In many respects, we're on the same journey. In that we live in the same world."

No, they didn't! She had no idea where he'd been since they'd last seen each other, and what had he meant when he said he'd been watching her? That simply didn't happen in the here and now, she knew. But what about his?

Reminding herself that this place, wherever it was, was his

domain, she ached to take in her surroundings, but of course she couldn't see anything.

"You have no idea how long I've waited to see you like this," he muttered, his breath feathering along her right temple. She shivered but didn't move. "To touch you again."

Something warm slid over her belly. When the gesture was repeated, she realized he was caressing her with his cock. Maybe he wanted her to open herself to him, but much as she needed to do that one thing in life, she waited on trembling legs. Obey, that's what she needed to do for him, obey.

Sensing yet new movement from him, she prayed for patience and self-control. "I'm kneeling at your feet, looking at you," he said.

At my pussy.

Fresh hunger flooded her. Fascinated by the liquid running from her, she surrendered the last of her hope that she might keep anything from him. He'd tethered her sex because he could, and she'd bow before him in gratitude if he freed her. Then he cupped her hips and drew her toward him, and she hoped he'd keep her tied forever. Head back, all but hanging, she prayed the sight of her pleased him.

"Mine." He ran a finger over her labia. "Your gift to me."

Yes.

His second gliding touch made her jump. Much as she tried to relax, she couldn't. She prayed he was still on his knees, but because she couldn't think beyond her own needs, he could have stood without her knowing. More of what could be minutes or seconds slid over her to envelope her in need. She couldn't remember ever wanting anything except him, or feeling so alive; ever been prouder of her body or more a slave to its desires. He called her his slave, but the word went far deeper, burrowing into her core and setting her on fire.

Fire!

She'd jumped and tried to close her legs before she realized he'd touched her labia with his tongue. Certain she wouldn't survive, she struggled, but he clutched her buttocks, forcing her to remain in place. When she quit resisting, he rolled his tongue over one labial lip and then the other. Nearly exploding, she could only wonder if he'd also tongue-tested the difference between her hot, wet flesh and the unyielding rope.

Sinking into the existence he'd created for her, she willed her cunt to both soften and endure this latest assault. He started slow and almost hesitant with a brief wet touch here, a quick probe there. Moment by moment, however, his pace quickened until she bleated with each intrusion, every invasion.

Something that might have been an orgasm popped deep within her when he released her buttocks and drew her labial lips apart. The pop came again when he ran his tongue into her, only to die under nearly frightening rapid-fire movements. Much as she hated the sounds she was making, she couldn't stop. Neither could she keep still.

His hot breath! Washing her cunt!

Her mind filled with the image of this remarkably powerful man with his face hard against her pussy. Her legs gave way, but how could she send any strength to them when everything revolved around her hole and what claimed it?

She was still hanging when he pulled his tongue out. His hard, quick breath said he'd enjoyed this almost as much as she had—maybe more than he'd wanted. Silently begging him to be honest, she went in search of her feet and managed to get them under her again. Still, she was drifting somewhere, with her body belonging to someone else. She was heat, wet heat, nothing else.

"Do you remember where we are?" His voice told her that he was again standing.

Thinking of the jungle, reconciling herself to the end of his pleasuring her, she nodded.

"I was taking you to my home, my city. We'll get there soon. But this is all the farther we'll go tonight."

Did he really expect her to understand what he was talking about?

"A parting gift."

No, don't go!

He kicked at her ankles. Angry and upset, she debated trying to kick him back, but before she could make her decision, he slapped her pussy. Jerking upright, she waited. Instead of striking her again, he tugged on the back of the crotch rope, and it slid off her. Fresh blood flooded her.

There was nothing light or teasing about his next slap or the one that came after. Over and over, he tattooed her with his open palm. Each quick contact sent an electrical impulse deep into her sex and maybe beyond. The pace kept accelerating, and she gave brief thought to how long he could keep up the pace. Then, because the impulses were backing one upon the other, she lost the question.

And she danced, danced on his tether and under his direction, her pussy weeping for both of them and her clit short-circuiting, jumping, climbing, reaching. She had no thought of trying to escape, but her legs didn't know that as they kept trying to back away from him. At the same time, she strained toward him and dove headfirst into his assault.

Heat was everywhere and everything, rolling throughout not just her sex but down to her toes and up to her fingertips. She'd never felt anything like this, never guessed pussy slapping could lead to a climax.

But it did—and the climax went on and on, living off and breeding from his all-knowing palm.

13

Hayley had finished her shower and was reaching for the moisturizing cream before she could force herself to look at her wrists. Faint purplish marks ringed them, but studying the indentations gave her the courage to acknowledge what she'd discovered while soaping between her legs—her pussy was swollen and sensitive. Then she stared in the mirror at the slight abrasions on either side of her mouth.

"Why, Mazati, why?"

Her familiar image faded, and at the edges of a cloud that seemed to have taken over the mirror, she spotted a solitary male figure hunched over something she couldn't make out. The man had to be Mazati; who else could it be? But she'd never seen him looking like this. Instead of the strong and commanding presence she expected, his bare shoulders slumped, and his hair had fallen forward, obscuring his features. He was on his knees, his body bent forward as if trying to protect something, maybe his heart? After a moment she saw what appeared to be a spear on the ground next to him. Although his fingers were near it, he made no attempt to pick it up. He was naked with a vulnerability that made her long to hold him to her.

Heart heavy and pounding, she leaned closer and blinked repeatedly to clear her vision. Her hand strayed to her collar as she locked on to an exhausted and lonely man. It was raining wherever he was, large, heavy drops pelting his exposed back and running off his glossy hair. He seemed unaware of his surroundings, and for too long he didn't move a single muscle. Then he stretched out the hand that had been near the discarded spear and touched a lifeless figure that had been nothing but shadow and blur before.

A naked woman lay on her side with her legs tucked up near her belly and her arms draped over her knees. Like Mazati, her hair was long and ebony and rain drenched. She was so small that for a moment Hayley thought she was a child, but the outline of high, full breasts nearly hidden by her upper arm changed her mind, as did the swell of hips. She wasn't naked after all, not completely, because a leather collar circled her long, slender neck.

Mazati's woman? His lover, wife?

Jealousy and pain roared through her, but she forced the emotions away because the woman was too limp and unmoving. Dead.

Who had she been, and did Mazati love her?

Although Hayley hadn't been inside the local community college for at least five years, the physical layout, sounds, and smells inside the library felt the same as it had before. What took some getting used to was how young some of the students looked. Fortunately, there were a number of middle-aged men and women hunched over the tables, so she didn't feel ancient. Because she was no longer a student, she wouldn't be able to check out any of the books, which was why she'd brought along her laptop. Another change, she acknowledged as she placed her pile of books on the table next to her laptop: pen and paper had given way to technology.

Fortunately, the library's history section was among its largest, but she wished that so many of the texts on the Aztecs hadn't been checked out. She hoped she wouldn't have to return later, that she'd learn everything she needed to in a single session.

Instead of opening the first book, she took a moment to gather her thoughts and emotions. Insane as it was, she no longer questioned Mazati's ability to track not just her comings and goings but her emotions as well. For all she knew, he was here right now, the *here* being up to interpretation. And if he was here, he certainly knew what she was doing.

It couldn't be helped. Bottom line, she had to learn everything she could about him.

The Aztec Nation: Culture and Cruelty. Well, she assured herself, did she really expect the author to soft-pedal the title? Although she knew little more than that the ancient Aztecs practiced a bloody form of human sacrifice—was there any other kind—if she'd written a book on them and wanted it to sell, she'd go after sensationalism herself. She was beginning with this text because a quick thumbing through it had revealed that it included a number of photographs of what little remained of Teotihuacan, an ancient city that was once home to an estimated 200,000 people before its deliberate burning. What had caught her attention the most were the Sun and Moon pyramids.

Tracing her fingers over the ruins, she soon determined that what Mazati had introduced her to wasn't either of these pyramids, and yet the similarities were unmistakable. The longer she studied the once great city, the stronger her conviction that she was looking at Mazati's roots. As far as she could remember, he'd only spoken the word *Aztec* once, but that coupled with what he'd shown her and the things he'd said had been enough.

This was his origin, the place of his birth, where he'd grown into manhood. And although much of his culture and the rest of his people had been lost, he was still alive.

Shaking off what had begun as disbelief but she now accepted as truth, she dove into the text. What both chilled and angered her was why much of what had made the Aztecs great no longer existed. During an eighty-five-day siege in 1521, the Spaniard Hernán Cortés and his invading army had cut down some two-thirds of the people living in the Aztec capital of Tenochtitlan, but that had only been the beginning. Evidence of their intricate religion, highly evolved symbology, icons, shrines, literature, math, even a number of the cities, had been destroyed, often deliberately, by those who followed Cortés.

Fortunately, the Franciscan friar and missionary Bernardino de Sahagún had devoted fifty years of his life to studying what little remained, particularly a series of drawings known as the Florentine Codex. Later historians had expanded on his work, and as a result, a partial picture of what it had meant to be Aztec had emerged.

Her high school history–fed memory had been woefully incomplete, she acknowledged some three hours later as she stood and stretched her aching spine. Inadequate fragments, because she hadn't cared back then.

After taking a walk down several aisles and getting a drink of water, she returned to her laptop and skimmed over what she'd jotted down. Because religious sacrifice had been a dominant topic in all of the books, she made more notes than she wanted to on the subject. Not that she'd needed the graphic details, but several books had included artists' renderings of what had taken place daily in what was known as The Temple of Death.

The gods had been responsible, that's what it all boiled down to. For reasons she, a modern woman, could barely comprehend, the Aztecs had been fearful of their gods, particularly the God of Sun, Huitzilopochtli. In an effort to give him the necessary strength to fight the frightening unknown of night so the Aztecs would continue to live and prosper, they'd performed daily human sacrifices by cutting out beating hearts. Amazingly, death wasn't always something to be feared, and warriors going to battle apparently embraced the possibility of being killed because that allowed them to join the Land of the Dead, which was considered the Aztecs' common home. Captured warriors from other tribes sometimes chose being sacrificed over freedom because the act guaranteed them a place in the afterworld.

This was the world that had given rise to Mazati. Aztec belief and practices might appall her, but he'd never known anything different—at least during what should have been his lifetime.

Running, bare feet slapping hot, wet earth. Countless branches tore at her rough and unfamiliar clothing. The sound of yelling from behind her accompanied the heavy footsteps that were coming closer, closer. Terrified beyond all reason, Hayley tucked her arms against her body and turned off the narrow path, praying that the jungle would hide her. But before the thick growth could envelope her, a great weight slammed into her back and knocked her to the ground. Before she could catch her breath, her captor lashed rope around her arms and wrists. Other ropes that went over and under her breasts sealed her helpless arms against her body, while yet more restraints secured her thighs, calves, and ankles. Only then was she rolled onto her back. The man standing over her was a stranger, naked except for a loincloth. He was armed with a long knife.

"Foolish savage. Why did you leave your village unprotected and alone, not that that would have saved you." Grabbing her hair, he pulled her into a sitting position. "Did you so much as suspect that the Great Warriors would find your people's village and attack? We did." When he laughed, although she didn't know what he was talking about, she felt heartsick because she had no doubt that innocent people—people he believed she was one of—had been killed. "It is a good thing you were not among them; you have far greater value alive, slave."

That's what Mazati had called her, but this man with his rotting front teeth wasn't him. *No*, she wanted to scream, she already belonged to someone; but not only was she too confused and unnerved, she *didn't* belong to anyone. Up until now, her so-called dreams had revolved around Mazati. With that anchoring element gone, she felt adrift. Scared.

When the man continued to study her, she was certain he'd rape her. Instead, after a few minutes, he stood and threw her over his shoulder. Unable to see where he was going or to lift her head except briefly, she had no choice but to hang limply. Before long his breathing became labored, and he slowed. Blood rushed to her head; she wasn't sure, but she might have passed out.

The journey took much of the day, during which she drifted in and out of consciousness. No matter how she worked to free her mind from what she needed to believe wasn't reality, she couldn't. At length she knew they were nearing their destination by the increased sounds. Countless people were talking, their voices accompanied by hammering and other sounds that signaled construction. When she looked around her as best she could, she noted that her captor was walking her down a wide, packed earth and stone street with what she believed were stone masonry shops on either side. Many of the prosperous-looking shops were decorated with wood that had figures and designs painted on it.

More smells than she could begin to identify assaulted her, as did the great array of colors. Of particular note was the number, size, and height of the buildings. Beyond what she assumed was the commercial district or marketplace were many flat-roofed houses clustered in groupings of three or four. Because of the design, she couldn't tell what was in the middle; maybe some kind of common area. A pair of what must be stone warriors stood at least twenty feet high at the end of the street she was on, the carved detail both breathtaking and intimidating. This was indeed a city.

During her stint in the library, she'd concentrated on aspects of the Aztec world that would hopefully shed some light on Mazati's role in that world. Now she'd give anything to know which of the several cities she was in.

Almost everyone was barefoot, although some had decorated their ankles with leather strips to which feathers had been fastened. The people weren't particularly tall, and the majority appeared to be young. Despite the effort, she again lifted her head, determining that clothing or the lack of it wasn't of particular concern. Almost all children were nude, and men either had on something resembling a diaper or had decorated their penises with feathers, bits of painted leather, or other decoration. Women wore capes or shawls that ended near their knees, and many of the capes were fastened in front like dresses.

There was a definite pecking order, with those wearing clothing decorated with feathers and shells and other colorful adornment, in addition to jewelry made from turquoise, jade, and other stones, either ordering the plainer-dressed around or ignoring them. This dovetailed with what she'd learned about Aztec social life, which placed priests in the role of supremacy.

After the priests, of which she saw none, came nobility, warriors, craftsmen, and others valued for their contributions to the whole. At the bottom were farmers and slaves. From what she could tell, she was of little if any interest to anyone. Most disconcerting, she couldn't understand a word they were saying.

Finally her captor put her down, positioning her so she was leaning against something hot and hard with her bound legs bent under her. If not for the rough support, she would have toppled over. Several men approached her captor and spoke to him in that unintelligible jumble that separated her from everyone else.

Tearing her attention away from her immediate surroundings, she studied what she could see of her world. The marketplace she was in took her breath away. Among the goods for sale were gold and silver, copper, tin, brass, and lead, even what she believed was lime and both finished and unfinished stone. Other construction material included adobe bricks, tiles, and wood. Available in the food shops was everything from corn, beans, tomatoes, chili peppers, and a number of fruits to fish, frogs, turkeys, ducks, pigeons, parrots, rabbits, and other small animals. In one place barbers were at work. Another shop held what she thought were medicinal herbs and roots, and two shops were devoted to household items such as cooking pots and bowls, reed mats, brooms, and baskets.

Instead of running around, even the smallest children stayed close to their mothers and seemed well behaved. Although the mothers were young, their bodies looked worn down and tired, most likely from repeated pregnancies and hard work. Even with one shop where people were bathing themselves from huge wooden bowls filled with soapy water, hygiene wasn't up to modern standards. Too many of the men bore signs of injury ranging from canes to bandages to open wounds, and clenched teeth and furrowed brows gave away the pain they were trying to hide. By their spears and knives, she took those men to be warriors or soldiers.

Other men, their drab clothing and hacked-at hair seeming to indicate lesser status, carried massive loads attached to their foreheads via wide straps. Equally humbly dressed women were also taking the role of beasts of burden although, thank goodness, their loads weren't as large. Those people all had a lost and despairing quality about them.

Was that what was going to happen to her? She'd be expected to labor for as long as her body held out?

Desperate to distract herself from that terrible possibility, she looked beyond the people to a massive building in the distance she'd dismissed before because she'd wanted to take in her immediate surroundings. This was no high-rise apartment, no commercial establishment. No doubt about it, the imposing structure was a pyramid, maybe *the* pyramid in this particular city. She was far enough away that she couldn't be certain whether it was the one Mazati had introduced her to. It seemed to be larger at the base but not quite as tall as she remembered, and several people were doing something on the top. Judging by the sharp sounds, she guessed they were carving something out of the great chunk of stone that had somehow been hauled up there. Either the top and the stair closest to the top were in shadow or the material used to make it was stained.

A sudden and horrible thought froze her. The stains might be blood. What did she mean, *might* be? Hadn't her research left her with no doubt of the central role sacrifice held in their culture?

Maybe she wasn't destined for life as a slave after all. Like too many of those the Aztec had captured from tribes living nearby, her heart would be cut out to feed the gods' bloodthirsty demands. Oh god, what had she read? Something about women being sacrificed during a harvest festival in the fall. Was it fall here?

Fighting terror, she swiveled as best she could so she could look behind her. She determined that she was leaning against a number of stone chunks stacked one on top of the other. Was this, could this possibly be, the beginning of another pyramid?

I want out of this nightmare, she longed to scream. *Stop it, just stop it! Give me back my life!*

Instead she remained silent because something had caught the attention of those around her, and she wanted to be invisible. Men lowered their heads; a few even bowed. In contrast, the one who'd captured her positioned himself beside her and pulled on her hair, forcing her to sit as upright as possible. Struggling not to think of herself as a sacrificial lamb, she looked in the same direction the others were. A trio of tall, robust men were striding toward her, ignoring those who were obviously trying to get their attention by demonstrating their subservience. The trio wore sturdy sandals, colorful albeit scratchy-looking shirts made from a material she couldn't identify, and short skirtlike garments that barely covered their upper thighs.

What fascinated her the most was their wooden headwear. From the stiff way the three held their heads, she imagined that the helmets, if that's what they were, weighed many pounds. The headwear resembled hawk or eagle heads complete with open mouths and long beaks. They'd been constructed in such a way that the wearer could slip the reddish-brown object over his head and look out through the open mouth. If their intention had been to frighten children and force reverence from adults, they'd succeeded. Even as she wondered why any sane and free man would agree to wear something so cumbersome, the message became clear. The wearer belonged at the top of the pecking order.

"Welcome, my gods," her captor addressed them, his English as unaccented as when he'd first spoken to her. "My gift to you awaits. Her blood will run red and true, her heart beating even as you cut it from her body."

Too horrified to make a sound, Hayley just managed not to wet herself. Unfortunately, she didn't realize that one of the three had indicated he wanted her brought to her feet, until her captor grabbed her arms and hauled her up. Although she managed to stand, she'd probably lose her balance if he released her. The smell of her fear assaulted her nostrils.

"It is her," the man in the middle said. "*Her.*"

"What are you saying, my god?" her captor asked. "You know this creature?"

"Yes." Mazati's voice was even deeper than she remembered.

"You approve? You will take her as your slave sacrifice?"

By way of answer, Mazati grabbed the rope that went over her breast and yanked her toward him. "As my slave, yes. As sacrifice, no. She is too valuable for that."

"Valuable? She is a savage! Barely human."

"Look at her hands with their long, strong fingers," Mazati countered. "They are gifted. Under my leadership and control, her skill will spread everywhere, and endure."

Lost in Mazati's intensity, she hardly noticed that her surroundings were becoming hazy. By then, Mazati, too, was fading Only the word *endure* remained, working its way into her heart.

"What are you doing at home?" Saree demanded when Hayley picked up the phone a little after 8 a.m. "I thought you said you had to go to the salt mines come hell or high water. Don't tell me you quit that shit job."

"No."

"Hey, are you sick? You sound weird."

"I'm fine." *Except for having been sucked into yet another weird dream and losing my mind.* "I decided to take the day off."

"Shit, he isn't there, is he, Mr. Strange and Stranger?"

"No, he isn't." *At least I don't think so.* Shaking off the thought, she studied the opals spread out on her work space. In her latest dream or delusion or whatever, Mazati had praised her hands or rather what they were capable of. If he was right, *if*, her work would endure long after she was dead. What she wished she understood was why that was important to him. "I'm creating like a madwoman, as if someone else is guiding my hands. I'm afraid to stop because the creativity might dry up."

"Not going to happen. You haven't called for over a week. Are you sure you're all right?"

I'm not sure of anything. "Don't you have to go somewhere and get tied up?"

"As a matter of fact, I'm on my way to my own version of the salt mines. Look, what are you doing Tuesday night? You want to check out a new club with me?"

"I don't know. I—"

"No excuses. Besides, if I don't keep an eye on you, who will? Oh, one more thing. When are you going to make something for me, maybe a killer necklace I can wear at one of my shoots?"

For the first time since she'd picked up the phone, Hayley truly paid attention to her sister. "Are you joking?"

"About a lot of things, yes. About this, no. It belatedly occurred to me—a flash of brilliance—that my sporting a creation from my one and only sibling might be a great way to get the buzz really going about Night Fire. What do you think?"

"I think I love you."

"I'll take that as a yes, you adore your one and only sibling, the source of all things amazing. Now, what's it going to be?"

Closing her eyes, Hayley easily brought up an image of the impressive marketplace she'd been in during her *dream*, but although inspiration had all but poured in around her since then, nothing jumped out at her right then. "I don't know. Give me a little time."

"Not much time. My strokes of genius demand to be acted on now!"

14

The tree's bark was much smoother than she'd anticipated, thank goodness. In fact, the feel of it against her back reminded her of the velvet she placed her finished jewelry on. Was that his intention, to treat her as she did one of her creations?

At the sound of footsteps on packed earth, Hayley cast off the life she existed in when Mazati wasn't with her and accepted his reality. The last she'd remembered, she'd fallen asleep in her recliner after dragging home in the wake of twelve hours at her job. Now she was no longer in her house but crouched at the base of a tree Mazati must have selected. Going by the quiet and clean smells, they weren't back at the city she'd been carried to as a prisoner of war or whatever she'd been. Even with all the emotions and sensations she went through whenever she was with him, she wanted to be alone with him, to ask some of the questions that had been haunting her.

She was naked from the waist down. True, she still had on the top she'd selected this morning, at least she thought that's what she was wearing. Blindfolded, it was hard to be sure. Like the tree bark, the blindfold was soft albeit firmly in place and just thin enough that a little daylight penetrated.

She crouched, oh yes crouched, with her butt barely off the ground, her knees deeply bent, and her legs widely spread to keep from losing her balance. Warmth on her inner thighs and crotch kept her awareness of her intimate exposure high. She would have done something, anything, about her position if her arms weren't being forced back and her wrists secured via something that wrapped around the tree.

Back to being Mazati's sex slave, his personal slut.

Back to feeling so alive she thought she might explode.

Although he didn't say anything, she knew he was standing over her and imagined him looking down at her. Maybe he'd kneel or crouch and tease her cunt into awareness, not that she wasn't already abundantly aware of the purely sexual nature of her position. But although she waited and breathed and gave up denying the heat chasing through her, he didn't touch her.

Oh god, not that! Anything except being left alone. She needed him, in ways she hadn't dreamed were possible.

"Please," she moaned, "please."

"Who am I?"

About to gasp his name, she swallowed the sound. Right now he wanted obedience and subservience from her; her questions would have to wait. "Master. You are my master."

"Why?"

Ah, his voice was midnight silk, fine whiskey, and promise. She could drown in those tones. "Because—because it's the way we both want it."

"You too?" he asked after a brief silence. "This is what you truly need?"

Her legs were starting to burn from the awkward position, but that wasn't why she rolled her pelvis from side to side. "Yes, yes."

"Why?"

"I don't know!"

"Yes, you do."

Her earlier thought that he was forcing his superiority on her with his questions faded, replaced by an understanding of how deep he wanted to take her emotions. "I've never connected with anyone the way I have with you. You're taking me places I've never been before, the time and richness and mystery of the Aztecs, the richness of what my body's capable of. Please, master, I need you."

"What about when I free you? Will you say the same thing? Will you stay here?"

I don't know. I'm afraid of both of us.

"Your silence speaks for you, slave. You aren't ready to turn ownership of your body over to me, are you?"

"Not just my body, my mind and soul. Do you have any idea what you're asking of me?"

"Yes."

Just yes, nothing more. "What do you want from me?"

"What I must have." He stroked her cheek, then slid his hand over her collar before resting his fingers on her shoulder. "I love the way your muscles feel here, the way your mouth stays open. Tell me, slave. Why can't you close it?"

"You know! You know."

"Do I? Just as you're learning about me, I'm still trying to work my way through your layers. How does it feel to be half naked and to know I can see your sex while you can't see anything of me?"

It's driving me crazy! "Damnation, do you want me to beg you to fuck me? I will. All right, I will! Whatever it takes."

"And when you're free?"

He'd already asked her that question, and yet she still couldn't answer him. Yesterday she'd shaved her scant, pale pubic hair for the first time in her life, which might be why he'd displayed her like this. But why hadn't he exposed her breasts or let her see him? Even more important, what did he mean by saying he was doing what he needed to? What were the stakes for him?

"Do you want your freedom, slave?"

Before she could begin to make sense of the question, he placed his hand over her pussy and lifted her a few inches before letting her sink back down. Throwing back her head, she waited. His hand remained in place as he took hold of the hem of her top and slowly pulled it up over her bra. She filled her lungs with oxygen but forgot to let it out until her chest started to burn. "No! I don't want freedom! I want to stay here with you."

"So I can do this?" He rubbed his forefinger against her labia.

"Yes! Yes!"

"And this?" Knowing fingers tugged her bra upward and exposed her breasts.

"Yes!"

"You want to be fucked?"

On the brink of another screamed *yes*, she fought her way past what he was doing. In her last dream or whatever it had been, she'd been presented to the warrior Mazati, who'd clearly been of a higher social class than the majority of Aztecs and confident of his power and position, like now. But before that, she'd seen a man alone, a lonely man with a dead woman beside him. Were they two different men or two sides of the same thing, the solitary one something he didn't want to reveal to her? Was that why he treated her like his possession, so she couldn't walk away from him?

"Master?"

"What?"

"I had a vision of you—and a dead woman."

"Did you?"

"Who was she? You were mourning her, looking so lost."

"Not lost. Facing my future."

"Who was she?"

"My wife, my slave-wife."

"Did—did you love her?"

"Not when I captured her but later. The Spanish killed her."

Before she could begin to think what to say, he slid his fore-finger inside her. Whimpering, she clamped her pussy muscles around him. Then she leaned forward and offered her newly exposed breasts to him.

"What is this about?" she demanded with an explosion only a few heartbeats away. "I'm supposed to replace her? You trained her to see you as her master, her god, and you want to feel that power again?"

Because she'd already determined that silence was his way of dealing with questions he didn't want to answer, she forced herself to remain still while waiting him out. Despite her out-burst, if she could have touched him, she would have cradled his head against her breasts and whispered comforting words while he laid the story of his marriage to his slave at her feet. Maybe he'd also explain why he'd shown her an ancient and thriving Aztec city, but not until he was ready.

"I hope you'll understand one day," he said at length. "And that there's more between us than what we have now, but . . ."

"But what?"

"True closeness might not happen."

Don't scare me! Determined to reach him in the only way he seemed to care about, she struggled to suck his finger deeper into her, but although he didn't resist, neither did he press his claim on her.

"Do it!" Frustration powered her words. "Whatever you were planning to do when you tied me like this, do it. And when you're done, maybe you'll tell me why. And if you don't . . ."

Although he withdrew his finger, he didn't leave her hot and dripping. Turning his attention back to her labia, he lightly but rapidly rubbed the wet surface. A heady yet familiar wave raged to life to separate her from everything except being manipulated. He was feeding her bits and pieces of energy and heat, teasing nerve endings until blood rushed to her cunt.

"Damn you, damn you," she chanted. She should tell him she hated his power over her, but she didn't, she couldn't. He knew her far more intimately than she did, knew the raw creature who thought and felt and maybe even loved with her pussy, and saw her own body as a giant electrical current. "Damn you."

Clamping his fingers over her left breast, he drew on it while increasing the tempo of his cunt massage. "For doing what you want?"

"Yes! Please, please, please!"

"You're dancing again, slave. Your mind might hate me, but your body belongs to me."

"No!"

"It's open and honest."

"No!"

"Isn't it, slave? Isn't it?"

Movement on her pussy slowed, stopped, ended. Equal amounts of terror and frustration filled her when he abandoned her, but seconds later when he pressed the heel of his hand against her sex and gripped her right breast, she envisioned him as a deep, dark pool of water she'd dived into. She might fear the unknown depths but was helpless to withstand the pull of danger and excitement, of life.

Release nipped at her, the sensation shaking her and causing her to thrust her pelvis at him. As she did, she became aware of a manageable but warning pain throughout her left thigh. Desperate to avoid a full-blown cramp, she tried to straighten her leg, and as she did, the impending climax rolled out of her grasp. Grunting in frustration, she nevertheless had no choice but to concentrate on her leg muscle. Maybe Mazati understood because with a single tug he freed her arms and helped her to her feet. Crossing her wrists in front, he held them as he massaged away the knot in her thigh. When she sighed in relief, he flattened her hands against his chest. No fabric stood between him and her fingertips, and he didn't stop her from running her fingers over his hard belly and from there to his erection.

"You're naked," she breathed.

"Yes."

"Thank you." She started to cup his cock only to have him draw her hands off him and spin her around. Maybe she could have twisted out of his grip, but when she realized he intended to tie her hands behind her, she sighed and relaxed. As he slipped cords around her wrists, she questioned not just his insistence on treating her like a possession but how easily and fully she embraced the role. Maybe she was afraid she'd lose him if she insisted on being a modern, liberated woman.

Modern? Is that what it all boiled down to? She lived in the present while he came from a time so far in the past that she couldn't comprehend it, a time and place where men saw women as chattel, as slave-wives?

No, that wasn't right. True, from what she'd read, Aztec men were the rulers, but women's contributions were acknowledged. While boys learned to fish and handle boats, girls were taught how to spin thread, grind maize, and operate looms. Even more important, both sexes went to school. As adults they filled vital roles as mothers, farmers, merchants, soothsayers, jewelers, even slave-courtesans. So did he see her as a jeweler or his slave-courtesan?

And which role did she want to fill?

When he turned her back around so he could look at her, it took her a moment to realize she still wore the blindfold. Being unable to read his expression pulled her into herself. Limp with wanting, she offered no resistance as he guided her onto what felt like thick moss. Then he released her and she sensed him stepping back. Free and yet not, she ran her fingers over what she could reach of her ass. If only he was doing this!

"Mazati, what is this about?"

"I'm waiting for you."

"To do what?"

"What you want."

Her response was a sharp laugh that startled her. "That's a hell of a thing for you to be asking someone you've stripped naked and tied up and blindfolded. In case it hasn't occurred to you, I can't exactly walk away."

"Would you if you could?"

She sensed he was staring at her; her hard and hurting nipples left no doubt of where his scrutiny was directed. Seeing herself for what she was, his willing possession, she embraced her role by widening her stance. Hot jungle air slid over her fevered core. "For you to fuck me, master. For both of us to forget that what's between us is insane."

His long sigh made her wonder if he felt the same way, but she didn't have the courage to ask. As the juices clinging to her thighs dried, she admitted what she had to: her body was all she had to offer him, all she wanted to. Unsure whether getting fucked or facing a long and honest look at what existed between them came first, she threw back her shoulders and lifted her head. "You like what you see, don't you? Like having me at your disposal."

"Yes."

"Is that all? You don't want or need anything else from me?"

"What about you, Hayley? What do you want from me?"

Everything and nothing. "Isn't it obvious? Look at me. I reek of sex, or rather, my body's response to what it wants. I'm standing here with my nipples so hard it's driving me crazy, and my cunt is hot and wet."

"You want my cock, then."

"Yes, damn you, yes!" The moment the words were out of her mouth, she would have given anything to take them back. There was so much more to him than what was between his legs, such as his rich past and his willingness to share pieces of it with her. And yet right now she couldn't think beyond what made him male. "We aren't getting anywhere, are we? Every time we're together, it comes down to sex. Then no matter what form it takes, whether we both get off or you push me over the edge, when we're done, we each go our own way. I stay in the only world that existed for me before you came into my life, while you—" She didn't know she was going to cry until hot tears bled into the blindfold. "I don't know enough about you when I need to know everything."

"You will, soon."

Both afraid and excited, she again jerked upright. One thing she'd learned about Mazati, he refused to be pushed any farther or faster than he felt safe doing, which is why she didn't ask for a timetable. At the same time, there was no denying the relief spreading over her. He was promising her more than this moment and this master/slave relationship, wasn't he? How could she do anything except give him what he needed right now, what they both did?

Weak and strong, she sank to her knees and lowered her head to the ground. Sun-heated air slid over her exposed ass, but the weight of her hanging breasts and tight belly made it impossible for her to concentrate on a single part of her anatomy. In her mind, she saw herself for what she was: a willing and complete submissive offering everything to her master, maybe as his slave-wife had once done.

Her experience with ass play was limited to a little short-term wearing of a small butt plug prior to Cal's disastrous attempt to take her back door. She'd blamed the failure on her inability to relax and his insistence on attempting to plunge in before she was ready. Today she would accommodate Mazati any way he wanted; the choice, like her body, was his.

"Master, please, accept my offering."

He hadn't moved; she was certain of that. Neither had he taken his eyes off her. As for what was going through him—a yank on her hair stopped her question. He kept her upper body parallel to the ground as he ran his free hand over her useless arms much as if she was a pet he was training. He had to be proud of what they'd both accomplished, didn't he?

"Master?"

"Quiet. I need to study you."

Admitting she was far from being at her most graceful or attractive, she tried not to shiver as his fingers trailed over the small of her back, up her spine to her shoulder blades. When he reached the base of her neck, he released her hair and pressed down on the back of her head. Sagging down again, she settled her temple against the soft ground and waited. Anticipated.

She wasn't sure whether he was standing or on his knees when he reached under her to cradle her left breast in his big palm. She, who'd always had to fight not to pull back when Cal roughly massaged her breasts, slipped into a narrow tunnel of sensation where nothing existed except her owner's expert handling. True, he did little more than cup her weight, but the promise and power was there. As in everything else where her body was concerned, her breast existed for him.

Once done with that part of his lesson of mastery and maybe caring, he turned his attention to her ass and flanks. He walked his fingers over her straining thigh muscles, over the curves of her knees, along her crack and from there to her labial lips. She thought he was on his knees as he cradled each fold between a thumb and forefinger and lightly but steadily drew them down. Sparks flashed throughout her, freeing a moan. Increasing his hold, he rubbed her lips together. Trying to bring her legs together without lifting her head was next to impossible; and she lacked the strength and will to straighten.

"Master, master, master," she chanted, a whimpering bitch in her man's hands.

"Damn you," he ground out as he transferred her hot juice to her puckered ass. "Damn you."

"What do you want? Please tell me. I'll—" A quick slap to her ass silenced her, but she couldn't stop shaking as he worked her fluid into her butt. Thoughts of what he had in mind filled her mouth with moisture. When she managed to widen her stance a little, he rewarded her by repeatedly slapping her pussy and ass with the flat of his hand. Bleating like some needful animal, she rolled from side to side. Much as she wanted to speak, she couldn't remember how to put words together, not with her entire body burning, aching, crying.

Ah, his juices-wet hands firm against her buttocks, spreading her there and exposing her crack. Mouth open and drooling now, she sucked in air. The touch of his cock head against her ass nearly brought her off the ground, but, sobbing in anticipation, she tucked her legs even farther under her and lifted her ass as high as possible. His cock kissed her again, the contact holding, promising, torturing.

"Fuck me, please! Fuck!"

Keeping his cock against her aching ass, he repeatedly slapped her buttocks. Although he put little strength behind the contact, she guessed her usually pale skin was turning bright pink. Wondering if he was leaving a handprint fueled her imagination, and for the first time in her life, she believed she could come from ass penetration.

By hooking his hands at the join of pelvis and thighs, he easily drew her closer. As he did, her butt muscles relaxed and then gave way. In he slipped, barely penetrating but there, commanding. "Ah, ha," she moaned.

"Slow, slow. No." A firm stroke of her buttocks stopped her from trying to push back against him. "Let me do this."

In another time and place, when she'd regained her sanity, she'd ask him where his knowledge came from, but right now she was content to be his pupil. Just the same, she had to fight her body's natural instinct to fight by clenching her teeth and knotting her useless fingers.

He'd prepared her well by greasing her with her body's fluids. What he hadn't told her was how his cock filling her ass would feel. Words or rather fragments of words skittled through her, shattered her mind. She clung to overwhelming, helpless, powerful, surrendering ownership, primitive. Swallowing his cock one cautious and controlled thrust at a time caused her thighs to catch fire and now those flames licked along her belly, the heat originating in her cunt, sparked by her clit.

How was that possible? He hadn't touched her pussy and yet—

In! He was all the way in her now with his balls pressed against her buttocks and his hands against her pelvis as he lifted her into an upright position. Spreading her buttocks as best she could with her tethered hands gave her something to concentrate on. At the same time the effort distracted her from her straining, stretched butt muscles, and she had no inkling before he pulled back only to plunge deep.

"Ah!" she gasped.

"Haah."

If it wasn't for his grip on her pelvis, his strength would have sent her sliding, but with him offering the necessary support, she turned her upper body to the side and planted her right shoulder against the ground. Now anchored, she concentrated on moving with and in counterpoint with him, careful and measured. Whether she rocked in time with his tempo or allowed him to nearly slip out made no difference. Everything felt wonderful, as if she was now part of him, no longer a separate human being. A burning sensation between her shoulder blades only added to the fire. Her breasts shook and her bra pressed against the top of her mounds, making them feel as if they were as imprisoned as the rest of her.

But she didn't care. Everything had become movement and heat, his cock seemingly gliding throughout her, the invasion complete.

In the past she'd learned to recognize an impending climax by the sense that she was drawing in upon herself, tucking her pussy deep inside her, maybe to protect her against the coming explosion. But she didn't sense this one coming, had no warning, no defenses, nothing except power. Freedom!

There wasn't enough air in the world! She was going to pass out, maybe die with her whole body twitching. Then, maybe understanding her need, he gripped her arms and pulled her up to where oxygen waited. Still holding her, he rammed at her, rammed and rammed again.

"Coming! Oh god, it won't stop!"

He said something, a flow of hard sounds played out as his powerful body and hot cock shattered her. She might be screaming, might have started to cry. Like a roped wild horse she fought not her bonds and his hands but her own out-of-control body.

And like a masterful rider, he rode her.

All Hayley knew for sure was that the swimming back to the here and now had taken a long time. Even now, with her system satiated, she couldn't look at Mazati without bits and pieces of their lovemaking/sex/fucking/whatever-the-hell-it-was intruding on her barely there brain. He scared her. Hell, she scared herself. And, although she didn't know how she was going to survive, she needed for him to back off.

"Why is it this way?" She indicated the marks left behind by the restraints he'd recently removed. "Do you think I won't want sex if bondage isn't part of it? That I need the fantasy of being forced to keep going?"

He'd been stretched out on his back with his hands supporting the back of his head but now he rolled over onto his side and studied her. "I have my reasons."

"Shit!" She punched his shoulder. "You keep so damn much from me! What are you afraid of revealing?"

"If only it was that simple."

"What are you talking about?"

"What I keep to myself is beyond your comprehension, the stakes more than I'm willing to risk, now."

"That tells me nothing." She waited until she was certain she had his full attention. "Maybe you don't trust me. You think the only way this—this whatever we have is going to work is by keeping me sexually indebted to you. Is that it?"

"No," he said, but his tone lacked the conviction she needed to hear.

"Do you really get off on tying me up?" she blurted in frustration. "That's the only way you can—forget I said that. I know it isn't that for you." About to flop back down, she sat up and stared at his prime body. She hadn't often been in the superior position, if that's what this was. "You're wrong if you believe I'm locked into BDSM or whatever you want to call it. I'm an average, normal woman. Sex in all its forms appeals to me." *Especially sex with you.* "Sometimes I want to be your equal. Can you understand that?"

"That isn't possible."

"What isn't?"

"Us as equals."

"Why? Because you were born who knows how many hundreds of years ago and never got around to dying? Because you have the ability to direct my dreams and take me back in time with you? Just because I don't understand and can't explain those things doesn't mean we don't speak the same language."

"I speak English because I need to communicate with you. Otherwise, you wouldn't understand a word I say."

Like the Aztecs in her latest dream/time travel. "Why me? Of all the women in the world, why did you select me for—for whatever this is?"

Yet another of his silences left her with too much time to try to answer her own question, and to again face how little she truly knew about this amazing and mysterious man. Not only didn't she have any idea where he lived or how he filled his days in the present or the continuum of his life since his beginning, she couldn't begin to guess what he was thinking right now. Maybe his thoughts didn't go farther than her accessible and too-easy-to-control body. That's why they were together? She was an easy lay?

"Until we've bonded, I have to take things one step at a time."

"Bonding? Damn, damn!" Fury and frustration forced her to her feet. "I'm so fucking tired of your word riddles. If you think all I have to do is sit around waiting for you to storm into my life and turn it on end, you're beyond mistaken. I don't want this!" She tugged at her collar. Of course it remained in place, which suddenly and inescapably scared her. "Are you some kind of sicko? Am I?"

"Neither of us are."

Still propped up on his elbow, he gave no indication that he thought she might bolt and that pissed her off even more than she already was. Oh yeah, his little bondage puppet. His latest entertainment. "I'm not so sure," she belatedly told him. "And unless you start giving me some answers, I don't want you touching me again, do you get it?"

"I don't have a choice."

When he started to sit up, she jumped back, hands outstretched as if that could ward him off. Ignoring her, he concentrated on getting his feet under him. That's when she turned tail and ran.

*   *   *

Let her go. Don't make her part of your obsession; she deserves better.

But even before Hayley was out of sight, Mazati knew he wouldn't walk away from what he'd begun with her. How could he turn his back on his determination not to let his way of life die with him? This woman who understood the language of opals as intimately as he did represented his connection with today's world. Before he was done with her, her mind and body would belong to him, and his dream of revealing the truth about the Aztecs would be reborn through her creativity.

That was the only thing that mattered, not either of their hearts, not her freedom—or his. He'd bond with her in the only way he'd ever bonded with a woman. Before he died, she'd know as much about his world as he did.

Otherwise why was he still alive?

15

―――――――

"Have you been drinking?"

Forcing a laugh, Hayley fought the urge to hang up on her sister. "Not in the middle of the day. Why do you ask?"

"Because you sound, I don't know, like you're on something. You aren't taking drugs, are you?"

"Not a bad idea, but I can't afford them. Why'd you call except to ask how I'm coming with *your* jewelry, which I'm not? I thought you were subbing for another girl today."

"I am." Saree's throaty chuckle made Hayley long to watch, although given her sexual frustration, she'd probably embarrass herself as soon as the shoot got started. "They're messing around getting some equipment in place so I'm killing time. You should see this *little* toy I'm going to be strapped to."

"Spare me." Despite her attempt to sound disinterested, Hayley's vision blurred and her hands heated. As if she wasn't having enough trouble concentrating on the bracelet she'd been working on for hours, Saree had to call and pull her completely out of the mood for work—and into another mood.

"You know those medieval racks they used to tie people to?

Then the goons would stretch the captive or prisoner or whatever until their bodies were pulled—"

"I said, spare me. I know they're not doing anything like
that to you."

"Fortunately, no. But the results are going to be killer because this rack'll bow me back so my boobs'll reach for the sky.
When it's fully engaged, it's like having my arms and legs
strapped to half a circle, pussy totally exposed for all kinds of
fun while I pretend I don't want what I'd lick a boot for. Shit, I
can hardly wait. Randy said he's going to keep after me until
I've come at least four times."

Randy was one of Saree's favorite riggers; he didn't make
hollow threats, or should she say promises. "That's what you
called for, so I'd know how you'd be spending the afternoon?"

"No." Saree turned serious. "We really haven't talked for
about a week. Are you still seeing what's his name?"

"I, ah, I told him I needed some space."

"So you could work or because he's too intense?"

Saree, you know me so well. "A bit of both."

"You want to talk about it?"

"I don't know." She sighed. "What you said about his intensity pretty much hits the nail on the head. It's kind of like being
in a horror movie that scares the shit out of me without being
able to leave the theater."

"He won't let you walk away?"

Those who only knew the superficial Saree called her some
pretty unsavory things, none of which had anything to do with
her intellect. However, those people were missing a great deal.
"He hasn't been, ah, around since I told him I wanted breathing
room, and yet, hell, it's as if he's sitting in a corner watching me.
That's part of what's so unnerving about him; he pops in and
out of my life. And when he snaps his fingers or whip, I dance
to his tune like some damn puppet. I can't—"

"What was that about a whip?"

"No, I didn't mean that," she said, although she wouldn't be surprised if erotic whip play was around the corner if she allowed their relationship to continue. "Just because that's the way you play—"

"Play nothing. It's business, and you know it. Look, I need to get myself revved up, if you know what I mean. Okay, so you're taking a break from Mr. Intense but are you really putting any space between the two of you?"

She hadn't been having any of those *dreams*, not that she was about to tell Saree about them. "What are you talking about?"

"I have to spell it out?

Hayley didn't know or care how long she'd been sitting at her workbench with her head in her hands, eyes closed. She also couldn't say with any degree of certainty what she'd been thinking; mulling over the conversation with her sister, of course, but there had to be other things bouncing through her brain. Finally, she stood and walked from her shop into her house and from there into her bathroom. Turning on the light, she leaned over the counter so she could study the leather around her neck. The longer she stared, the more bizarre, the more obscene it looked. No way would anyone call this a necklace. It was what it was: proof of ownership.

"Why, Mazati, why?"

Half expecting to hear one of his nonexplanations, she waited. When his voice didn't break the silence, she ran less-than-steady fingers over the collar. This, in addition to the opals, was her link to him, unshakable proof that he existed and had singled her out for—for what? Other men gifted women with flowers, jewelry, dinners, trips. Hers locked a slave collar around her throat and then confused the hell out of her by hinting about some dark secrets.

That was sick.

Wide eyed now, she returned her stare in the mirror. The time to hide from the truth, to play whatever the hell game they'd been playing, was over. Yes, he'd ruled her with his powerful body and mastery of her hungry one, but that was sick and not exciting, as she'd been trying to convince herself. Unhealthy. Dangerous.

There, that was the word she'd been avoiding since that first day. Bottom line, what she'd allowed Mazati to become in her life was dangerous.

Deliberately shutting down emotionally and intellectually, she opened the top drawer and pulled out the strong, sharp scissors Cal had bought after seeing it advertised on TV. Surprisingly, it had lived up to its billing as being superior to all other household scissors. Pulling the leather as far as she could away from her throat, she slipped one blade under it and started squeezing. At first she wasn't sure she was making any headway, but tackling the sturdy leather a little at a time made the difference. As the slit increased in length, her emotions wavered between relief and regret. Was she losing contact with Mazati this way? With his deeply personal gift no longer adorning her body, would he believe she didn't want anything to do with him?

Rocked by the thought, she steadied herself by leaning against the counter. Then, although her head still wasn't clear, she turned the question on herself. Was this the end of whatever existed between her and the mysterious man? Didn't she need to move on with her life, to regain ownership of her body and consequently her soul?

Yes. No.

"Give me some time," she compromised. "Time for me to be me without you getting in the way."

Although she wasn't sure whether time and distance was what she truly needed or wanted, she returned to her task. This time the leather gave way with almost no resistance, and less than a minute later, it slid off her to land in the sink. Feeling as if she'd lost something both precious and dangerous, she picked it up but couldn't bring herself to drop it in the trash. Instead, she took it into her workshop and placed it near the supply drawers to the right of her work space.

Turning on the stereo, she selected a rock station and dove into the hard-rolling music. Even when her ears started throbbing, she refused to turn down the volume because if she did, she'd start thinking. This way there was nothing but her fingers and tools on her latest piece and her mind skating. When she finished the bracelet she'd been working on when her sister had called, she stretched and rubbed the back of her neck. Her plan had been to get started on another bracelet, but what had happened to her preliminary sketch?

She was at loose ends, that's all. It was as if her weekend date had called and cancelled at the last moment, leaving her with nothing to do and the sense that he'd blown her off because he'd gotten a better offer.

No, it wasn't that. What ailed her went deeper than a girl's ego. Although admitting it was hard, the fact was that having leather caressing her throat had served as a minor but continuous turn-on. Now there was no buzz, no subtle reminder that Mazati would show up when it served him and put her through her paces, paces that had culminated in climaxes that loosened her teeth.

Damn it, she needed her teeth loosened.

"Are you responsible for my mood?" Picking up the collar, she shook it as if punishing it would punish him. "Hanging around in whatever netherworld you exist in, watching me, impacting me in ways that make no sense?" Not giving a damn what he might think if he was indeed here in some form, she spread her legs and ran the collar over her pussy.

Alerted by the zing shooting through her, she clamped her knees together. No way was he taking her back to where he'd taken her before, no way!

Still, she couldn't let go of the collar.

Compromising, she stretched it out on her work space and started caressing the leather. From the beginning she'd decided that Night Fire's signature would revolve around the marriage of opals and silver, not leather. Besides, a delicately colored opal would be lost in the harsh contrast. But if she could fashion silver in some way to make it resemble leather—no, not leather but the whole collar concept.

Excitement snaked up her spine. Just because everything she'd created so far had carried out a delicate theme didn't mean she couldn't broaden the concept, at least in subtle ways. Most women, especially the well-heeled ones who could afford to buy Night Fire, didn't want anything to do with the simulated dog collars seen on mall crawlers, but what if she used silver strands to create a graceful, lightweight chain necklace imprinted with her signature opals? What about a high-class, in-your-face takeoff on a slave collar?

Long hours later, Hayley forced her aching spine into an upright position. With her vision on its way out, she had to rely on memory to truly see what she was looking at. The necklace that had evolved out of her surge of creativity most closely resembled medieval chain-mail mesh. Two inches wide, loose and flexible, it would cradle and caress the wearer's throat. She'd randomly woven a half dozen opals of nearly the same size into the mesh and had thought she was done until, guided by something she didn't understand or question, she'd braided three silver threads about four inches long to the front of the necklace and topped that off with a magnificent black opal designed to rest in the hollow of the wearer's throat. She'd have to put an obscene price tag on it if she was going to make back her investment, maybe more than anyone would be willing to fork over, but damn it, this was a wonderful creation!

Smiling in weary satisfaction, she locked up and staggered into her house. Fortunately, she had some leftover Chinese, which she popped into the microwave. It went down with a glass of white wine. Leaving the dish and glass in the sink, she planted herself in front of the TV and stared without comprehension at a drama. She thought she'd made it through that show, but had obviously fallen asleep because the next thing she knew, the eleven o'clock news was on. Maybe she should catch up on the world, but that took a brain, didn't it, something she'd lost.

As she crawled into bed, she acknowledged that working herself into the ground had accomplished something valuable—she was too tired to have any libido left, too spent to do more than remember Mazati's name.

Good, she thought, as the dark haze of sleep sucked her in. She'd begun the process of putting him out of her life.

As for her heart . . .

Images and impressions flickered through her mind. Caught by the vibrant colors, Hayley nestled deeper into sleep and willed the sights to continue. She had no awareness of herself as a human being; nothing existed except the sense of drifting while one object or another came into view. She stared, barely comprehending, at an intricately carved circular stone some twelve feet in diameter. The longer she studied it, the more detail she could make out in the carvings. The center depicted a face with round ears and protruding tongue. Outside that was a circle, and within the circle's boundaries, a number of symbols. One looked so much like a jaguar head that she half expected it to attack. Other symbols depicted fires, rains, and hurricanes, although how she knew that she couldn't say. More detailed circles were beyond the first, but she wasn't given time to try to decipher them before the great stone faded into nothing. Only then did an explanation for the center face come to her. Tonatiuh, the God of the Sun.

There, another object reaching up from the past to touch her with its terrible beauty. This was a nearly foot-long flint knife with an intricate, warrior-shaped handle made from several hundred small turquoise pieces. A disembodied finger she recognized as her own traced the three-dimensional warrior figure, and as with Tonatiuh, she understood that this represented an Eagle warrior and that the knife was used in sun-god worship ceremonies.

Next came a low circular platform where Eagle and Jaguar warriors sat during their initiation rites. In the middle was a detailed stone effigy of an eagle. Although no warriors were there now, she had no doubt that Mazati had once sat on the platform.

A mural, at least five feet high, exquisitely painted with bright-feathered birds, a great serpent, blooming trees. The colors, ah, the colors! Rust red and new-leaf green, sun yellow, and earth brown.

More turquoise, in the shape of a two-headed serpent this time. Thousands of tiny turquoise fragments represented scales. Both fierce and remarkable in its detail, it spoke to her of a long-dead but highly skilled craftsman.

Finally, a relief carving of what at first appeared to be a warrior woman with her head upturned, naked breasts hanging, fingers clenched, and a human skull on her belt. Then, as before, Hayley understood that this was the decapitated and dismembered Coyolxauhqui, the Moon Goddess, and that the Aztec had feared the evil woman who spoke to centipedes and spiders and transformed herself into a sorceress. Long after the image faded, Hayley continued to shiver because Mazati had once feared Coyolxauhqui.

"What is this, Mazati?" she asked the night. "Where are you taking me now?"

Into my world. My beauty and danger.

He stood over her, shadow and substance coexisting in the same body. She thought she was in her bed, but with her attention focused on him, she couldn't be sure. Instead of being afraid, she locked onto his loneliness, his solitude. In her mind she clearly saw what he'd been doing before intruding on her world and life.

He'd been wandering through a maze of rock-covered mounds, only, judging by his expression and the pain radiating from him, she'd known they were more than random formations; they were graves. Much as she'd longed to join and comfort him, she hadn't been able to find the window between his world and hers. Hurting for him, she'd begged him to join her. He had, as witnessed by his presence in her bedroom, if that's where they were.

"Where were you?" she asked, looking up. "All those graves, were they your friends? Relatives?"

"They were my life."

Shock sent strength to her muscles, but when she tried to sit up, she discovered that several leather belts had been cinched around her. One pressed against the top of her breasts and over her upper arms, trapping them by her sides. A much smaller length lashed her wrists together behind her. Another was around her thighs, while yet another just above her knees assured that she couldn't separate her legs. The final belt caressed her ankles. She was naked. "Why, Mazati? Why did you do this to me?"

"So you couldn't leave today."

His reasons went far deeper than physical restraint; she was certain of it. "Is this because of what I did to the collar?"

He didn't answer and the dim lighting made reading his expression difficult. "You can't keep doing this to me. It's no way to form a relationship. I don't understand why you insist—"

"Maybe I should have gagged you."

"Even if I couldn't speak, you'd know what I'm thinking."

Once more silence flowed between them. When he'd first started restraining her, she'd been so trapped between erotic response and fear that she'd been unable to think beyond those emotions, but familiarity had bred a certain comprehension that she now pulled around her.

He wasn't a man who feared anything, so she didn't believe he relied on ropes and leather because he was afraid she'd run away. Neither was he motivated solely by her personal fantasies about being a submissive, if indeed he'd been able to tap into them. Instead, unless she was badly mistaken, a master/slave relationship was all but inbred in him. This was how he related to woman and how he believed women wanted to be handled. After all, his wife had also been his slave.

"You keep throwing up barriers between us," she softly told him. "I tell you I don't want anything to do with you, but you intrude on my dream or wherever we are right now. You force your way into my life, take away my freedom, and give me glimpses into something I might never fully comprehend, and you believe that'll forge a link between us that goes far beyond opals. But you're wrong, Mazati. Women need more than physical response and playacting. We need emotional connection."

When he ran his fingers over her exposed and vulnerable flank, she had to struggle to concentrate. At least he understood that tenderness was a core component of the man/ woman relationship.

"Don't," she said. "Sex isn't enough. That's what I've been trying to tell you; there's more to life than fucking."

Rolling her onto her side, he slid the flat of his hand between her ass cheeks. "You don't want this?"

"Not *just* this, damn it!" She squeezed her buttocks together.

"I don't believe you." Making no effort to remove his hand, he leaned down so he could pull her breast into his mouth. She started to melt as his moist heat surrounded her, briefly fought the sensation, then surrendered. He knew her well, damn it, knew so much about the sensual creature she usually kept so deeply under wraps that she barely knew of that creature's existence. But the animal came to life under Mazati's leadership, and she loved him for it.

No, not love! Gratitude and surrender, yes, but a lifetime away from love.

Marginally satisfied with her amendment, she mentally and emotionally returned to her body. He still sheltered her breast but was no longer simply holding it inside him. Instead, he pressed his tongue against her nipple, causing it to become so hard that it bordered on the painful. Taking advantage of what he'd created, he drew back an inch at a time until only her nub remained inside him, but before she could decide whether to try to free herself, he closed his teeth over her nipple.

Heat sparked. Somewhere between panic and wonder, she stared at him but saw nothing beyond the damnable dark shadow he'd become. His hand was still against her butt in a statement of control and intimacy she couldn't possibly deny. No longer trying to punish him with her ass muscles, she acknowledged what she'd again become: his. Willingly his.

16

"**I** missed you," she admitted. "I didn't want to, but I did."

His response was to bathe her burning nub in his wet heat, and despite her restraints, she arched toward him in abject surrender, and yes, trust. Not being able to move freed her from responsibility; as before, he was in charge of everything that happened between them.

But what was that *everything*? "Mazati? Damn it, what's with these straps?"

"You don't like them?"

Quite the opposite, she loved the sense of being cradled by his restraints, but that wasn't the point. "There can't be any sex this way."

After patting her cheek, he straightened and looked down at her, his hands limp at his side. Staring up at his equally naked frame, she wondered why she hadn't noticed his nudity before. Maybe he'd been dressed at the beginning? Anything was possible. "It's on purpose, isn't it." She demonstrated by trying to separate her legs. "What? You want me to be frustrated?"

"No. It's me I don't trust."

The unexpected admission silenced her. If Mazati didn't epitomize the confident, in-control male, who did? From the beginning, he'd directed the course of their relationship, directed her body and mind, in fact. About to tell him she didn't believe him, the memories of him standing alone in a graveyard and mourning his dead slave-wife returned to her. "Why don't you?"

Unfortunately, the dim lighting prevented her from reading his expression, but his slowly clenching fingers told her how hard answering her was. Although she tried to ready herself for his emotional distance, she reverently hoped their time together had taught him that he could trust her.

"So much depends on what happens between us," he said at length. "The stakes . . ."

Not that again. "Stakes? For who?"

"Me. I thought you understood that."

Yes, he was vulnerable after all, the truth clearly spelled out in a few words. "I, ah, I saw something the other day," she said. "An image of you standing in what looked like a burial ground. Maybe you were really there; maybe I picked up on a memory. Whatever it was, I sensed your sorrow, your aloneness. The same impression hit me with that earlier *memory* of you beside your wife's body."

He left; just like that, he was gone. There was no turning away, no footsteps, no door opening or closing, nothing except sudden and complete loss. Although she'd become conditioned to his disconnect with the physical world she understood, his leave-taking shocked her, not because she was helpless, but because it said too much about his inability to open up.

"You're still here," she said to the empty air. "I know you wouldn't abandon me like this. What is it, Mazati? What are you so afraid of? It can't be me; you wouldn't have reached out to me in the first place if I represented danger. You wouldn't be giving me those incredible opals if you didn't believe I was worthy of the gift or taking me into your world, and you wouldn't have spilled yourself in me if trust wasn't involved. Mazati? Listen to me, listen! Whatever we've started, it can't continue without honesty."

Because he'd shown her his thoughtful nature, she steeled herself for a long wait, and because he sometimes kept everything from her, she didn't dare hold out much hope for the truth. Still, a man who stripped and restrained a woman owed her something in exchange, didn't he?

Although the straps did a more than adequate job of keeping her in place, he'd managed to do so without leather or metal pressing against her flesh. As a consequence, she sank back into the cocoon he'd created for and around her. Granted, the hot hum between her legs was inescapable, but she was content to drift in sensation. To think of wrapping her body around his and feeding off it.

He'd return, pick her up, carry her to wherever he'd been. He'd set her down and stretch her out on a grassy carpet. Then he'd free her one slow and sensuous strap at a time, caressing and massaging where the leather had been while her skin sang and danced and her mind whirled in heat. When only her wrist restraints remained, she'd push him to the ground as she'd done before and straddle him with her core open and waiting. And then maybe he'd position her so he could bury his tongue in her cunt.

A ragged moan brought her back to the *real* world, and in the aftermath of her fantasy, she realized her mind and imagination had pushed her upward and a climax waited at the top—a climax she couldn't reach while restrained. Even with her legs pressed together, her hard clit made its presence known, compelling her to try to satisfy herself by rubbing her thighs together. Damn it, she needed Mazati, not this!

Him!

How she knew he'd returned wasn't important; maybe because the very air seemed to reach out to welcome him. As she waited for him to become form and substance, she mentally asked where he'd been. By way of answer, he *showed* her an image of him back at the gravesite, only this time he wasn't simply standing alone among the dead. Instead, he was digging a deep trench. Sweat streamed off him, and when he straightened and turned, she saw he'd been wounded in the side. Fresh blood mixed with his sweat to run over his naked flank and down his leg.

If he felt pain, he gave no indication. Except for the infrequent occasions when he glanced at the inert body behind him, his concentration fixed on what he was doing. When he studied death, grief fought with and won over his anger. Was he responsible for all those graves? He'd buried other men and had been left alone to grieve?

"Mazati?" she whispered, trying to make his name a caress. "What are you showing me?"

"All I can."

With the simple and inadequate explanation swirling around her, she didn't realize he was becoming reality until his magnificent form again stood over her. She no longer resented her bonds because they prevented her from masturbating; instead, she struggled because she desperately needed to touch him, to comfort, but the straps had no give.

"Who are those men? How did they die and why are you burying them?"

"The invaders killed them, sometimes by cutting off their heads. They left the bodies to rot in the sun, but I found them."

"My god! How—you mean the Spanish, don't you?"

"Yes."

"Why weren't you killed?"

"I don't know. I should have been. I prayed to die alongside my fellow warriors but . . ."

"I'm so sorry. What you've been through—I wish you'd told me earlier."

Reaching out, he brushed her hair off her forehead. "Trust takes time. I had to be sure you could handle the truth and know what to do with it."

Much as she wanted to melt into the touch, she clung to his words. "That's what everything between us has been about? Bringing me along so—so eventually I could join you at that graveyard?"

"No."

She'd said all she could, pushed her courage as far as she dared for today. If only she could talk to her sister! The connect with reality, specifically with Saree's pragmatic nature, might keep her from wondering if she was going insane. "Where is the graveyard?" she asked because it was a question her sister would ask. "Where did you bury them?"

"In the past."

"Everything about you is part of history, isn't it?"

"Except what's lost."

"Yes, of course. The Spanish destroyed so much, killed so many—"

"Not fully destroyed. Not fully killed."

Before meeting him she would have laughed at such nonsense, but she couldn't because he'd shown her that the past still existed.

"I'm scaring you, aren't I?" he asked with his knuckles on the valley between her breasts.

"No, not scared but unnerved."

"I'm sorry. I didn't want to do this to you."

"Why did you?"

"Because of who you are and what you do."

Oh, damn him! What was this, riddles? Before she could fling her question at him, it flowed away under his fingers.

"You've turned my life on end," she admitted, although he already knew that. "I can't remember who and what I was before you came into it."

Leaning low, he licked first one nipple and then the other, causing her to squirm and arch toward him. The night continued to hold him, but she sensed she wasn't the only one who'd been drawn into whatever spell had encompassed this dark space. "Do you want back what you were?" he asked.

No, no, no! "I don't know. If—if I didn't know better, I'd say you'd drugged me."

"I'd never do that."

Because I mean too much to you? Damn, damn, what's happening?

The universe shifted again, a reddish haze descending until it encompassed her. Then, bit by bit, she was able to make sense of what she was seeing. The pyramid was there in all its just-built perfection. A large number of people were gathered around its base but with enough space between them and the pyramid that she wondered if they were afraid of it. Looking where they were, she saw five men climbing the steps. The two leading the way had long gray hair held in place with red bands around their foreheads. They wore predominantly white capes that extended to their knees and under that an even longer dresslike garment. Both carried large knives held up so everyone could see.

Because of the dark stains on the knives, she couldn't tell what they were made of; and she didn't want to think about what had caused the discoloration. Behind them trudged two young men with bronzed skin whose only clothing consisted of multicolored loincloths. They each had a hand on the naked, stumbling figure between them. From the way the man in the middle was acting, she guessed he was either drugged or had been wounded. His hands were tightly tied behind him.

A sacrifice.

"I don't want to see this!"

"It was part of my world."

"Did you ever question this insanity?" she demanded. "Who are the men in front, priests? That's what their knives are for, isn't it? So they can butcher—"

"Not butcher. Our belief was that the war god Huitzilo-pochtli needed the daily nourishment of human hearts and blood. Otherwise, he wouldn't have the strength needed to battle the forces of night."

"I don't want to hear this!" she snapped, struggling to free herself from the touch that had nourished her in many ways just moments ago. "It's barbaric!" The *sacrifice* lifted his head and seemed to look straight at her. His eyes swam with helpless fear and resignation. She could smell his sweat and urine. "Everything the Aztecs stood for was obscene!"

"No!" Grabbing her shoulders, he easily kept her in place. "Not everything. Much of what we accomplished was good. Our language and math, our creations."

"Creations such as a two-headed turquoise serpent; a great circular stone that depicted what was important to your people such as jaguars, fire, rain, and hurricanes; Coyolxauhqui, the Moon Goddess. I appreciate being shown those things, but I still don't understand why you went to the effort."

Although he stopped pressing on her shoulders, she made no effort to move. Instead, she sought to find the core of the man through the current now passing between them. The world she'd always known was concrete and traffic, bills and gas heat. She'd never believed in things that went bump in the night, but now she accepted that Mazati's reality was far different from hers.

Maybe she had from the beginning.

"I hand you my truths, Hayley. I can't tell you what to do with them."

"I know you can't." Eyes wide open, she welcomed him

into her heart as fully as she'd welcomed him into her body, if only for this moment. "But why me? If you've—if you've somehow survived all these centuries, have there been other women, other collars and ropes?"

"No."

Nearly drowning in relief, she rolled onto her side and drew up her legs as if trying to protect her core. At the same time, she continued to gaze at what she could see of his face. Not long after getting married, she'd had to work late and then drive home after dark on a densely foggy night. Disoriented and isolated, she'd clung to sanity by thinking ahead to opening her front door. Her fingers gripped the steering wheel as she inched along, and she feared the dark curtain that obscured everything except the few inches her headlights were able to penetrate. At the same time, she cradled a clear image of her brightly lit living room with her loving groom waiting for her.

This moment took her back to that sense of being in two places at the same time. Mazati was offering his incredible body and knowledgeable hands, promising pleasure and release as she'd never experienced. But much as she longed to embrace the moment and him, only him and not his past, he was unlike any man she'd ever known, dark and mysterious, maybe deadly.

Beyond her comprehension.

"No other women during all those years," she finally thought to say. "Then why have you chosen me?"

"The gift in your hands, and the opals."

"What about the opals?"

"They speak to both of us. Before the gods guided me to them, I was only half alive, drifting in nothing, trapped in the past. They brought warmth to my heart and allowed me to hear it beating. I no longer simply wanted to be dead. Then, through the shared language of opals, you and I found each other."

The language and life-giving properties of opals? What was

he talking about? And yet didn't the multicolored stones tap into her creativity as nothing else she worked with did? "We didn't find each other. You walked into my world, intruded upon it. You've tied me up and forced yourself on me. Why?"

He was on the brink of answering; she could sense the change in him. But although she prayed he'd tell her, he didn't. Instead, he unfastened the belt around her thighs followed by the ones anchoring her calves. Her ankles were still restrained, but there was no doubting his message. He was returning her sex to her.

"It's back to that, isn't it, Mazati?" she said around tears and need. "The one thing that truly keeps us together."

"It should be enough."

"No, it shouldn't!" Despite her awkwardness, she managed to sit up but then had to lean forward a little to keep from falling back. "All right, I'm not going to lie and say I don't get off on some of the things that go on between us, and my sister makes a damn good living as a bondage slut, but that's not what keeps a couple together into their golden years. What about buying a home, careers, children? What about who takes out the garbage and who sorts the mail?"

"First comes need," he said and pushed her back down. "Once that has become part of us, you'll accept what I truly need of you, your mission." Straddling her with his hands near her shoulders, he lowered his buttocks until he was practically sitting on her. "You know about need, Hayley."

It was happening again, this disconnect from everything except his power over her and how much she craved that power. Feeling as if she might melt into him, she allowed her body to relax, to sink into the ground, to absorb him. No matter how firmly she told herself that he was only doing what she was willing to let him do, that was only part of the story. She'd called Saree a bondage slut, but it was Hayley who craved this unequal relationship. He knew more about her than she ever had, the knowledge making him believe she felt most complete when he controlled her.

"It took a great deal of strength of will for you to remove your collar," he said. "But you aren't fighting today's restraints."

Damn that seductive and knowing voice of his. "How can I? You're smashing me."

"I wasn't before, and even now you could tell me to let you go." Rocking back, he cupped her breasts and lifted them. As he did, she melted even more. Boneless and nearly nerveless, she saw herself for what she was: his. "Say the words, Hayley. Order me to leave you."

"You—you know I can't."

"Because your need is as strong as mine."

There was wisdom in his words, wisdom and more. But whatever that was would have to wait for when the heat radiating out from his heart didn't bleed into hers. And when hunger had been satisfied.

"At least free my hands. I need to touch you."

"I know you do, but I can't let that happen yet."

"Yet? When? Damn it, when?"

"When I've made you ready."

Oh yes, he could do that; she'd already memorized the lessons borne out in the now-teasing fingertips tracing circles around her nipple. Rocking her head from side to side provided her with an output for her energy but did nothing for longing. He was smiling; despite the night, she clearly saw that rare and precious expression. Knowing she was responsible for his lightened mood and the rod scraping along her belly infused her with a power that made a lie of her helplessness. Being under him and within his control was good and necessary.

Smiling back at him, she traced an awareness that began in her temple and ran throughout her, pooling in her fingers and toes and threatening to spill out of her cunt. He was still simply exploring her breasts, but his weight settled over her hips and his cock along her belly said he'd claimed all of her. He hadn't asked permission; she hadn't given it. Instead, in their own ways, they'd each known this was what should be between them. For now.

"What do you want?" he muttered. "Tell me."

"I want to be licked," she said without embarrassment. "To feel your tongue on my pussy."

"Where else?"

Ah, what an incredible question. "Down my spine. Slow. Even if I scream and beg, I want it to be slow. Only when I've lost my mind do I want you to turn me over and spread my legs."

"Not just your spine," he said after completing yet another circuit of her nipples. "Your shoulder blades and buttocks."

The thought made her shiver, that and the sensual tickle that made her nipples ache. "You—you would do that?"

"Yes, because you want it."

She did, oh god, she did! And although an instant of fear locked her muscles as he rolled her onto her stomach, she concentrated on relaxing. She'd turned her head to the side, and if she put all her strength into it, she might be able to roll onto her back again, but her arms were useless and unneeded, her legs worthless. She belonged to him, didn't she? His to handle as he saw fit, to restrain even more if he believed that's what she needed.

"Have you always been this slender?" he asked, positioning himself at her right side.

"What? No. I lost some weight when, you know, when my marriage fell apart."

"When you stopped trusting a man. Now you have to learn how to do that again."

"I—maybe I do."

"Listen to me." Something, a fingernail probably, began tracing her spine starting with the base of her neck. She jumped, her muscles tightening. "Relax, Hayley. Relax. And listen to me."

Impossible as long as he was doing that! Impossible as long as the promise of sex punctuated the night. And yet when he reached the end of her tailbone and started up again, tension seeped out of her. Hearing herself sigh, she wondered if she was responsible for the change. Maybe along with everything else he held control over her muscles and nerves.

It didn't matter, she admitted when he released her wrists. The belt around her upper arms and over her breasts was still there, but she might be able to free herself, not that she would. This moment was for believing she belonged to him, for turning her body over to him.

For, maybe, learning why he always approached and commanded her this way.

After massaging her hands, he settled her arms by her side. She was wondering what he was going to do next when his teeth scraped along the back of her neck. Shivering, she started to lift her head but fell back down because he'd sucked the strength out of her. He used his teeth, tongue, lips, and saliva to stake his claim on that part of her anatomy. Quivering, she whimpered.

"You taste incredible," he said as he straightened. "Like a woman."

I've never felt more like one.

"I love the way you look stretched out before me. Knowing it's what you want only makes it better, different."

"Different?"

"From how it was with my slave-wife."

"That's the way things were between the two of you?"

"I was her master."

"She was also your wife."

"She didn't want to be. She wanted her freedom, but I couldn't give her anything except the pleasure that came with my ropes; she loved that and worshipped me for it. In the end, death freed her."

"What do you mean you couldn't let her go? You were a warrior. No one could tell you what—"

"The priests did, and our gods."

Much as she wanted to learn more, she couldn't form the words. He'd told her so many things, and now she needed time to absorb them before taking on anything more. Besides, she was in his embrace.

Thinking he'd return his attention to the back of her neck, she concentrated on trying to relax her muscles. As a consequence, she wasn't ready when he slipped his hand between her knees. Mouth dry, she prayed he wouldn't head for her crotch since she'd probably go off like the proverbial skyrocket. Maybe he knew how close she was because, although he ran the back of his hand up and down her inner thighs, he stopped short of her sex. When he shifted hands and repeated the gesture, she wasn't sure which was worse, waiting for the moment of contact or fearing it wouldn't happen.

"Lick me," she whimpered. "You promised."

"Eventually."

The word had weight and substance, heat even. And much as she hated being teased, the anticipation caused her inner juices to heat. Trying to increase his access to her pussy accomplished nothing because her ankles were too tightly bound. She was biting down on a fevered curse when he pressed on her inner thighs and spread her a little. She sensed a shift in his position, a curling down around her body.

Something zinged through her, a hot spark as if she'd touched a live wire. Not until the current backed off did she realize he'd dragged his tongue over her labia. "Oh god, god."

"Feel, Hayley. Feel your body's power."

What power? she wanted to ask when he invaded her again. She was a wet noodle, a butterfly trapped in a spider's web, this man's sexual plaything. Trembling so that she wondered if she was cold, she clenched her jaw to keep from screaming because he'd bent her knees so he could bathe her at his leisure. Having her head lower than her heart was making her lightheaded, but what did it matter; she didn't want to think anyway.

This was her, this tethered and submissive creature with her buttocks sticking up and his fingers spreading them. He was indeed bathing her, his tongue hot and wet and real, working quick and strong, hard even. Nothing was sacred, not her entrance or clit, not the scant space between pussy and ass. If he wanted to lathe her puckered butt, she wouldn't stop him. And if he was content tongue fucking—

What about her spine? Wasn't that what she'd asked for?

Didn't matter. There was only him over her, controlling and claiming her, drinking in her fluids and replacing them with his own. Her head hot and roaring, she struggled to make herself even more accessible. And when he rewarded her efforts by pressing against the base of her spine with the heel of his hand, she screamed.

Climax! He'd hauled her to the top and thrown her into space. A sudden and deep fear that her need had already been spent caused her to try to look back at him, but he ran his lips down the backs of her thighs, stripping her of everything except wanting.

When he took hold of her ankle restraints and bent her knees, lazy anticipation stole through her. She couldn't say she fully trusted him with her body; maybe she'd never reach that place with any man. But he'd demonstrated his wisdom of her needs, and for now that was enough. Massaging her right instep with one hand, he kept her wonderfully off balance by applying equal attention to her left calf. By turns he was gentle and strong, the shifts coming when she least expected them. A long stroke up her calf made her quiver while repeatedly pressing against and releasing the pressure on her instep calmed her. How many times had she likened her responses when she was around him to floating, swimming? It was happening again, a weightlessness caused by his ability to cradle and support her entire body while touching only a small part of it.

She should be doing this to him, sometime. He deserved the same attention eventually. But until she could pull herself together enough to tend to him instead of luxuriating in his gift to her body, she'd lie on her belly and breasts with her useless arms by her sides, trusting.

"Belonging to me isn't all about giving up control, Hayley," he said as he lowered her legs.

"Belonging? I—"

"The owner is also owned, don't ever doubt that."

"You aren't my owner. I . . ." Whatever else she'd been about to say evaporated because he was pressing the heel of his hands along the outsides of her thighs, slowly working his way up to her buttocks. More than swimming or floating, oozing out until nothing except sensation remained. Yes, yes, he deserved the same. Later.

"Right now I am your owner, Hayley. It's the way I believe it has to be so I can move beyond what I was, but it's also right—for both of us."

Before she could begin to make sense of what he was telling her, he flipped her over onto her back. She could only watch and feel while he strapped her wrists together in front and then bent her legs as much as the ankle restraints allowed, so her sex was open and ready and hot for him. And when he lifted her legs into the air and stretched out under them so her feet now rested on his back, she understood; he was staking his claim on *his* woman's pussy.

His woman.

With that, no fight or will remained in her, only this aching hunger; she belonged to him. She might never understand why he needed it to be like that. As his possession, her role was to please and be pleased, to dance when he told her to and come when he brought her to that place.

He was doing that now.

Pulling herself back to this moment's reality took too much time, and by then, his tongue was on her clitoris. Only his grip on her hips kept her on the ground. Although maybe she should have known better, known her place as *his*, she grabbed fistfuls of his hair and held on. Rode the currents his damp, warm tongue created. Her upper body arched without her mind having issued the command, and she could no more still her cunt's twitching than she could stop breathing.

Again, again, and yet again he brought her to the summit. Each time, believing she'd fly over the edge, she embraced that great and wonderful space, but he gave her no rhythm to cling to, no cadence or tempo, no promise beyond one second at a time, so while he teased and licked and even cupped his lips around her hot nub, she waited.

"Please, please, please," the savage he'd turned her into chanted. "Let me, let me, let me."

No, he replied by abandoning her core. *No*, he insisted by giving her nothing more than his moist expelled breath.

"Please, please, please." Grinding her hips into the ground, she all but tore his hair out. "You're killing me, Mazati, killing me."

"Call me master."

The woman she'd once been would have hurled the title and a string of oaths back at him, but that creature had disappeared, maybe died.

"What do you want, slave?" His breath seemed to catch on her soaked labia. "Say it. Beg it."

"Let me climax, please, master," she said with her eyes on

the stars, her fingers now caressing her master's scalp, and her thighs against his shoulders. "Help me, bring me—"

"Is this mine?" He pressed damp lips against her pussy. "Given freely."

Free? He'd tied her up, turned her onto her back, forced himself on—"Yes. Yes!"

"Why?"

"No questions, damn it! I can't think."

"Yes, you can." Again he sealed his lips to her center, this time drinking of her offering. "Go deep, slave, deep to where the truth lives. Why are you willing to surrender yourself to me?"

Can't think, can't think. Then don't try, she ordered herself. Feel, and let what you find speak for you. "Because, damn it, because I want it so bad."

He didn't rush his response, instead collecting her juices and then spreading them over her perineum as if he had every right to do something so intimate—which he did.

"Beg for it."

Sudden and unexpected anger froze her muscles. An instant later, he pressed his nose against her mons and the emotion flowed out of her to be replaced by helpless need. "Please, master, take pity on this slave. I want only one thing of you, to be— be allowed to come."

"You're ready for me to grant your request?"

"Yes, if it pleases you, master."

"What about later?" He pressed his chin against her mons. "When you have nothing left to feel or give, will you still understand that everything you are flows into me?"

Despite everything he'd done and was capable of doing to her, she was still a modern woman, and the words spoke of a slavery of the soul as well as body. And so she fought her body and denied the impact of his mouth, tongue, and teeth on her sex. The battle tore at her, forcing out small helpless whimpers.

Her legs and feet were still off the ground and his hands kept her from writing about and strength had fled her fingers so she could no longer grip his hair. Everything she believed about his ability to make her float was being spelled out in liquid reality as he ran his tongue deep into her opening. Her whimpers became louder and more frequent, and again she climaxed, a small sharp shudder that came and died so quick she wasn't sure.

"Enough, please, master, enough. I can't take—"

"Yes, you can."

"No, no."

"Listen to me." Every word flowed over her cunt. "We've come too far on this journey to abandon it now. I don't dare. And I can't do it without you."

She didn't want him to be alone. Reminded by memories of those haunting images of him surrounded by death, she knew she'd do whatever she had to to keep him from returning to the half life that had followed those deaths. "Why me?"

"You're my only hope."

Before she could decide whether she dared ask what he was talking about, he slid out from under her. His hands remained on her, and she wasn't surprised when he once again turned her onto her belly. He elevated her buttocks by tucking her legs under her and left her wrist restraints alone but loosened the one around her upper arms enough that she was able to lift herself onto her elbows. Then she waited with her eyes downcast and her hair obscuring her vision.

"Beautiful," he whispered as he stroked her buttocks. "Precious." He drew a series of curves over her flanks with his fingernails and chuckled when she bleated like a lost lamb.

"I belong to you." Her whisper was no stronger than his. "Take my gift, master, please."

His only response was to rest his hands over her tailbone, fingertips twitching slightly. The faint, hot sensation slid through her, and she lifted her head and whimpered. Maybe she called him master again; maybe she only thought it. But the word imprinted itself on her mind and in her heart. He needed her and she was his.

There. Leaning closer, his cock seeking entrance. Opening herself as much as she could, she thanked him with tears when he spread her buttocks before doing the same to her hot and starving cave. Fluid dripped from her, some of it running down her inner thighs, some landing on the grass. Ready, ready for her master, her owner, her reason.

"Now," he told her with his tip against her clit. "Now."

Her body knew to shift slightly, to soften even more, to open wider. And his cock knew where home waited, knew to dive deep and true.

There. Him. In her. "Thank you," she muttered, drooling. "Thank you, master."

"My beautiful slave, my beautiful and incredible slave. My salvation."

She wanted to be his woman, not this other thing she couldn't comprehend at the moment, but she didn't care about anything except the shaft buried in and filling her. The union between them defined not just her but their entire relationship. She hung on to him with all the strength her cunt possessed, only belatedly realizing she was hampering his ability to move. Relaxing with an effort, she turned inward and became her pussy and what claimed it. If her nerves were trying to speak, she couldn't hear them. Neither could she concentrate on the music playing deep within her until the heated drumbeat slid along her inner walls to blend with his rough, urgent thrusts.

He'd sacrificed to bring her pleasure and subservience, denied himself while giving her everything. And now he was paying for his self-control; they both were.

Why?

How could she be his only chance, and for what?

Digging her elbows into the ground, she managed to withstand his assault, but each attack threatened to flatten her. It didn't matter! If she fell, he'd ride with her until grass and soil supported them. They'd continue to fuck animal to animal, grunting, growling, one and maybe both of them sobbing.

It was happening again, that lifting up and out that signaled release. Screaming into and with her climax, she willed herself to explode. And take him with her.

"Thank you, thank you," the beast she'd become whimpered. "Thank you, master."

"No, thank you."

17

"You did what?"

"You heard me. I had sex with him again. You've heard of that, I trust."

Head cocked to the side, Saree stared at Hayley, or more precisely, at the abrasion on her right cheek. "Hmm. And how did you get that? Forget to put fabric softener in the rinse cycle?"

Wondering but not really caring if she was blushing, Hayley ran her hand over her cheek. Bad idea; it stung. "You want me to say it? We weren't in bed."

"No shit." Saree's what-the-hell expression sobered. "We've been over this relationship you and Mazati have and I don't want to rehash old territory. I'm also the last person in the world to lecture anyone about acceptable and unacceptable behavior, but sis, the man scares me." Frowning, she hugged Hayley.

"I'm learning a great deal about him that goes beyond sex. Things are pretty intense." The moment she'd said the words, she regretted the understatement.

"No shit. And no, I'm not talking about such things as fucking on the front porch or the hood of your car or in the woods or wherever the two of you got it on. It's the man himself."

Fighting the urge to drop her gaze, Hayley shrugged. "So you've said."

"Are you going to argue the point?"

Hayley had been in her workshop taking pictures of her latest creations when Saree unexpectedly showed up. Although it was after 9 P.M., Hayley, accustomed to her sister's work schedule, hadn't been surprised. Sometimes after a particularly successful bondage session, Saree was too wired to sleep for hours. This time she'd brought a bottle of wine, which the two of them were going through at a rapid pace.

"I'm not going to argue anything with you right now." Hayley held up her nearly empty glass as evidence that she was less than clear headed.

"Point taken." Saree downed the last of her drink and reached for the bottle. "I thought you weren't going to see him anymore, after getting rid of that damn collar thing."

"Guess I was wrong."

"You guess? How'd it happen? He show up like I did and you opened the door?"

How had it gone? If her less than reliable memory was serving her at all, Mazati had simply appeared.

"I know what it was." Laughing, Saree punched her shoulder. "I bring wine. He brings a ready-to-go cock. Hell, who can ignore either of those gifts." Again she turned serious. "Look, I'm about as grounded as it can get. None of that otherworldly, paranormal crap Aunt Reggie kept trying to pour down our throats for me. And I always thought you felt the same way."

Sensing where things were going, Hayley could only nod.

"But the stud in question defies laws of logic. You're not going to try to deny that, are you?"

"No."

Leaning against the work table, Saree sipped. "You haven't told me everything that's gone on between the two of you; I understand and respect that. But what I'd like to know is if any of it makes sense."

"Sense?"

"Don't make me try to explain myself. My head's not on squarely enough for that. You know, bump-in-the-middle-of-the-night stuff, walking through walls, disappearing in a puff of smoke?"

Much as she wanted to laugh and make light of the question, Hayley couldn't. "No walking through walls, but sis, I've been to an Aztec pyramid with him." *Seen what happens right before a human sacrifice.*

Eyes wide, Saree turned her full attention on her. "Shit. You mean it, don't you."

"Yeah. Look, I'm not in shape to tell you more than that. I wasn't going to say anything, but I can't keep this to myself." She closed her eyes but opened them again when her head started spinning. "I don't know where he lives, or when."

"Huh?"

"Present, past, sliding between them. Look, I don't blame you if you don't believe me, but I'm starting to believe he exists in a kind of continuum that started when the Aztec nation was at its height."

"Oh shit. For real?"

"For real. Not that I'm sure what's real anymore."

"Are you all right?"

"I don't know. I feel more alive than I've ever been, scared and fascinated, hurting for him because he's all alone."

"Alone?"

"The last of his kind. The only Aztec still alive."

"Shit, shit."

Saree's tone and expression coupled with the shock of having actually said what she just had was too much for Hayley.

Waving off Saree's next question, she took a too-healthy swig of wine and deliberately turned her attention to the jewelry display. One piece stood out from the others, and she ran suddenly cold fingers over it. "Grounding," she muttered. "What I need to do right now is to stay grounded. You said that collar I wore was ugly, but it was the inspiration for this."

Saree used her well-toned hip to shove Hayley aside so she had a clear view. "Shit."

"What?"

"This." Demonstrating no regard for the effort Hayley had gone to in arranging the chain-mail and opal necklace in its box, she picked it up. "Holy crap, it's incredible."

Saree had always admired her work but *holy crap* signified top-of-the-heap admiration. "I rather like it myself," Hayley said.

"Like?" Looking wistful, Saree put it on and turned toward Hayley. "Ah, feels as if it was made for my neck, and the way that single opal dangles down nearly to my boobs—talk about erotic. It has substance, an I-dare-you-to-ignore-me substance, and yet it's so light." She marched not quite steadily over to a wall mirror. "Come over here. You gotta see."

"I already did, and it looks great on your long, tanned neck." Rocked by a flash of inspiration, Hayley grabbed her digital camera. "Let me photograph it on you, please. It shows off much better on you than just sitting there in the box."

By the time Hayley joined her sister, Saree had pulled down her neckline to expose her flawless flesh, but instead of starting a debate about where she should stand for the best lighting, she pasted on a smile Hayley knew all too well. Her sister's wheels were turning. "Let me wear this during a shoot," she said.

"I thought the piece I sent you last week—"

"It's fine but doesn't have this one's bling. We've got to get people buzzing about Night Fire, right?" Caressing both the necklace and the hollow of her throat, Saree turned back toward the mirror. "If this doesn't do it, nothing will. Membership at the site is growing by thousands each month."

"That's good."

"For both of us. Look, there's that narrative at the beginning that goes with each video. I'll make sure everyone knows where they can buy your stuff. Of course, that means you need to get cracking on finishing your Web site."

"Are you sure the owners will let you—"

"What's the matter? You having second thoughts about my offer? You gonna wait until some Paris model wears it on a runway?"

"Like that's ever going to happen."

Demonstrating that her career had caused a fundamental shift in Saree's idea of modesty, she whipped off her shirt, exposing nothing but skin from the waist up. "The members will notice." Smiling, Saree stroked the single hanging opal.

"They're looking at your boobs, not your jewelry."

"Quit selling yourself short. Trust me, this'll knock their socks off."

Saree was right, damn it, 100 percent right. The marriage between absolutely flawless skin and the best work she'd produced so far was incredible. And if a rigger snapped clips onto Saree's nipples or wrapped them in rope, that would draw even more attention to that part of her anatomy. "Can't argue with that."

"Of course you can't. Look out, sis, I'm gonna put Night Fire on the map. This"—she indicated the necklace—"demonstrates a new boldness in your work. You're opening up, pulling out all the stops. *He* has something to do with it, doesn't he?"

"He's keeping me supplied with opals, you know that."

"I'm talking about a hell of a lot more than that." Leaning close, Saree hit Hayley with an intense gaze. "So you got it on with him just before you came up with this, didn't you?"

"Ye-ah."

"You went off like a Roman candle, didn't you?"

"What are you getting at?"

"How many times did you climax?"

"I wasn't counting."

"But more than once, right? You're the one who always maintained that once a session was all you were good for or interested in."

"So?"

"So a hell of a lot has changed since he slid into your life. Because I love and am worried about you, I'm on a mission to get to the bottom of it. I'm guessing you're asking yourself if he's responsible for the jump in creativity I'm seeing in your work. Maybe you're thinking you couldn't do it without him."

Maybe. Even more important, there's something he believes he can't do without me.

"Well, if that's where your thinking has gone, you're wrong. This is where the creativity comes from." She tapped Hayley's forehead and then over her heart. "You let Cal know that you weren't his damn puppet. Do the same with Mazati, while you can still think for yourself. Otherwise . . ."

"Otherwise what?"

"I don't know. Maybe I'll have to declare you incompetent, legally insane, something. Become your guardian, whatever it takes to keep you sane."

The opals hadn't been on her work space when she'd left for work, which meant Mazati had come in while she was gone. Sitting down and leaning back, she imagined him wandering around the converted garage. She hoped he'd looked through her sketchbook filled with preliminary and otherwise drawings of what she wanted to create, but even more she hoped he'd approved. He must have, or he wouldn't have left so many of the fires for her to work with.

Silently thanking him, she started sorting through the nearly one hundred stones. What he'd been supplying her with couldn't be duplicated in quality, let alone exceeded, but he'd more than outdone himself this time. Not only were they so large that if she wanted, she could design a complete necklace or bracelet around a single opal, but she'd never seen such depth of color.

They were all blacks, and yet ranged from some that were so dark they made her think of a panther's coat, to a deep gray. She could create an elaborate piece using a single predominant shade or mix them for variety and hopefully excitement.

Mind churning with possibilities, she played with different groupings. As she did, she had the sense that she was hovering above her working fingers watching, appraising, approving. Mazati had said something about her talented fingers. They were long and slender, deceptively strong, and although she kept her nails short, that didn't detract from the overall appearance. Despite the work she subjected them to, both while pounding a keyboard and when creating jewelry, they gave no hint of wearing out. If the gods were with her, the rest of her body would surrender to Father Time long before her hands stopped being the most valuable part of her body.

Her hands, not her sex.

Brought short by the thought, she laced her fingers together. Mazati had done such an incredibly thorough job of focusing her concentration on what lay between her legs that she'd taken the basic tools of her trade for granted. Fortunately, like the expensive tools her father had taught her how to use when she was a girl, they thrived under constant use.

Smiling at the memory of leaning against her father while he demonstrated what each item was used for, she placed three opals in the palm of her right hand. Her parents might be dead, but they'd left their legacy for her to tap into. Her father had been a woodworker in his spare time, her mother the possessor of the neighborhood's greenest thumb. From her father she'd learned to appreciate craftsmanship; from her mother she'd embraced nature's beauty.

And now, from Mazati, she was learning things she'd never before comprehended. What had he said, that she had a mission in life? Closing her eyes, she slipped back in time and experience until she found the junglelike terrain he'd introduced her to. Feeling as if she was floating, she skimmed over a narrow and twisting path until she reached a mountainous area. Intrigued because up to now everything she'd experienced through him had been on ground level, she began climbing. At length she reached several structures against the side of a hill. To her amazement, she realized they'd been constructed from the living rock itself. Two of the seven were fronted with masonry, giving everything a strong masculine feel. Slowing, she listened intently but caught no sound indicating anyone was around. It was impossible to determine how long ago this hillside community had been built.

Catching sight of what appeared to be a central gathering area, she approached it. She had no difficulty imaging warriors meeting here to discuss whatever it was warriors discussed, maybe how to go about attacking one of the Indian tribes that had been living in Mexico when the Aztecs arrived.

Did Aztec men talk about other things, maybe plan ceremonies? She vaguely recalled that several musical instruments such as flutes and drums had been found among the ruins. What an incredible experience it would be to sit here while ceremonies and songs lost to time and deliberate destruction came back to life!

Filled with a sudden and deep need to discover at least a tiny part of the Aztec heritage on her own, she started wandering around, her attention fixed on the ground. Paths ran from one structure to the other, obviously made by countless feet over countless years. Although she had no doubt she was alone, she sensed something, the ghosts or spirits of those who'd once lived here.

What Cortés and his followers had done had been monstrous! Not only had they murdered countless Aztec men, women, and children, they'd also burned their homes and smashed artifacts. Yes, modern archaeologists had managed to uncover and decipher pieces of the past, but massive chunks of a complex and rich culture had been obliterated.

She was brushing away tears when it all fell together. A complex and rich culture resided in Mazati, the last of his kind, but he couldn't share his knowledge with a disbelieving modern world without someone from the present introducing the past to people of today. He or maybe the gods and opals had chosen her to help him, to somehow reconstruct the past.

Overwhelmed, she tried to shake off the thought. She was only one woman, a beleaguered cog in a large company, a jeweler with a dream.

Yes, she acknowledged, she had a dream, a compulsion, and a goal, just as Mazati did.

The sense that she was in over her head faded away to be replaced by renewed appreciation for where she was standing. She'd take everything Mazati gave her, every bit of insight and knowledge. And when she'd gathered everything she could, she'd decide what to do with it and how to begin sharing what she'd learned with others.

When she dropped to her knees and picked up what she'd first thought was nothing more than an interestingly shaped rock, she knew, absolutely knew, that Mazati was responsible. Far from a simple stone, she was holding an impressive replica of a conch that had been carved from a rock.

"Tell me about it," she whispered to Mazati. "Please."

Life comes from the sea.

"This symbolizes life?" she asked, her voice deep with awe.

Life, creation, and fecundity.

Shaking, she cradled the conch in her palm. Then she looked at the ground again, discovering that a trio of tiny fish figures made from what appeared to be mother-of-pearl lay where a minute ago nothing had been. She picked them up and wasn't surprised to find them warm.

"What about these?"

They were created to honor Tlaloc.

"Tlaloc?" she gasped, struggling to control her revulsion. "The Aztec made sacrifices to the God of Rain."

He was more than that. He also held dominion over the world's seas, lakes, and rivers, and he was responsible for the clouds that nourished farmers' land with rain.

"Tlaloc was all powerful?"

And much more complex than the people of your today know.

Acknowledging that Mazati and only Mazati knew Tlaloc's complete story, she rubbed the small fish against her shirt to clean them. Now the delicate mother-of-pearl coloring came through to give the fish figures a richness they hadn't had before.

If she put her own creativity to her new finds in the form of jewelry, maybe by incorporating opals into the pieces, and if she included text with the finished product that explained the link between the modern and ancient Aztec—

"This is why you made contact with me, isn't it. Because you want and need me to keep your heritage alive."

Not keep: restore, honor.

"But what if I can't do it? What if I fail?"

No answer.

"What if I don't want to be what you're determined to turn me into? I have a life, Mazati, dreams of my own."

A nude woman was on her knees, her arms stretched behind her and fastened to a four-foot-high wooden stake. Two shorter stakes on either side of it held her feet in place. The collar and rope securing her via yet another short stake forced her to stretch out her neck. Naked and glistening, she studied the approaching man.

At first Hayley, watching from an unlit area to the woman's right, had thought the man was Mazati, but now his slender build told her it was a stranger. In contrast to the woman, he was dressed in colorful knee-length loose shorts and an equally bright orange shirt. In addition he had on an elaborate feathered headdress that forced him to walk stiffly.

Frightened for the woman, Hayley turned her attention back to her, but instead of the helpless fear she expected to see, the woman's eyes were alive with adoration. She straightened as best she could so the regal-looking man could see more of her breasts.

"You wait for me, do you, my slave?" the man demanded, his tone cool and distant.

"They made me ready for you. I pray you are pleased."

"I will see." Keeping his head immobile, he paced around her, turning so Hayley could see the thin switch in his right hand. Wincing, Hayley covered her mouth when he ran the switch over the woman's back, but the helpless creature's only reaction was to lower her head.

No doubt about it, the line of the woman's body was pure artistry. Young, slim, with dark skin and long, ebony hair, she would be considered a prize to any man who valued a female slave.

"I claim you," the man said.

"Yes, master."

"And do you understand that the priest who owned you before you were given to me has no right to you, that you exist to serve only me?"

"Yes, master."

Still circling the now-quivering form, the man continued to

run his switch over his possession's flawless flesh. "Your former owner has not branded you."

"He, ah, he said he intended to sell me as soon as he could arrange it and wanted to keep my value high."

"Of course. And before he did that, he repeatedly took you, didn't he?"

"Y-es, master. I, ah, I had no choice."

Smiling faintly, the man lifted his prisoner's head by pulling on her hair. "And why was that, slave?"

Amazingly enough, even though the woman's eyes were dark, Hayley could read her every emotion. She was afraid of her new master; that was obvious. But she also eagerly anticipated this time with him. "He kept me tied."

"As I ordered done with you now?" He tugged on one wrist restraint, forcing her to lean to that side.

"Not like this. He preferred me on my back with my legs in the air. Sometimes in the time I was with him, not often, he let me kneel at his feet with his organ in my mouth while he ate or conducted his priestly activities."

"I know." The man continued to keep her off balance. "That's where I first saw you. So you learned to service his organ well, did you?"

"I pray my talents will please you, master."

"I imagine you do, because otherwise you will be punished."

Working efficiently despite the headdress, he snapped the switch against the woman's buttocks. Because he'd released her hair, she was able to move about a little more, but of course her restraints prevented her from escaping the repeatedly falling instrument of torture and dominance.

"Master, please, master, please."

"Silence, slave! You know this is necessary." Slap, slap, slap. "You must learn your place."

"I do, master!" She nearly fell trying to watch the switch

and get away from it at the same time. "My place—my place is to do everything you command."

"And it's what you want, isn't it?"

Instead of giving Hayley what she needed to hear, the woman dropped her head and let her wrenched-backward arms take the bulk of her weight. She continued to twitch whenever a blow landed, but was no longer trying to get free. And because she'd somehow been given access to the woman's thoughts, Hayley understood that deep down this is what the naked and helpless slave wanted. For reasons Hayley wondered if she'd ever understand, the sweating creature needed this from her master; she was fulfilled.

What was it she'd said, that her place was to do everything her master commanded her to? Oh shit, did Mazati expect the same from her? No! No way!

"I'm not your slave-wife, Mazati! You didn't buy or capture me. Enough. Get it? Enough of this!"

18

"Mazati, where are you?" Hayley demanded. She was sitting up in bed with the too-vivid dream still playing out in her mind. "You're responsible for what I just saw, I know you are."

A firm believer in getting sleep right, she kept her bedroom as dark as possible, but although no moonlight penetrated her curtains, she sensed she was no longer alone.

"Why?" she demanded of the darkness. "Why did you show that to me?"

Because it's part of what I once was, my world.

"Don't do this to me! I need to talk to you, see you, not have this damnable voice in my head. If you're not going to reveal yourself, I'm going back to sleep."

I'm here.

"*Here* is subject to interpretation." Fueled by her anger, she sat up, only to realize she was naked. Had she forgotten her nightgown or was he responsible? "I not only understood what they said to each other, I knew what she was thinking. That was deliberate on your part; I know it was! She loved pain. It turned her on."

"Would you rather not know that about her?"

Ah, a real voice now. And although she hadn't pulled back the curtains or turned on a light, she saw the familiar form standing near her bed. He was naked, of course, honest and pure in his nudity. "Don't expect me to be able to answer that, all right? You've thrown so much at me, expected me to accept so many things. I'm on overload, don't you understand that?" Marginally calmer than she'd been when she'd begun her rant, she took a deep breath. "Is that how you treated your slave-wife?"

"I was a warrior. Warriors who had proven themselves in battle were rewarded with slaves who loved their roles."

If only Saree was here. Surely her grounded-in-reality sister could make sense of everything that came out of Mazati's mouth. Maybe. "Did you beat her?"

"Sometimes, if it was what we both wanted."

"That's sick!" Or was it? Didn't her sister embrace bondage and erotic pain and didn't Hayley sometimes get off on that fantasy herself? But that's what it was for her and Saree: fantasy.

Settling himself on the side of the bed, he stretched out an arm to support himself. His fingers, although several inches from her knees, seemed to be touching her. "It's time for you to understand more of why I do what I do around you."

Shit, oh shit! But if she said no, it might all end between them. "All right."

The room shifted, tilted a little, spun. Disoriented, she reached for Mazati, but when he clutched her to his heat, she didn't know whether to be grateful or afraid. Just the same, she clung to him until the spinning stopped and the curtain lifted.

Of course, they were back at the pyramid, or more precisely, within sight of it. Looking around, she spotted the raised platform she'd been standing on when he'd purchased her—or she'd dreamed or imagined or fantasized he'd paid for her. There was no sale going on, but apparently one was scheduled for the not-too-distant future, as witnessed by a line of tied prisoners being led to it. There seemed to be an equal number of men and women, and some of the dirty, disheveled men looked as if they'd been in a battle and lost. In contrast, the women were in much better condition, and instead of looking as if they feared being killed, they looked around, and some were talking quietly. Unfortunately, she couldn't understand what they were saying.

"They are Pzal, a people already here when the Aztec arrived. These were captured in a raid and will make serviceable slaves."

"Serviceable? Like mules pulling plows?"

"My people were conquerors. They did what they chose with those they'd vanquished. Your archaeologists believe that most of our slaves became so because they were too poor to pay their debts. They sold their services to those willing to settle the debts. Others had been convicted of crimes and this was how they were punished."

"But that's not the whole story, is it?"

"No. Look. These creatures are hostages, prisoners of war."

"That doesn't bother you, does it."

Although she needed him to tell her she was wrong, he didn't. Neither did his eyes hint at revulsion, but then why should they? Conquerors and the conquered had once defined his life; it was all he'd known.

Stunned by an awful thought, she dug her nails into his forearm. "Will they be sacrificed, their hearts cut out?"

"To appease the gods, yes, some."

No wonder the men looked so defeated. "And the women?" She forced the question. "They'll become sex slaves, won't they?"

"Some, yes. That's some of what your archaeologists and historians didn't know about us. Some females were taught to embrace their sexual captivity and feed off it. They did so because it was better than the alternative."

Instead of arguing with Mazati about the primitive and savage practice, she concentrated on the women. The ones past late teens or early twenties looked as if their existence had been defined by hard work. There were scars and bent backs; teeth in need of repair; dry, shallow skin; and thinning hair. No wonder, since for most of the natives, life back then must have been a backbreaking existence, with disease, war, and accidents taking a terrible toil. Next to their primitive lifestyle, the magnificence of an Aztec city must have looked like a gift from the gods, whoever their particular gods were. Even if they spent their lives as slaves, at least their bellies were full and they had roofs over their heads. And they were considered desirable.

"What you just showed me of that tied woman and the naked man, is that what it meant to be an Aztec sex slave?"

"Unless he chose to also make her his wife."

"Oh. Oh. Mazati, I've been avoiding something for way too long, doing everything I can to avoid asking the most important question. You were alive before Cortés and his army showed up, weren't you?"

"I was a seasoned warrior the day the Spanish conquistador arrived with six hundred soldiers and sixteen horses. I watched as Cortés imprisoned my ruler, Montezuma. Two years later, I fought alongside my brother warriors as Cortés's men and countless Indian warriors destroyed Tenochtitlan, city of my birth. I should have died when the others did, but I didn't."

"Instead, you're still alive in the twenty-first century."

"Yes." He didn't look at her.

"How is that possible?"

"Eternal life was both my reward and my punishment."

A sudden stab of pain tearing into her brain forced her to shut her eyes. Punishment? Not this incredible man! "I don't understand."

"I don't know if you can."

"Give me a chance, please."

"A chance." He sighed. "Yes. Huitzilopochtli cried for and blessed me when he saw me burying my brothers, but I didn't want what he gave me, eternal life, alone. I prayed to Coyolxauhqui to release me from my hell. She allowed me to remain in a half life for many years, but finally I begged to be released from that as well. Coyolxauhqui granted my request but only after I'd promised to share what it was to be Aztec with the modern world. Like you, I will grow old and die but only once I've fulfilled my promise."

"By using me."

"The opals—"

"To hell with opals! What about me, Mazati? What if I don't want to be your ticket out of this hell you're living in?"

Despite her throbbing head, she sensed equal parts acceptance and anger in him. Cupping her face in his hands, he lifted her head. "You are a gift. I'll do whatever I must to keep you with me."

"Oh Mazati, you can't do that anymore than I could keep you with me. Neither of us are slaves, possessions. If I want to walk away, you can't stop me."

"Yes, I can."

"No!" she snapped and broke free. "Damn it, damn it! I get crazy every time I'm around you; I can't think!" She started to turn her back on him, only then noticing that the image of the newly arrived prisoners was fading, and she could no longer see the pyramid top. Empowered, she spun around and faced his strong, nude body. Forcefully dismissing the power and promise in his cock, she slapped him. "I'm sick of this! How dare you think you can do whatever you want to with me."

Giving no indication that the blow to his cheek so much as smarted, he reached out as if to stroke her left breast. Damn him for thinking a touch would bring her to her senses, and to her knees. Backpedaling so she wouldn't be tempted to, again, turn herself over to him, she indicated between her legs. "This is *mine*, got it, Mazati? I don't care how Aztec men treated their women, and I care even less how they handled their slaves. I'm neither of those things."

Shadow was overtaking him, closing down around him as if sheltering him from her outburst. If darkness stole him from her and she never saw him again, could she survive? But was sinking farther into the spell of a man from another time and culture, a man who did things that had never been done to her body, any better? A man who should be dead?

She'd found the courage to leave Cal. Once she had, she'd called on even more courage and determination to make good on her vow to get out of the debt Cal had imposed on her. If necessary, she'd do the same with Mazati.

If necessary.

Even if he was forced back into his lonely solitude and endless life.

"Take me back to my bedroom," she insisted. "But don't come with me."

"You'll be alone."

"I won't be the only one."

Floating was easy, a weightless, fog-surrounded drifting that seduced with promises of oblivion, even death. But experience had taught Mazati that the act of moving from past to present and back again always brought pain.

Now, back in the land and time of his birth, he shook off the remnants of that fog and forced himself to face his latest truth. Every time he returned to the only place he'd once believed his heart would beat, he discovered that he'd lost yet a little more. The buildings and pyramid were still there, but with their edges blurred. Sounds were less distinct, colors muted, the distance between him and his fellow Aztec greater. Everything was fading; eventually nothing except the land and forgotten graves would remain.

When he'd first faced what was happening, he'd railed against the cruel march of time. Whatever it took, he'd vowed to the gods, he'd keep his world alive. But he'd been given so few tools, only lessons and beliefs from a time that now existed only in his heart and mind. Yes, the god-given opals had allowed him to find a woman who shared his love for the stones, but it wasn't enough.

Not enough, he repeated. His lessons and beliefs, along with the memories of his relationship with his slave-wife, hadn't been enough to bond Hayley to him. Yes, the fucking had been good; they'd both loved it, but she'd needed more, and he didn't know how to give her those things, didn't fully comprehend the missing pieces.

Settling himself on his knees beside his slave-wife's grave, he shut his eyes. He was so weary, a warrior with no more battles left inside him. Hayley had said it so well. Fucking, the master-slave fucking he'd tried to give her, wasn't enough, wasn't what she needed.

"Take back your life," he whispered to the image he carried of her. "Your life, not the one I tried to force on you."

Although he opened his eyes, he didn't try to focus on his surroundings. How long before nothing remained, how long until only he existed, a cool mist faintly heated by memories?

He'd failed not just himself but his gods. And he was too tired and resigned to care any more.

"Embrace tomorrow, Hayley. And if a part of me remains with you, I pray it will help feed your creativity."

To her relief and regret, Mazati had granted her request. Unfortunately, her erotic dreams over the next two weeks had made sleep all but impossible, and she'd worn out all the batteries in the house and broken two vibrators.

When she wasn't squirming under the sheets, she either suffered through her day job or risked wearing out her eyes and fingers making enough jewelry to replace the Night Fire stock that was all but flying off the shelves at Porters and from her Web site. As the owner/buyer had said when he told her about Night Fire's popularity, "Sometimes lightning strikes. Sometimes the stars are all in a line. Whatever it is, Night Fire is becoming *the* jewelry for this city's in crowd. Send me everything you have; we'll sell it."

As excited as she was by the speed of her success, she couldn't devote all her free time to Night Fire after all, because every time she sat down to sketch or work, images of the conch and tiny fish she'd found or Mazati had given her intruded.

Night before last, she'd given up trying to pretend they weren't calling to her. It might have been after midnight when she started shaping a thumb-sized piece of silver to duplicate the mother-of-pearl fish. She'd used opals for the eyes and black wire filaments to outline fins, scales, and the tail.

Last night had been devoted to the conch. The end result was a broach that just fit into the palm of her hand. After careful study, she'd used several small opals to highlight the long eye stalks. A single large opal enhanced the pointed, sickle-shaped foot. Black wire spelled out *life, creation,* and *fecundity* while the word *Aztec* ran along the highest point in flowing, black cursive. On the underside, she'd fixed a note explaining the importance the Aztec accorded anything that came from the sea. What frustrated her was not knowing any more than she did, but the one man who could tell her the full story wasn't here.

Studying the original items along with what she'd created, she had absolutely no doubt that she'd just started on a new journey. These pieces weren't the same as the rest of her Night Fire collection, and as such, they deserved their own unique identification. No matter how obscure the references she had to consult, she'd learn everything she could about Aztec art and beliefs and incorporate the jewelry that evolved out of that self-education into—into what?

Aztec Fire.

At 6 A.M. on Tuesday morning, wired from a dream/fantasy that had tangled her nightgown and soaked her sheets, Hayley turned on her computer for the first time in she didn't know how long. Among a virtual mountain of junk e-mail, she found no less than three from her sister. Two were forwarded jokes. The other said that the bondage session with her using the Night Fire necklace had been shot three days ago. Both the video and stills were so hot yesterday that the Webmaster had posted a teaser on the home page. *Take a look*, Saree had written. *It's going to pop your cherry, or it would if you still had one.*

"You're right," Hayley muttered as she watched the clip showing Saree wrapped in red rope from the breasts down. In contrast to the webbing, the collar-inspired necklace truly caressed her sister's flawless throat. And yet something more than the artistry of the scene held her attention and something had its roots in the dream/fantasy that had ruined her sleep. Closing her aching eyes, she tried to concentrate. Before long an image of her standing spread-eagled at the entrance to one of the mountainside buildings that made her cunt ache forced her to straighten. Ignoring the time, she dialed her sister's number.

"Lousy timing," Saree muttered. "Suffice to say, I'm not alone."

"Oops. Look, I'll call back later."

"Never mind. We were done. Besides, I was going to call you in a couple of hours. You will never, ever, in a million years, guess who got ahold of me via my place of employment. You did get my e-mail, didn't you?"

"What? Yes." Even with her eyes wide open, Hayley couldn't shake the images left behind from her last *dream.*

"Well, it's amazing who subscribes to our site. Go on, guess."

"The president?"

"Hmm. Wouldn't that be a hoot. Nah, but Jas Farr does."

"The actress?"

"Actress, globe-trotting celebrity, model, multimillionaire all rolled into one and probably a bunch of other accomplishments I can't think of at the moment and in the satiated state I'm in. She called yesterday afternoon. And in case you think it might be a hoax, there was no doubting that voice. She even gave me her agent's number, which is where she was, for verification."

"Why'd she call?"

"You don't sound particularly interested. Are you sure you want to hear this?"

"Of course. I'm just—I had a pretty vivid dream, that's all."

"Let me guess. Mazati was in it, right? Never mind answering; I already know. Oops, what?" A muffled conversation ensued. "Ah, sis, I guess my friend here isn't as used up as I thought he was. To cut to the chase, Jas Farr was interested in one thing."

"What? Your rigger's cock size?"

"Wrong. What she wanted was *your* phone number, or more specifically, the name of the amazing talent responsible for the necklace I was wearing. She couldn't say enough about how much she loved it, and she knew her friends in the biz were going to feel the same way. She's going to call you; I know she is."

"Jas? Call me?"

"Bingo. This is the break we've been after, sis. Night Fire is going to be big; big!"

Hayley's mind swirled, a dizzying collage of colors and images, but what she saw wasn't dollar signs and the words Night

Fire being praised during the Academy Awards. Instead, she saw a nearly deserted mountainous collection of ancient structures, and in the middle of it, herself, watching Mazati approach.

"Hey," Saree broke in. "Where'd you go?"

"I'm here."

"No, you aren't. It's him, isn't it. Tell me."

"You're busy."

"He can wait, can't you, loverboy? Oops, no I guess he can't. One thing before I go—or come. Any chance I can use your fantasies for inspiration at work?"

Hmm. Maybe. The words started tumbling out of her almost without her being aware of them, and she told Saree that she'd been standing on her toes—naked, naturally—with her arms tied behind her at the elbows and wrists. Ropes wound around her breasts and behind her back to keep the ropes from sliding off her artificially rounded mounds. A single strand at the top of each breast had been fastened to something overhead and enough pressure applied that she had to remain on her toes to keep as much strain as possible off her breasts. Mazati was there, sheltered by shadow as he studied what had to have been his handiwork, although she couldn't remember being wrapped into the crazy position. She'd woken up as he walked toward her.

"Holy shit," Saree spluttered. "Damn, I can see it now, me tied and tethered with all this rope on my upper body but free from the boobs down, going nowhere. Sis, how do you feel about it?"

"It was a dream."

"Was it? You've been pretty close mouthed for days and too busy for us to get together. It's not just your work schedule, is it? Some serious shit's going on between you and Mazati."

"I haven't seen him for two weeks."

"You haven't?" Saree said after a brief silence. "Except when he plows his way into your mind and under your skin and between your legs, you mean."

"Go entertain your guest," Hayley insisted, determined not to touch her sister's last statement. "We'll talk later."

"You're damn right we will. After all, when it gets right down to it, you're the most important thing in my life."

"What about studly?"

"That's all he is, a stud who happens to be taking a leak as we speak."

"Do you think he might become more?"

"Not him, and not anyone else I've met since I got into this line of work. Guess I can't find anyone interested in more than my neck down."

"Saree, I'm sorry."

"Don't be. This isn't about me. Take care. I love you."

Standing, Hayley took the first step toward the bedroom so she could get ready for work, but couldn't force herself to take the next one. Awash in restlessness, she headed outside. Because it was summer, daylight had already slipped over this part of the world, making it easy for her to see the small lawn and massive old oak tree. This place had been a space to park her belongings; walls and a roof where she'd hidden out following her divorce. Even before Mazati had walked into her life to change everything, time had started to work its healing ways, so much so that she'd been contemplating getting in touch with Cal.

She'd begin by telling him she was making headway on the bills he'd left her with. Then she'd ask how he was handling prison, and if he didn't ask about her personal life or utter a word of apology, she'd put an end to the conversation. It might be wishful thinking on her part, but she'd love to describe what Night Fire was about and know he gave a damn. She wouldn't try to explain what had given rise to Aztec Fire.

Aztec Fire. So far it consisted of nothing more than a couple of pieces and the desire, the need to bring Aztec art out of oblivion and up through the years.

"Mazati? It's a beautiful morning. I hope you're enjoying it."

Surprised by the sound of her voice, she debated putting contemplation behind her and throwing her energy into going to work, but she didn't. What did people call it when they took chances because they believed in something? A leap of faith.

"I'm making a leap of faith, Mazati. Trusting the signs that Night Fire is going to support me. I'm quitting my job." She gripped the railing but the expected dizziness didn't materialize. Instead, she surrounded herself with what she'd just blurted and made it her truth. "I didn't know I was going to say that, but it feels wonderful!"

Hugging herself, she smiled, trusting that the man who'd changed her life could both see and hear. "There'll be times when I'm scared shitless, but hopefully I'll know to slap myself upside the head and keep on taking it one step at a time. Do you understand what this means? I'm actually going to do something I've dreamed about since I was a teenager." Closing her eyes, she went deep inside to where the truth lived. "You're responsible."

How.

Answering took time because she first wrapped her emotions around the sound of his voice. How long since she'd last seen him? Only a couple of weeks as far as the calendar was concerned, but much longer in every way that counted.

"The opals, for one. Remember what you told me, that we connected through them. How's this for some pop psychology? You restrained my body but left my creativity free. Maybe being tied up and wearing that collar made it possible for me to concentrate on what I had some control over, my imagination."

Your talent was always there.

"I appreciate you saying that. Mazati, we need to talk." Strange that she should emphasize talking, when always before their relationship had revolved around sex—hadn't it?

It was nothing more than a brush of air, a sigh in the morning breeze, and yet when she opened her eyes, she knew he'd be here. Tense and anticipating, she waited for a touch of rope, forceful hands on her, gags and collars. If he did that, it would be the end to everything between them.

He came to her as an Aztec warrior. A two-horned helmet covered with countless pieces of turquoise, mother-of-pearl, malachite, and pink shells left her with no doubt that he'd been more than an ordinary warrior. Because there were so many intricate carvings on the broad blade, his obsidian-edged sword struck her as more ceremonial than practical. The carvings included a number of figures that reminded her of the Aztec codices, which served as a vital pictorial record of their history and had filled so many gaps. Maybe the codex on his sword told his personal history. In his other hand he held a lance that was taller than he was. Like the sword, hard wood was edged with sharp obsidian.

His armor—at least that's what she believed it was—covered his chest from the neck down and extended over his cock, and was made from a thick, tightly woven material. Over that he'd placed a feathered tunic, the large, colorful feathers arranged to resemble an eagle's head. Most impressive was a towering object strapped to his back by means of a shoulder harness. A basketwork for lack of a better term, it was decorated with feathers, turquoise, opals, silver, and gold. She could think of no practical use for it beyond making him easy to identify, perhaps so his fellow warriors or soldiers could spot him in a battle. Was that it, he'd been the equivalent of a general? Maybe that explained why he'd believed he had every right to dominate her.

"Incredible, " she breathed. "Magnificent. And intimidating."

"But worthless against the Spanish. Their weapons and fighting skill turned us into deer being chased by panthers."

Nodding in response to his somber tone, she clenched her fingers to keep from touching him. How strong and remote he looked, an ancient warrior with a single role: to protect his people. Only, as he'd pointed out, colorful finery was no match for the Spanish army's superior weapons. Someday she might ask him what pitting himself against Cortés's men had felt like, but not now. Neither would she tell him how fragile the bond between them was, because surely he knew.

"Opals." She indicated what was on his back. "Why didn't I see them in any of the pictures of Aztec artifacts?"

"Because so much was lost to time and destruction. Archaeologists and others believe they know everything about what we once were, but they're wrong."

Ah, they were back to that, were they? Unless and until he told her everything he remembered, she'd remain as ignorant as everyone else, but she'd thrown up a barrier by refusing to be the only kind of woman he'd probably ever known, a possession. "You alone know what it truly meant to be Aztec. As long as you're alive, it isn't really lost."

"Isn't it?"

Because he couldn't do it alone. Things were coming together, insight about why he'd tried to dominate her life. Only, she couldn't concentrate on that because he was standing so close, real and warm, and she was suddenly on fire after being without him for too long. "Alive but alone, that's what you're saying."

Although he didn't respond, she saw the truth in his eyes. God but he was incredible! Not incomprehensible, because she now accepted him for what he was, a gift from the past, and if she had the courage, part of her future. That's what she needed, not his collar and ropes, not even the gift of orgasms. True, those things were part of the fabric of what they'd been to each other, but it could be so much more, if they trusted each other as equals.

"Thank you for appearing dressed as you once were."

"I wanted you to see the truth about me."

"Did the Spanish laugh or make fun? They took one look at Aztec warriors and knew you could be defeated?"

"Yes."

"I'm so sorry." She indicated the armor beneath the light-weight feather tunic. "What is it made of?"

"Cotton that's been quilted and soaked in brine to make it impenetrable. Even the Spanish used that technique."

"Oh. And the feathers? What's the meaning behind them?"

Squaring his shoulders, Mazati looked down at her. Damn the beautiful dark in his eyes! Just acknowledging the color sent a current through her. "That's important to you?"

"The Aztec used feathers for so many things; I kept noticing that. Maybe it's just because they were beautiful and plentiful, but I can't help but wonder if there wasn't another reason. Maybe they symbolized something."

"Tloque Nahuaque."

Struck by the reverence in his voice, she studied him to see what else she might learn, but felt only her growing hunger. "What's that?"

His gaze softened until the man began emerging from the warrior. "One of our rulers, creator god of the first pair of humans and ruler of the first four ages of the world."

"Then—all that use of feathers was to remind the Aztec of their origin?"

"And that in many respects Tloque Nahuaque was our father, and we could never fly like birds so we had to live in harmony with the earth."

"Harmony with the earth? A lot of Native American belief is based on that. Mazati, that's an aspect of the Aztecs I didn't come across in my reading."

"Because we lost much of Our Father's wisdom. During the first four ages, the ancestors carried his truth in their hearts, but over time we became warlike. Tloque Nahuaque shared a great deal with me when it was just me and the gods."

"Just you and the gods. My god, Mazati, when I think of everything you know—"

"Knowledge that will die when I do."

Certain she'd never heard that resigned tone from him, she struggled to clamp down on her awareness of his body. This was important. The knowledge he carried was *him* as much as her craft was part of her, maybe more. "I'm glad you were able to connect with Tloque Nahuaque because so many of your gods were involved in or concerned with war."

He nodded. "Respect for and worship of the earth faded from our hearts as survival and conquest became more and more important. And because other gods such as Huitzilopochtli compelled us to perform human sacrifice."

"And yet the use of feathers never went out of style."

"No, they didn't. Maybe because, as you say, they're beautiful."

She'd been growing warmer and warmer since they started talking. Needing to control her internal temperature and response, she took a moment to fill her lungs with the coolest air the day would offer. By then she'd managed to filter through what she'd just learned. "What you just told me, that's part of what all the historians believe has been lost."

"A small part."

How much, how much! "But vital if people are going to truly understand what the Aztec were about. All this focus on the brutal aspects of . . ."

"Is that what you think, that I'm brutal?"

The way he was looking at her, she half believed he knew what she was going to say so hurried her response. "You were a warrior, a chief or general or whatever they called their leaders. You weren't thinking about the god who created your people when you trained your slave for sex or dressed for war."

"Wasn't I?"

Peace and war in the same body? "Don't do this to me! You're throwing so much at me when I—hell, when I can't stop staring at you."

"And thinking about what I've done to you."

"Yes. Yes."

Dropping his weapons, he stepped toward her. She took a step herself, then stopped. How far had he come since that fateful and horrible time when his world had crumbled? Next to that incomprehensible journey, reaching out to her should have been a simple thing, and yet he'd been alone for so long. And before that he hadn't seen his wife as his equal. Maybe he hadn't acknowledged anything approaching love for her, but following her death, he'd tried to take out his anger on the invaders— and lost.

Would he lose again with her? Would they both?

"Come inside," she said. "I have neighbors."

"I don't see them."

"Maybe not, but I want you to come into my workshop with me." Not giving him time to respond, she headed for it. As she opened her door, she acknowledged that she was inviting him into much more than the place where Night Fire and Aztec Fire had taken root. She was bringing him into her world, her life, much as he'd begun to introduce her to his.

Fortunately, the morning sun poured in through the single window because she lacked the concentration needed to head for the light switch. It seemed both strange and right to be in the same room with a man dressed for battle.

Although she wanted to examine his attire in detail, now

wasn't the time. Being apart from him had honed her awareness of his body and its potential. Her sessions with her toys hadn't done enough to blunt her need for sex—with him.

And yet that wasn't why she'd brought him in here, not the only reason.

Walking over to her work space, she picked up the two pieces that constituted the beginning of Aztec Fire. "You're responsible for these. If you hadn't let me go to where I found the shell and fish, I'd have never had the inspiration. Was that on purpose?"

To her surprise, he shook his head. Shrugging out of whatever it was he wore on his back, he extended it toward her. His other hand was out, indicating he wanted to see her latest creations. Without touching they made the exchange.

His war ornament was too bulky for her to hold so she leaned it against her work space and ran a finger over the turquoise and opals. "This is wonderful. I'm thinking maybe I should incorporate some turquoise into my work. After seeing pictures of remnants of what once made the Aztec rich, I'm delighted to be looking—these aren't black opals."

"No."

"Why not?"

Looking up from his study of the fish and conch jewelry, he stared at her for a long moment. "Blacks were sacred. Only the priests could make use of them."

Sacred, and yet he'd willingly supplied her. "Was that part of a legend, maybe one of the gods—"

"Some of our beliefs went so deep that even those who were alive when the Spanish came didn't know the origin, and even when it was just me, the gods kept that to themselves. I grew up hearing that fire opals had been created in the waters of paradise. They called them quetzalitzlipyollitli, the stone of the bird of paradise. Blacks were the eyes, most sacred of the sacred."

"That's beautiful." *And perfect to add to my information sheet about opals.* "I keep saying this, but when I think of how much you must know, legends and stories—"

"There's more than old stories and legends, history and craftsmanship." He paused, black eyes seeping into her. "Hidden cities lost to time, burial grounds, caves where some of what was precious to us remains."

Thoughts of what that might entail, coupled by eyes darker than any opal, weakened her. "I wish I could but I don't see how I can help you with that. I'm not an archaeologist."

"The gods trust you with quetzalitzlipyollitli. You see more than stones with fire in them."

Even weaker than she'd been a moment ago, she started to sit. Then, because he was who he was, she stepped toward Mazati and touched his tunic. The large, multicolored feathers were absolutely beautiful but nothing she was familiar with, making her wonder if the birds responsible for them had become as extinct as the Aztec. Even with the body armor under the tunic, she could feel his heat.

In her eyes and heart he was still a warrior, a leader of men, but the strength and courage that went with that word were being buried under the weight of everything he'd been carrying inside himself. Determined to relieve him of a little of that burden, she took hold of the tunic's hem.

He didn't try to stop her as she drew it over his head. His armor was held in place with ties on both sides and releasing that called for her full attention, but finally she'd dispensed with it, too. All that remained were the marks left on his strong and naked chest. She ran her forefinger over one of them, reminding herself that before this morning, he'd been in control of everything that happened between them. He'd carried the ropes. He'd placed the collar on her. And he'd touched her when and how he wanted.

Today was for her. "You're alive, Mazati. That's all that matters, you're alive."

"Barely."

Taking his hand, she began stroking his fingers. They were strong and competent, trained for battle and exploring a woman's body, but had he ever surrendered himself to a woman's strength? The longer she traced the lines in his palm, the more convinced she became that he'd never truly opened himself to what a woman was capable of.

"I want you to simply feel," she told him with her fingers laced through his. "To have your nerve endings tell you what it truly means to be alive. To trust."

A fine measure of tension ran through him so she brought his hand to her mouth and kissed the pulse at the inside of his wrist. "It's incredible when you think about this," she said, her mouth now inches from his flesh. "Bone and muscle representing what it means to be a warrior and yet a man is so vulnerable here." She made her point by running first her teeth and then her tongue over the dark vein.

Studying his reaction out of the corner of her eye, she slid her teeth along the inside of his arm until she reached his elbow. He again tensed when she nibbled him there but soon relaxed. "Not used to having that done, are you?"

"No, never."

"Do you trust me?"

"Yes."

That single word was everything, so she let him know by slipping her arms around his waist and resting the side of her head against his chest. He started to reach for her, but she forced his arms down by his sides. "I'm not sure you know the full meaning of the word. You understand one kind of surrender, but I want to show you another." Stepping back, she pulled off her top and dispensed with her bra. "I did this"—she lifted her breasts—"because I wanted to, not because you made me. Do you see the difference?"

Nostrils flaring, he leaned toward her. Much as she ached to respond, she held back. "You think of yourself as Aztec first and foremost. Of course you do; what you represent is precious. But before everything else you're a man."

"I wouldn't exist if I wasn't Aztec."

"I realize that, but I want you to see yourself as a human being, a male human."

How, his eyes asked. She found at least the beginning of her reply in his naked chest. Wrapping an arm around his neck, she brought her breasts within an inch of his ribs. Instead of continuing to try to keep his hands off her, she shivered as he ran his fingers down her spine. Instead of allowing him to move down to her buttocks, she distracted him by kissing his chest with her already hard nipples. His hold tightened, prompting her to push back and shake her head.

"Easy, easy. My pace today."

He gave her a puzzled nod, and although his grip relaxed, he didn't let her go. Fine, she could work with that. Mentally putting herself in his place as much as possible, she alternated between standing flat footed and lifting herself onto her toes so she could run her breasts up and down his chest. He was going into himself, concentrating on sensation, maybe learning something new about his body.

"Sex isn't always about lighting flames. Sometimes it starts with a little heat."

Fortunately he didn't question her understatement. After all, she was experiencing more than a simple matter of heat, and he was already aroused. Stepping back, she placed his hands on her shoulders, giving them a pat to let him know he was to leave them there. Hopefully he'd honor her desire to be the teacher this time. After making sure he understood what she had in mind, she spread her hands over his hip bones. When he sucked in a breath, she rested her finger pads against his skin until she sensed that he was relaxing, at least a little.

"You're much more than a cock, Mazati."

"My cock—"

"Is wonderful. Never doubt that. But that's not the only thing I want from you because it isn't the only part of your body that speaks to mine."

Again his expression said he wasn't sure where she was taking the conversation. Determined to find a wordless way to explain, she began massaging his belly using small, firm, and yet gentle circular strokes. At first tension roped him, but she kept the pressure constant and was careful not to tickle him, and he gradually relaxed. "I love the feel of your skin here, the softness and beneath that muscle and bone."

"Soft?"

She couldn't help laughing. "Don't take it the wrong way. Not every part of a man's body has to be like sandpaper. Behind your ears, under your arms, the backs of your knees and insides of your elbows . . . where else?" she muttered, not particularly caring whether she finished. Her body was undergoing a softening of its own, a gentling. Accustomed to feeling like a tightly strung bow around him, she wasn't sure what to make of this sensation, but she didn't want it to end. "Sit down." She indicated her work chair.

"What?"

"Sit down, please."

Looking doubtful, he nevertheless did as she'd commanded. Once he was on it, she stepped behind him so she could massage his shoulders and the base of his neck. Being where she couldn't study his expression made it easier to concentrate on pleasuring him. Having never given serious thought to the nuances of a professional massage, she could only go by what she'd like to have done to her. His shoulders were all strength and power, barely sheathed muscle and bones that were much larger and denser than hers, but when she moved her fingers to the base of his throat where his lifeblood pulsed, she amended her observation. The human body was comprised of such amazing contrasts. Even the most seasoned warrior was deeply vulnerable. Leaning close again, she let her breasts trail over the tops of his shoulders.

He looked back at her on a hiss of breath. "I didn't expect that."

"Like it?"

"Yeah. Yeah, I like."

"Good," she said and ran a hard nipple over the curve leading to his upper arm. At the same time, she closed a hand over his throat. "Do you trust me?"

"What—"

She tightened her grip. A little more and she could rob him of oxygen. "Trust, Mazati. Do you?"

The familiar tension she recognized as instinct ran through him so she waited him out. *Yes,* his slow relaxation said, *I trust you.*

"That's the way I felt when you put your ropes on me. Beneath everything else I was feeling, I knew you wouldn't hurt me. Without that, we wouldn't have anything."

He responded by pulling her around so she was standing in front of him. When he released her wrist, she made a fist and repeatedly thumped his chest. Again he rewarded her with a quick smile. Her body was humming, singing softly, alive and acutely interested in everything about him. "Playing you like a drum," she explained. "Listening to the sounds we make together."

Suddenly embarrassed by her corny lines, she braced herself against his knees so she could lean forward and press her lips to his nose. His expression said he thought she was losing her mind. "Didn't your people ever do that?"

"No."

"How much I have to teach you. Did you know, Eskimos kiss by rubbing their noses together."

"No, they don't."

"Yes, they do. At least that's what I've always heard. Do you want to try it?"

Taking his baffled look as her cue, she presented him with her nose, and after a brief hesitation, he brushed his against hers. Eyes at half mast, she tracked her reaction. Not bad but not nearly as exciting as lips against lips. Arching away but with her hands still on his knees, she turned her head to the side. He must have known what she had in mind because he did the same, and when they closed in on each other, the alignment was perfect.

Kissing, simply kissing, bodies barely touching and heat bleeding into heat. Even with the strain in her back, she might stay like this forever while their mouths spoke to each other. She couldn't tell whether he'd had much experience with kissing and maybe she'd ask him—later—but he seemed to know what she needed. By turn he gifted her with a feathered brushing and sealed power, frequently changing tactics and keeping her constantly interested, forever wanting more. Whether open or closed, his mouth was a current telegraphing not just passion but something deeper. Something she'd needed from the moment he'd walked into her life.

At length, though, her back threatened to cramp. She started to straighten only to have him draw her onto his lap. Unfortunately, her chair was designed for one, and she didn't need to look around to know there wasn't anything better in here. "My house, my bedroom."

"Like this?" He indicated his nude and her nearly so bodies.

"Sure. Gotta give the neighbors something to talk about."

Not allowing herself time to chicken out, she jumped to her

feet and trotted over to the door. Only then did she realize he hadn't joined her. "What?"

"I'm trying to get used to this side of you."

"Hang on. We've got a long way to go." She punctuated her comment with an impatient head jerk. His smile holding longer than it had before, he stood. The sight of him closing in on her in all his naked glory made her doubt whether she could hold out long enough to get him on her bed. Counting her self-control in mini-seconds, she stepped into the sunlight. Not bothering to check to see if anyone was out, she sprinted for her place.

Laughing as she hadn't in too long, she slipped inside. The moment he closed the door behind him, she hauled him toward her bedroom, something she couldn't have accomplished without his compliance. A few tugs dispensed with the rest of her clothes.

Scrambling onto the bed on her hands and knees, she patted the coverlet. "This is where you belong, big boy. On your back and ready for servicing."

"Servicing?"

How wonderful he looked with his arms folded across his chest, head back, legs apart, cock ready, willing, and able. Hard pressed to remember what she'd just said, she licked her lips and gave him what she hoped passed as a come-hither smile. Either he bought into her act or had decided to take pity on her when he sat on the edge. He was still settling himself on the mattress when she pushed him onto his back. Hmm. Having him dangling halfway off the bed wasn't what she had in mind, compelling her to stand and heft first one and then the other of his legs up. "You aren't cooperating. And you're heavy as hell."

"You complaining?"

"Let me get back to you on that. Right now it's time for you to exhibit some self-control. Think you're up to it?"

"It depends on what you have in mind."

I'll let you know once I have it figured out. Fortunately, a few seconds of looking at him stretched out like that was all it took for inspiration to strike. She'd wanted this to be a gentle and emotional journey, but maybe lighthearted was better, at least for now. If his gods blessed them, they'd have more than this one time to explore the range of their relationship.

If?

Positioning his arms over his head, she acknowledged she'd never wanted anything more than she did this moment. One second after another would flow over them. That's all she could control, endless seconds chained together.

Perched on the side of the bed, she bent low and ran her hair over his chest. A series of twitches warned that she was close to tickling him so, after tossing back her hair, she placed a hand on either side of him and kissed first his right and then his left nipple. Hard, small, warm, they fascinated her.

She didn't blame him for running his fingers into her hair, didn't try to tell him to let her go. And his touch on her scalp increased her courage and commitment. This man, *her* man, was a gift from the past and from gods she hadn't known existed until he walked into her world. Those gods might have believed they were buying her with the opals, but they'd been wrong. He'd slipped into her life, he. He'd branded her body with his knowledge of what it needed and wanted, and now it was her turn to do the same to him.

Giving herself up to the task, she trailed her tongue and mouth from the base of his throat to within an inch of his cock, but even when he tightened his grip and arched his pelvis toward her, she resolutely left that part of his anatomy alone.

Gentle, gentle, gentle, she chanted as she moved out to his hips. Despite the echoing words, it took all her self-control and then some to focus on showing him lightness and love instead of diving into the waiting lust. Much as she wanted his cock to be in her mouth, she settled for touching and tasting his thighs, knees, calves, even the bottoms of his feet. Trying not to think about him stretching her core, she rolled him onto his stomach so she could nibble his buttocks. Lovely! Sweet flesh covering yet more muscle.

When he looked up at her, she had to back off and drink in all the air her lungs could hold. His eyes were heavy and dark with the same hunger that clawed at her belly, and she didn't try to hide her arousal from him. "This is about you," she managed as the scent of her readiness wafted. "What I want it to be for you."

"Why?" His nails dug into the coverlet, and when he breathed, she guessed that, like her, he had to work at remembering how something so complex was done.

"Because until now it's all been about me, pleasing me with ropes, blindfolds, a collar. I loved it." Struck by the honesty of her confession, she kissed one eyelid and then the other. "You reached me on an incredible level but different from the one I'm trying to reach you on."

"Why?"

Again she bought time by running her lips over his lids followed by his forehead, but when he lifted her head off him, she dug through the layers to what remained to be said. "There's more than one connection between a man and a woman, Mazati. More than master and slave."

He nodded, that's all, nodded; but with the gesture, the dam broke, and she cried. Then she smiled when he wiped her tears away with the side of his thumb. "Sex—sex doesn't always have to be fierce, and it isn't always fucking. Sometimes . . ."

"Sometimes what?"

"Lovemaking," she whispered. "Sometimes when a man and a woman come together, it's because they love each other."

Another nod, this time longer than the first. His eyes still gave off their ebony hue, but she saw something else beneath that. "Do you know what the word means?"

"Teach me."

And so she did. Her skin so sensitive it was almost painful, she nevertheless taught with mouth and fingers, with whispers about how much she loved his taste and why she was glad he'd been in battles because his scars provided roadmaps of his life. In his eyes, she told him, she saw his people and his gods, and his words filled her with images of what being Aztec meant. Placing her face inches from his, she gave him her breath and took in his and traced its journey deep into her lungs. Then she pressed her ear against his chest and learned his heart's tempo.

He stroked her back while she talked, and when she ran out of words, he ran his palm over her breasts but didn't take hold of them, and maybe that was harder and more electric than being held in his inescapable grip.

When he turned onto his side, she stretched out beside him so she could feel his skin against hers as she told him how hard helping her parents die had been and how the necessary task had brought her and her sister together. He said his father had died from a fall when he was a boy but his uncles had filled the empty spaces.

And when she expressed her concern that her sister might never find a man to share her life with, he drew her onto his belly and held her hard against him and told her that only Saree could travel that road. She was crying again before he was done.

Finally he whispered that his slave-wife had been pregnant at the time of her death, and she kissed his eyes and tasted his tears and knew as she'd never known anything that his heart was as fully human as hers.

"Maybe your child's spirit is out there somewhere," she told him instead of saying how sorry she was. "Wanting you to have the kind of life he didn't."

"Maybe."

"I know, I know. Too deep." She tried to rise up so she could study his expression, but he didn't let her. Looking toward the window, she wondered if they'd been on her bed for hours, getting to know each other. Listening to each other's bodies and heads.

No more listening.

As she slid off him, he rolled toward her, and she lifted her leg so she could drape it over his thigh. Her arms were around his neck, his fingers in her hair and on her buttocks, holding them close. She was looking into his eyes when his cock touched her entrance.

"Come home," she whispered.

He did, slipping deep and strong and warm into her. There was no tension this time, no insistent electricity assaulting her. Instead she melted into him and understood that his cock and more were becoming part of her. They were flowing together, sharing heat and life.

Even when he started thrusting and she pushed back, she remained gentle and sensed the same in him. They climbed together, sweating a little, breathing rapidly and in cadence with each other. She felt his climax a moment before it rolled over him, so held on to him and made it hers as well. Then as he began to relax, she dove into her own long, slow, warm release.

When it was over for both of them, she licked sweat off his neck, and he lifted her head so he could kiss her. He sighed, the sound as long and slow as her climax had been.

"You're home," she whispered.

"Yes."

"Alive."

"Yes."

"Thank you," she managed before falling asleep with her man still around and inside her.

And when they woke, he spilled inside her again and after showering together, he began drawing sketches of the birds whose feathers said so much about the Aztec origin, and she promised him that she'd make that part of Aztec Fire.

Celia May Hart's doing it
ONE MORE TIME!

On sale now!

1

Abby Deane nudged the yoke, banking her plane to the left. Looking out the side window, she spotted her new home, a sprawling ancient mansion dating back to the Tudor period, added to over the ages.

Her new home. Away from the pointless distractions of men, men who were so commitment phobic, wanting only a quick shag. Thank heavens for modern invention. She owned a potpourri of devices designed to please her. Who needed a man in the twenty-first century?

Ever since she'd given up on the heartbreakers, her life seemed less off-kilter. She hoped this new job would rebalance her life. The toys'd definitely help.

With a grin, she checked her instruments and glanced ahead, squinting in the sunlight even though she wore dark sunglasses. Puffy cumulonimbus blocked her vision of the private airstrip ahead.

Circling, she slowed the Beech Bonanza into its gliding speed. She guided the plane into its descent, checking the altimeter until she broke clear of the cloud cover.

She blinked. The airstrip had vanished. She glanced to the left and the right. Had she flown over the strip? Nope, nothing.

Just below the cloud cover, she circled, searching.

What the—A runway didn't just disappear.

This one had. All she saw were mown hayfields and green fields of grazing sheep.

The engine cut out, sputtering. She checked the fuel gauges. Not even close to empty. She throttled back on the engine and gave it power again, to no avail.

Her forehead tightened. She took a deep breath. No need to panic; she knew how to make an emergency landing. She'd practiced it before.

She leveled the wings, aiming for a mown hayfield. She lowered the landing gear. At least she wasn't far from the hotel. If she managed to land in one piece, she'd walk over. If not, someone from the hotel would see her go down and come to her aid.

Checking her seat belts, Abby glided in. The plane touched down, not skewing, but bouncing over the dirt ridges and truncated hay stalks.

The plane rolled to a stop. Abby sagged in her seat. Her seat belts relaxed their grip. A bone-deep ache radiated through her, a counterpoint to her thundering heart. Without further thought, she evacuated the plane. She stood at a safe distance, but the plane rested, still and silent.

She returned to the plane, reaching for her toolbox. She touched the right-hand engine and snatched her fingers back. Cold. That wasn't right.

Abby sighed. Both engines felt like they hadn't run at all. Weird. She'd never experienced anything like this before. She'd have to contact a mechanic to repair her plane.

She unloaded her luggage, hoisting the wheeled bags over the rich black dirt to the field's edge. Through a small gap in the tall hedge surrounding the field (presumably hiding the spoils of hay from the adjacent grazing animals) Abby spotted a dirt track.

That should take me to the main road, she thought.

Two bags, one laptop, a large purse, and a long tube holding her copies of the hotel plans. She sat on the biggest bag to wait for assistance to arrive.

And waited.

Half an hour later, Abby came into sight of the hotel, her future home. Her future home with useless staff to fire. It didn't matter that her boss had agreed to keep the original household staff. Someone must have seen her plane in distress. Why hadn't anyone come to her aid?

And this drive . . . Gravel made a nice crunch under a car's tires, but dragging heavy wheeled bags over it for a quarter mile was not so much fun. The other quarter mile had been nothing but dirt.

That had to be fixed. Hotel guests may not be inclined to travel to a boutique hotel all on dirt road. She thought of flying stones scratching a BMW's paint job and shuddered.

No, that had to be rectified at once. Well, once she'd hired new staff.

She noted the shuttered windows on the house and at once forgave the staff. Keeping the windows closed preserved the restoration's freshness. That's why they didn't see her go down, and her landing had been practically silent.

Speaking of silence . . . a breeze brought the sound of baaing sheep, the rustle of leaves from the giant trees lining the drive. No sound of civilization reached her ears. Not the dull roar of the M3 highway, which was only a couple of miles off.

Abby shrugged, shifting the tube strap on her shoulder. Maybe the house blocked the sound.

She reached the grand front entrance. Two giant oaken doors, formidable and highly polished. Abby nodded in approval. The staff were doing superb work. Such attention to detail.

Leaving her luggage at the foot of the broad stone steps, she slung her purse over her shoulder. She ascended and rang the bell, an old-fashioned pulley. Another nice touch. With the hotel's official opening, those doors would stay wide open and welcoming.

She leaned backward, surveying the facade, approving of the sparkling windows and pollutant-free bricks.

A creak warned of the opening door. They polished the doors but didn't oil the hinges? Abby repressed a sigh of irritation. So much to be done.

The door opened a crack.

Some welcome. Abby huffed. "Are you going to let me in?"

A deep baritone voice answered: "Who are you?"

"Your former boss if you don't let me in," Abby snapped.

The pause from his end only maddened her further. "A woman?"

She hauled the door open, ready to give him a piece of her mind, and stopped dead. Her jaw sank and she closed her mouth with a snap.

Before her stood a gobsmackingly handsome man. She registered that much before his odd attire caught her attention. Perhaps it was the dark vee of chest hair poking out from his crumpled white shirt. Or the supertight breeches that let her know, despite the buttoned-up flap, that he was a well endowed guy. Very well endowed.

She cleared her throat. "Definitely your former boss. You're fired."

"Fired?" The man might look gorgeous but apparently he lacked in the brains department. "I do not work for you."

That gave her pause. Was this Lord David Winterton's son? She modulated her tone. "If you are not on my staff, who are you?"

He smiled, a broad smile that must have broken many a heart. Abby steeled herself. Not hers. "I'm just passing through."

Her eyes narrowed. "Trespassing? And my staff let you?"

"There's nobody here but me." He surveyed her, wholly un-inclined to leave her property. His eyelids lowering, his stern gaze turned his brown eyes into angry dark specks. "You don't look like the sort who possesses staff."

Abby's blood boiled. "You bastard." She pushed past him and into the house. Where *was* her staff?

In the middle of the large hall, she stopped, her sneakers squeaking on the marble tile floor. She frowned, surveying the space. "Something isn't right . . ."

The idiot man came up behind her. "I'm glad you're ac-knowledging that at last."

Abby ignored him, looking at the tiled floor. "For some reason, I thought this was linoleum in the pictures, but it's real marble."

"Linol-what?"

Abby made a slow turn. "It's in awfully good condition for an ancient floor."

"Ancient." He sounded doubtful.

Along the wall stood a delicate side table. The piece be-longed in a museum, not a busy hotel hallway. On it, a single gold tray contained a scatter of ivory cards. Her breath caught in her throat. "That—that's not supposed to be there."

She reviewed the hallway. Had she gotten it all backward? "Where's the reception desk?"

"Madam, you are not making any sense." Abby turned and saw his tense stance, his arms akimbo. "This is not a hotel."

She frowned right back at him. "It is. I'm the manager."

"You?" His rich voice held a note of derision. "A woman?"

"Oh my God." Abby drew herself to her full height, a full foot shorter than he. "Just get over yourself. This is the twenty-first century!"

"It's 1807," he said, his voice quiet. His brown eyes pierced her.

She tried to ignore the discomfort. "Don't be ridiculous." She put distance between them, looking for a telephone. If this guy got dangerous . . ."I don't have time to mess about in some fantasy role-play."

"It's not a fantasy," he insisted. Truly, it was a shame someone so good-looking was also so deluded.

"Look, mister." Abby folded her arms and glared at him. "It's time you took a hike. You're trespassing on private property. Do you want me to call the police?"

The man didn't move. "You're a hard woman."

She'd heard worse.

With no phone in sight, Abby fished out her mobile, hitting speed dial. "I warned you." She ignored his sudden, ashen expression. If he did a runner, so be it. She put the mobile to her ear. Hearing nothing, she frowned. "Hmm, must've lost the signal."

"What . . . what is that?" His stilted voice broke into her musing.

So he hadn't run. "Can you give the old-fashioned thing a rest, please?"

He sighed, throwing up his hands. He stalked off into another room and returned with a newspaper. "It's a couple of months old, but look." He thrust it at her.

She picked it up. "So the date is 1807. It's a nice printing job. It's amazing what computers can do these days." She tossed it back at him.

He caught it one-handed. "You're not making sense."

Abby sighed. "You're still here? Let me find a landline . . ." She wandered off. According to her blueprints, they'd turned this room into an office.

A small sitting room, definitely feminine, greeted her. "But . . ."

What was going on? How could all the work she'd seen in photographs be undone? Had she fallen victim to some kind of scam?

She looked up. No ornate ceiling rose, no electric light. Only a few sconces with candles attached to the wall.

Abby trudged back into the hallway. "I—I don't understand . . ." Her intruder crouched by her bags. Bags she'd left outside. Her eyes narrowed. "What are you doing?"

"Trying to figure out how to open these trunks."

"That's my private property." Abby advanced, pausing when he stood his ground.

"I merely sought to discover your identity. You need your family."

"I need you to leave this house." Abby sucked in her breath. This house where nothing seemed right. "Why have all the renovations been undone? What's happened?"

"Madam, I am sorry for your insanity, but it seems you've regained your senses for the moment. I can see you know there is something not quite right with you. Who are your family? Where do you live?"

"I'm supposed to live here," Abby replied dully. "This is supposed to be my new home." She took a deep breath. "Is it really 1807?"

"I showed you *The Times*," he replied.

The breath whooshed out of her. "I'm not insane. Look in my bag. You'll see that this is 2007."

Crouching, he grinned up at her. "You are an extremely stubborn woman. Although, I will admit you do have unusual items in your possession." His voice sounded strangled. "I'm almost inclined to believe you. That . . . thing . . . you spoke into."

"My mobile?" She tossed it to him, still keeping her distance, and he examined it.

"What is it made of?"

"Plastic and metal, mostly. Are you going to open my bag or what?"

He shot her an annoyed glance. "How *do* you open this thing?"

Abby knelt beside him, at once aware that this stranger was no skinny geek. He was built. The muscles practically popped from his thighs. He seemed so . . . so big.

"It's a zipper," she told him, demonstrating its function by opening the bag partway. "I think it was invented in the twentieth century."

He grunted, tugging on the other zipper. He flipped back the lid. White shirts lay in neat stacks, in between which lay flat navy blue shoes and impeccably rolled black trouser socks.

"Don't even think of rifling through my underwear."

"Wouldn't dream of it, my dear," he murmured, lifting and setting aside her shirts with precision. His lips curved. "Well, well, well . . ."

Abby wanted to curl up and die. She shut her eyes, sinking back on her heels. Why hadn't she stopped him? Because she thought he had her other bag. *Oh, no no no no.* What a way to get started with her staff—or whoever this person was.

"I recognize this," he said. She cracked open one eye to see him squeezing a large synthetic dildo. "Not made of this stuff though. Wood or ivory, yes." He cocked his head. "Do the other items serve similar purposes?"

Her cheeks burned and she nodded, not daring to look at the extensive array of toys she'd brought with which to amuse herself.

"Interesting."

That was the understatement of the year.

"Never seen the like of these before."

"Just . . . just put them back," Abby gasped with a weak wave at her bags.

He chuckled. "Well, now that we've discovered that at least your luggage is from the future—"

"You are a very stubborn man." Her words didn't have their usual force.

"—I believe you may stay."

"So very kind of you," she muttered, tossing her shirts back into the bag and zipping it up. Standing, she hauled the bag upright.

He rose also. "Perhaps it's time we introduced ourselves, given that we lack a common acquaintance to do it for us. Very well, twenty-first-century woman. Do they have names in the future? Mrs.? Miss?"

Abby gave him her best level glare. "Ms."

"Mzz?" His forehead creased.

"Ms. Abigail Deane," she told him, choosing to ignore his puzzled expression. "And you are?"

"Mr. Hardy, Myles Hardy. At your service." He sketched a brief bow. "Now, what are we going to do with you?"

She had no idea. *I don't belong in 1807. What's going to happen to me?* She eyed Myles Hardy. *Can I actually rely on him?*

"No need to look so scared," Myles soothed, stepping forward. He paused at her involuntary retreat. "There's nobody in this house except you and me."

"That's meant to reassure me?" she braved. She eyed her handbag on the floor. If she could just get her hands on that can of mace . . .

"It gives us time to figure it all out. How you got here; how we can send you back."

"What is this 'we' business?"

"I was about to add 'and help you fit in here,' but if you don't need my help . . ." He backed off.

Abby loosed a huffy breath. "Look, thank you, but how can I trust you?"

"You can't." His broad mischievous grin did something unexpected in her belly. She banked down the surge of attraction.

Not again, and certainly not now. "If you wish to manage on your own . . ."

"No, no," Abby said hastily. "I'm sorry. I'm used to shifting for myself."

"Must be some future." Myles grunted as he picked up her other bag. He set off down the hallway. "What is in the cylinder?"

"Blueprints." Abby slung the cylinder strap over her shoulder, followed by her large handbag.

"What?"

"House plans," she translated. What else didn't they have in this time?

Myles glanced over his shoulder, pausing for a moment. "You don't say," he drawled. "They might be most amusing to examine."

"Hardly amusing." She fired her patented glare at his back.

He caught her glaring, and his boyish grin widened. So much for cowing him. "Forgive me, but how often does someone get a look into the future?"

"Two hundred years into the future. Maybe I shouldn't. If you invented things before your time . . ." She dragged her suitcase after her, following Myles to the foot of the stairs.

He ascended the staircase.

Abby looked up. The dark mahogany wood stairs rose from the hallway floor, splitting at a landing to run along the walls on either side of her. "I don't suppose elevators have been invented yet."

He grinned, stopping to look back down at her. "No. Leave your trunk. I will carry it for you."

"No. I can manage." She gritted her teeth. She could rest on the stairs.

GREAT BOOKS,
GREAT SAVINGS!

When You Visit Our Website:
www.kensingtonbooks.com
You Can Save Money Off The Retail Price
Of Any Book You Purchase!

- **All Your Favorite Kensington Authors**
- **New Releases & Timeless Classics**
- **Overnight Shipping Available**
- **eBooks Available For Many Titles**
- **All Major Credit Cards Accepted**

Visit Us Today To Start Saving!
www.kensingtonbooks.com

All Orders Are Subject To Availability.
Shipping and Handling Charges Apply.
Offers and Prices Subject To Change Without Notice.